M000210796

Waiting Season

Waiting Season

a novel

✳ ✳ ✳

by Melanie Lageschulte

Waiting Season: a novel
© 2018
by Melanie Lageschulte
Fremont Creek Press

Kindle: 978-0-9997752-1-9
Paperback: 978-0-9997752-2-6
Hardcover: 978-0-9997752-3-3

Cover photo: JenniferPhotographyImaging/iStock.com
Cover design by Melanie Lageschulte

Web: fremontcreekpress.com

* 1 *

The last of the Christmas cookies waited on the snowflake-patterned tray, their frosting still bright but their corners starting to crumble. Auggie ripped away the plastic wrap and sighed. He put on his best business-owner smile and made a sweeping gesture with the plate.

"OK, everyone." His searching gaze swept the faces of his friends, who were gathered around the sideboard at Prosper Hardware, coffee cups in hand. Outside the frosted windows, Main Street was deserted except for the wind-driven snow flying about on this dreary January morning. "Two each should do it, and they'll be nearly gone. Almost there. Today could be the last day," he added hopefully.

No one moved. Auggie shoved the plate toward Jerry Simmons, the retired school principal now serving as mayor of the tiny Iowa town. "Jerry, come on, it's your civic duty. You get first pick."

Jerry only grimaced and busied himself adjusting the brim of his purple ball cap, which was embroidered with the local high school's mascot. "Sorry, Auggie, you're a week late to tempt me with those. Or at least, a day late. It's the second of January, you know."

"I sure do. That's why we need to wrap this up."

With his free hand, Auggie pointed at the glowing-white pages of the fresh calendar tacked up next to the sideboard, the one with pictures of antique tractors on the top and "Prosper Feed Co." boldly lettered across the bottom.

"Brought that spanking-new calendar in myself just this morning. Would've had it over here before today, but the dang things came in so late this year. I wanted to hand them out to customers down at the co-op before Christmas, even. But I guess you can't outsmart the postal service. Or beat Father Time, for that matter. He does as he pleases."

Auggie gestured again with the tray, then beamed when Frank Lange shrugged and took it from his hands.

"That's the way, Frank. Your heart doctor's not here to stop you. Besides, that one on the corner there has less icing. It's got your name on it, I'd say."

Frank picked up the star-shaped cookie and forced the tray on George Freitag, a retired farmer in his early eighties who was the oldest member of the coffee bunch. Auggie settled into his usual seat next to the coffeepot with a satisfied grunt, then adjusted his thick-rimmed glasses.

"Auggie, I've got to hand it to you," George pulled the edges of his wool cardigan closer together, despite the generous heat blasting out of the iron vents in the store's oak floorboards. "You just managed to sell us on some cookies while working in the meaning of life, and all before eight in the morning. Quite the accomplishment, I'd say."

Melinda Foster didn't always agree with Auggie's razor-sharp commentary about everyone and everything in this little community, but his assessment of time on this gray winter morning was spot-on. How was it already January? She paused in her polishing of the oak showcase that served as the counter for her family's store and took another, closer look at the calendar.

As she stared at the blank spaces that made up her future, she tried to remember what her life was like just one year ago.

It took a moment, as the sights and sounds of her former life in Minneapolis had grown fainter with each passing month. And then, she was there again: The bitter cold walks to the transit stop in her hip Uptown neighborhood, the snow-globe view out the fifteenth-floor windows of the advertising agency where she used to work. When a blizzard would blow in, it was hard to see the skyscraper across the street. On a day like today, the office would have been quiet, with some of her co-workers still on holiday break. Muffled conversations in this cube or that cube, the pitter-patter of fingers drumming on a keyboard, the *ding* of the microwave in the break room down the hall.

And then ... the jostling ride home on the bus, puffy parkas cushioning the riders at every stop; the slush pooling in watery lumps on the tiled floor of her vintage apartment building's lobby; the clang of the humming radiators as she fumbled in her fashionable tote for her mailbox key. The thump of her boots up the grand staircase, the creak of the front door to her cozy apartment, that happy moment when Oreo jumped down from the window seat and ran to greet her, purring.

Melinda felt the tears forming behind her eyes, a sudden stab of heartache lurching her back to the present. She hadn't thought of her dear friend quite so much during the past month, when the holiday rush had required so much time and effort. What little energy had remained went to caring for her sheep and chickens; cuddling Sunny and Stormy, her once-aloof barn cats; and curling up before her farmhouse's fireplace with Hobo, the sweet dog who had helped her open her heart again.

She blinked rapidly and reached for the comforting softness of the dust cloth, relieved her friends were too busy forcing those last Christmas cookies on each other to notice her reflective mood. She pushed her wavy brown hair out of her face, remembered it was nearly time to dye those pesky gray hairs again, and focused on rubbing out a suspicious ring that threatened the oak cabinet's still-glowing finish.

Her old life was gone, swept away by so many twists and turns that she could hardly believe it all happened in just eight months. How quickly it all unraveled, like a stray yarn on an old sweater: Oreo's seizure, the frantic drive to the emergency vet clinic, the sad echoes of her suddenly empty apartment. The weight of the severance package in her shaking hand, the sight of her vacant desk, the half-empty box of personal items left on its surface. Her mom's frantic call about Uncle Frank's heart attack, the rush home to be with her family, her decision to stay on through the summer.

Then more memories, warmer and brighter: Horace balancing a bucket of fresh eggs on the arm of his worn chore coat, the hope in his faded-blue eyes when Melinda showed interest in renting his acreage. Hobo's happy bark as he fetched a stick tossed toward the barn.

The wonderful day Sunny and Stormy set their aloofness aside to accept her hugs. The bounty from the garden, the clink of glass and the laughter of new friends as the canning jars were filled.

An autumn sunrise spreading golden light across the harvested fields. Her family gathered elbow-to-elbow around the farmhouse's antique table, her Christmas tree glittering in the corner.

"Melinda, we need your help!"

She looked up, startled, to see Uncle Frank approaching with the cookie tray in his hands. "You know I can't leave these alone, now. Be sure to take some."

"Half of my jeans already don't fit so great." She shooed the plate away. "And you know I have containers of cookies in my freezer at home." But then, that peanut butter one didn't have any frosting, it was sort of healthy ...

"As your employer, I'm offering you a special bonus as a 'thank you' for all your work during the holidays." Uncle Frank tried for a straight face, and failed, as he set the tray on the counter and nudged it toward his niece.

The peanut-butter cookie had a chocolate star on its top, too. She slid it off the tray and took a satisfied bite.

"Don't leave them here, OK?" she mumbled as she chewed, pleased the cookie was still fresh. Auggie's wife must have kept them in the freezer. "Pawn some off on Bill."

Bill Larsen, the store's other full-time employee, pulled

off his coat as he walked up the store's main aisle. Much to Melinda's relief, he eagerly reached for two cookies.

"I hope this is the last of them, Frank." Bill grasped both cutouts in his left hand as he poured coffee with his right. "Because my wife wants me to bring in some tomorrow."

Everyone groaned. Jerry slapped a palm on the knee of his jeans. "Bill, I promised mine I'd do the same. We'll be eating Christmas cookies until Easter, at this rate."

"Jerry, why don't you take yours over to City Hall?" Melinda suggested. "Maybe someone in cookie withdrawal will wander in to pay their utility bill."

"I wish I could," Jerry grumbled. "Nancy's already beat me to it."

Nancy Delaney was Prosper's city clerk and librarian, dividing her days between the two connected buildings directly across the street from Prosper Hardware. "She called me last night to say she has candy and cookies to share this week. 'Don't worry about bringing any in,' she said, like she was doing me some big favor."

"Nancy may be out of luck, anyway," Bill consoled Jerry. "I doubt she'll have many visitors. Other than your vehicles out front, there's maybe two other cars parked along the whole length of Main. It's only four blocks, but still."

Bill liberally spiked his coffee with sugar and powdered creamer, then took a hearty bite of his second cookie before he even made it to his chair. He was a stocky guy in his mid-thirties, just a few years younger than Melinda. Between lifting weights and bustling around in the store's back-room woodshop, he managed to eat whatever he wanted and yet avoid the rounded paunches that plagued most of the coffee group's older members. Only John "Doc" Ogden, Prosper's longtime veterinarian, had a lean, lanky frame. Doc was never one to turn down a cookie, but he was absent that morning.

Enjoy it while you can, Bill, Melinda thought as she adjusted the elastic waistband on her loosest pair of work pants. She'd be forty in two months, and her metabolism was already slowing down. That, or she'd been stuffing her face during the holidays. It didn't help that it was now too cold to walk the gravel road that ran past her farm. And the nearest gym was twenty miles away, at least. Dragging hay and straw bales around the barn and lugging water to the chicken coop wasn't going to cut it. She'd have to get inventive, and soon.

Taking down all of Prosper Hardware's Christmas decorations would burn off a few calories, she decided. And with the holiday shopping rush now past, there might be time today to get that done.

Maybe that's what she needed to get out of her rut: sweep away the residue of the holidays and get the store back to normal. Prosper Hardware, which had been owned by her mother's family since the 1890s, was charming all year long thanks to its pressed-tin ceiling, spacious windows and polished oak floors, but its Christmas displays turned it into an almost-magical place.

Melinda wasn't quite ready to pack away her farm's holiday decorations, however. The wreaths on the house's front and back doors were so cheerful on these gloomy days, and the larger evergreen wreath on the side of the barn brought a welcome touch of color and whimsy to the white-frosted yard. The colored lights on the enclosed front porch welcomed her home, glowing merrily in the near-darkness that slipped over the barren fields by five in the afternoon.

Next weekend was about as long as she could tastefully leave it all up, she decided, as that was when volunteers would remove the metal snowflake and tree decorations that had glowed along Prosper's Main Street all holiday season.

"Well, I might sort out the storage room if it stays this slow," Bill said to no one in particular. "I don't have any lumber orders to cut. Melinda, do you think you can get all these decorations down yourself?"

"Sure can." She was startled out of her reverie by Bill's spot-on comments. Someone else was looking to make a clean sweep, too. "I planned to start on them this morning."

"Hey, I've got an idea." Bill gestured around the store, his third cookie in his hand. "Esther's the one who went crazy and over-decorated. Why don't we wait for her to come in and help us put all this stuff away?"

Esther Denner, Frank and Miriam's neighbor, had rushed over to help at the store after Uncle Frank's heart attack in June. Retired from the local school district, she had been eager to take on regular part-time hours ... and to make sure the place was decorated to the hilt for every occasion that came along.

"Esther's not coming in the rest of the week," Melinda reminded Bill. "Now that the holiday rush is over, Miriam's asked her to work only on Saturdays for a while."

"I could help," Uncle Frank quickly offered. "The empty decoration boxes are stacked upstairs. I can bring them down for you." Since his heart attack, Frank's role in the business had been diminished to chief coffee inspector and door greeter. He was always looking for ways to contribute that wouldn't alarm Aunt Miriam.

"I know, I know," he answered Melinda's cautious expression. "I'm not supposed to lift heavy stuff. What if I let you haul the boxes and I'll just man the ladder?"

"It's a deal," she said over her shoulder as she poured out a cup of Auggie's strong brew. He still had a key to Prosper Hardware, having worked there in high school forty years ago, and prided himself on beating her in the door.

Melinda had everything ready to open at eight, and it was only seven-thirty. Uncle Frank's assistance meant that the un-decorating would probably be complete by noon. If things were really slow today, there was that seed catalog stashed in her tote. It had appeared on New Year's Eve in the battered metal mailbox at the end of her snow-packed lane, its cheerful colors and inviting photos a much-needed promise that spring would come again.

What might she plant this year? As she sipped her coffee, she recalled how her garden looked last summer, the way Horace had planted it before he left for the nursing home: Orderly rows of lush plants, their stems loaded with crisp cucumbers and savory green beans. The sweet strawberries peeking out from their canopies of leaves. And oh, those juicy tomatoes, sliced fresh off the vine ...

She yawned, then stretched her stiff right shoulder. They hadn't received that much snow last night, only a few inches. How had she injured herself smoothing the packed-down paths to the barn and chicken house? There were months of shoveling still to come. She'd better work on her form.

A relaxed silence settled over the store as the men sipped their brew. Bill's cobbled-together audio system was mercifully silent, no longer shuffling its digital decks of modern holiday carols and Christmas classics. Other than the sleepy *tick, tick, tick* of the round clock hanging over the store's refrigerated case, the only sound was the rumble of Bill munching his cookie.

Jerry was checking his phone, intently scrolling through his messages. Uncle Frank had his hands behind his head, staring at the Christmas tree. Melinda wasn't sure if he was simply enjoying its glow for a few more minutes or mulling the fastest way to dissect it.

Auggie had his feet stretched out, a crust of dirty snow still stuck to the bottom of his work boots. He was unusually quiet this morning. But the co-op had been closed for two days due to the New Year's holiday, leaving him without any fresh gossip to share.

Melinda wondered how Auggie was getting along with his once-estranged son and the granddaughter he barely knew, but wasn't about to ask.

Evan and Chloe's sudden arrival in Prosper just a month ago had triggered a rush of emotions for Auggie and then, just days before Christmas, a tentative reunion. And while he beamed when he shared the cute things little Chloe did or said, Evan was rarely mentioned.

She moved on to study George. Again today, he'd forgotten to remove his wool cap, the one with the ear flaps and the fuzzy lining. It was pulled low over his wrinkled brow, and his coffee cup tipped dangerously to the side. Thankfully, it was empty.

Jerry looked up from his phone, his gaze landing on George, and his shoulders began to shake with suppressed laughter. He glanced at Melinda, and soon she was giggling.

George's nose twitched. "What's so funny?" he muttered, then quickly sat up straighter.

"You, George." Jerry snickered. "Naptime already?"

"Well, I don't know about you young people," George adjusted his cardigan again, "but I've been up for three hours already. Decades of milking cows will do that to you. Mary and I moved to town years ago, but I just can't break the habit, I guess."

"So, I've been wondering," Melinda began, "what happens around Prosper this time of year?"

"Not a darn thing," Jerry answered, his attention already back on his phone. "People will head to Swanton when there's a basketball game at the high school. I'm sure the Methodist church is having their oyster soup and chili supper."

"That sounds fun." Melinda brightened. "When's that?"

"Dunno." Jerry shrugged. "Don't think they've decided yet. It's usually in February."

Auggie noticed her disappointment. "You might want to take up some sort of project. Do you knit? Like to put puzzles together? If you don't have a hobby, now's the time to get one. You'll lose your mind if you don't."

"Well, I like to sew. It's been a while, though. Maybe I need to get my machine out and make ... something. I love to read, too, I guess I can load up on books at the library."

"Nancy's got a shipment coming in next week," Jerry said.

Melinda glanced at the calendar again. The promise of new books, as well as an excuse to chat with Nancy, was indeed something to look forward to.

George lifted his coffee mug and shrugged out a fake shiver. "Melinda, I don't envy you one bit. By the time you keep those critters fed and that barn clean, and snow paths cleared from the house to the buildings and back, you'll be glad to just put your feet up. I sure miss the farm, but I don't miss breaking ice in a water trough when it's thirty below."

Melinda felt her stomach drop. The winter had been pleasant so far, with only a few rounds of measurable snow, but that was sure to change. She reminded herself that she was as prepared as she could be, right down to the axe that waited in the barn's grain room for the very trouble George just described.

"Oh, come on, now." Auggie waved away George's comments. "Thirty below? It's been years since it's been that cold around here. Don't listen to George. You're going to be just fine out there, even though we're heading into the toughest time of the year and you are, well, by yourself ..." his voice trailed off.

"Do you mean, *alone*?" She smiled knowingly. "I'm hardly that. There's a dozen sheep already, and several lambs on the way. I have eight chickens, two cats and, of course, there's Hobo. Ed and Mabel are just up the road. Angie and Nathan, too. John Olson and his family aren't much farther away. I'm less than ten miles from my parents' in Swanton, and my dad's eager to help whenever he can."

George seemed to consider something, then spoke anyway. "Ten miles is a long way in a whiteout."

She knew George was right, but tried to push that thought away. "Besides, you all know the deal I made with Horace. If I can make it through the next few months, he'll sell me the acreage come spring."

"What's he want for it?" Auggie jumped in, a shrewd glint in his eyes.

Melinda gave an exasperated sigh. "You know I'm not going to tell you. So quit trying to get it out of me. You'd have it spread all over the county by tomorrow."

Auggie laughed. Melinda knew him well, and he didn't mind. And thanks to the loan officer at the bank over in Swanton, she also knew Horace's price was only half of the acreage's market value. The kind of bargain Auggie wouldn't be able to keep to himself.

"Kevin and Ada and Horace and I are all on the same page," she continued. "Horace just wants me to be totally sure

I'm making the right decision before I set up my loan and sign those papers."

Ada Arndt was Horace Schermann's youngest sister. Kevin, Ada's son, was especially close to his ninety-year-old uncle, and had helped Horace find a renter so he could join his brother, Wilbur, at a nursing home last summer. Melinda had spotted the "for rent" sign the very day Aunt Miriam offered her a job at Prosper Hardware, and everything had fallen into place.

"You know," Melinda looked for a chance to change the conversation, "I wonder where Doc is this morning? He rarely misses."

"Must have had an early farm call." George took the bait. "Doc's another person I don't envy. Up all hours of the night, driving these snow-packed gravel roads. Good thing he's now got Karen to help him out."

Doc had been Prosper's only veterinarian for several years before he brought Karen Porter on as his partner. Karen, who was only a few years younger than Melinda, had become one of her closest friends. Both women were single, and new to the community.

They'd planned a low-key New Year's Eve celebration at Karen's house in town, complete with a few movies and some wine, but Karen caught a nasty cold at Christmas. Instead, Melinda had dinner with her parents and then fell asleep on her couch before eleven.

"Well, it's about time to open." Bill lazily rose from his chair. He clicked the deadbolt to the side and flipped the sign hanging in the door's window. "Doesn't look like there'll be a stampede this morning. Hey Frank, do you know if Miriam ordered more rock salt?" He eyed a pallet in front of the register. "That blue-crystal stuff is selling far better than I expected it to, given the higher price."

"I'll check with her when I get home." Frank deposited his empty coffee cup on the sideboard. "I know there's more of that garden-variety brand in the back if we run short. Depends on what kind of weather's coming our way."

Everyone stared at Auggie, who operated a reporting station for the National Weather Service in the co-op's main tower.

"Looks pretty calm for the next week or so." There was a hint of disappointment in his voice. Auggie's obsession with the weather was well-known by all his friends and customers. "I'll be sure to spread the word if that's going to change."

The morning was quiet, as expected, and only four customers came in. Frank was a great help, and explained how to pack all the decorations away so they'd be easy to organize the next holiday season. Melinda found herself breaking a much-needed sweat, and was glad to pause her trips upstairs long enough to ring up purchases. She was carefully lifting the vintage garland from the front of the oak showcase when her phone began to beep.

"Hey, Karen. How are you feeling? I've been meaning to call you, to see if you wanted to do lunch this week."

In Prosper, which had barely two hundred residents and only one eating establishment, "doing lunch" meant either a round of burgers and fries at the Watering Hole, or meeting in the break room at the vet clinic or Prosper Hardware to reheat leftovers.

"Well, it's been a tough morning." Karen sighed. "I wish I could do lunch today, but we're swamped with some unexpected patients. Do you think you could swing by here during your break, though? Doc and I could use your help with something."

"Oh, sure thing." Melinda had been pleasantly surprised at how her marketing skills continued to be useful, both for a corporate client in the Twin Cities as well as small projects around Prosper. A new creative project would be just the thing to help these dreary winter days fly by.

She wanted to hear the details, but the cheerful bell above the front door signaled another customer's arrival. "Sorry, Karen, I've got to go. But I'll come by the clinic at noon."

* 2 *

Prosper Veterinary Services seemed quieter than usual, at least from the outside. Melinda recognized Doc's and Karen's gravel-blasted work trucks behind the one-story building, which was clad in dark green siding with crisp white trim. But the small barn at the back of the lot was dark. No vehicles were parked in the diagonal spaces along the corner's curbs.

Her curiosity grew as she stomped the slush off her shoes in the clinic's empty vestibule, whose plain double doors were less concerned with offering a gracious welcome and more focused on preventing wild-eyed patients from escaping.

Based on the tension in Karen's voice, Melinda expected to find the waiting room packed with people gripping the leashes of nervous dogs o balancing cat carriers in their laps. But the lobby was vacant and silent, and no one was behind the front counter. A radio played softly in the background, its easy-listening station trying to counteract the medicinal smell that often put the clinic's furry patients on edge.

Melinda had removed her gloves and unwound her scarf by the time she spotted Karen hurrying down the hall. With her long blonde hair and petite frame, she didn't look like someone who could shoulder medical gear across a pasture or wrangle a sick horse or bull. But in the five months since she arrived in Prosper, Karen had silenced many of the naysaying farmers shocked by Doc's choice of a business partner.

"Hey, are you getting rid of your cold?" Melinda gave her friend a warm smile as she shrugged out of her coat.

Karen's nose and cheeks were red, and her eyes were puffy. She absentmindedly rubbed her cheek.

"Oh, sure, it's nearly gone. I'm feeling better but, oh, Melinda, we had a bad case this morning. I just ... I just can't believe it." Tears sprang into Karen's blue eyes and she reached in the pocket of her scrubs for a tissue.

Melinda's pulse picked up as she took in her friend's fresh tears and the too-silent clinic.

"Doc didn't show at the store this morning. We were wondering where he was." A terrible thought popped into her mind. "Doc's OK, isn't he?"

"Yeah, well, he will be, eventually. Right now, he's furious and upset. We're both so upset about this."

Karen motioned for Melinda to follow her down the hall, toward the exam rooms. "That's why I had to call you. I think we need a big favor."

"Whatever it is, just ask." Melinda had turned to Doc and Karen several times for advice on how to care for her sheep and chickens, and Karen had good-naturedly taken on the challenge of neutering and vaccinating Sunny and Stormy, who were still skittish around anyone but Melinda. She saw herself as deeply in Doc and Karen's debt.

"I'll do what I can. I thought maybe this was some marketing thing or something, but ..."

"How do you feel about fostering?" Karen blurted out as they paused before a closed door.

"I guess I've never thought about it. What ..."

Karen peeked through the steel door's small window, her chin trembling. "I'm sorry, I'm trying to hold it together, but I just can't. I found some kittens on the front step this morning. In this terrible cold and snow! I hurried them inside and called Doc. We got out the heating pads, tried to warm them up. They're very sick, Melinda. Their little eyes are crusted shut, they can barely breathe."

Melinda was so stunned, she couldn't speak.

"Come on, I'll show you." Karen opened the door to the exam room, where Doc hovered over a metal table piled with wadded towels. The bright overhead lights picked out the gray flecks in his sandy-brown hair and threw shadows over his sun-weathered face. Even from the doorway, Melinda could see his mouth set in a hard line and feel his outrage.

Doc was angry, but he had a careful touch as he massaged something wrapped in a towel. He didn't look up.

"What happened?" Melinda whispered.

"There's three of them." He reached for a cotton ball and dipped it in a shallow dish at his elbow. "Or at least, we had three an hour ago."

Melinda heard a soft "mew" somewhere behind Doc's arm, then a faint, answering cry from under one of the other towels. The third bundle, set apart on the corner of the table, remained silent.

"I can't believe people somedays," he said through gritted teeth. "Disgusting. Careless. Like life doesn't matter. Who would do such a thing? I never thought I needed to put up cameras out front, but maybe I should."

"Maybe they just wandered off?" Melinda suggested, but she instantly knew it wasn't true. "If they snuck out somehow, got away ..."

Doc just looked down and turned his bundle slightly to the side, his other hand still in motion.

"They were in a cardboard box," Karen whispered as she placed a stack of clean towels on the exam table. "The top was taped shut. A little air hole punched in one side."

Melinda gasped. "You mean ..."

"Yep. Dumped." Doc spat out the words. "Stuffed in a box and left out there on the step. Who knows how long? They were barely breathing, the snot on their little faces was frozen into their fur. The smallest one, we cleared his mouth and nose and got some air in him, but ..." Doc's gaze briefly flicked toward the silent bundle.

"We've run some tests." Karen picked up another towel, which began moving slightly, and cradled it to her chest.

"They have a severe respiratory infection. We can't keep them here at the clinic. It's too dangerous for our other patients."

Doc gently set his bundle aside and reached for the one in Karen's arms. Melinda saw the fuzzy tip of miniature black ear against the edge of the white towel.

"I know Stormy and Sunny don't come inside your house," he said, a pleading tone in his voice. "And your guys are healthy, unlike the cats that come through our clinic. It's a lot to ask, but I don't know what else to do. My son's allergic to cats."

"And Pumpkin would fuss over them so much they'd never get any peace." Karen tried for a rueful smile. Her collie instinctively herded any critter she met. "There's only two shelters within forty miles of here. They're overflowing, as you can imagine, and their quarantine wards are full."

"I already called," Doc said grimly. "Both directors begged me to not bring these kittens to them. I think you can read between the lines there."

He rolled back the corner of the towel, and two crusted, scared eyes peeked out at Melinda. The tiny kitten was a calico, with blotches of black and orange tabby on white, including a jaunty dark patch over the right side of her face. The baby was sure to have a long coat, given the way her thick fur stood out in all directions.

Melinda gasped in awe, but not because of the kitten's beautiful markings. Her fur was damp, thanks to Doc's efforts to clean her eyes and nose, and Melinda could easily make out the delicate lines of the baby's face. Under all that soft hair, the kitten was painfully thin.

"This one's a girl, being a calico, but I think the other one is, too." He unwrapped the second bundle. Melinda leaned in closer and saw a frail kitten with similar symptoms and more long hair, but this one had a brown-tabby pattern and tiny white paws.

"They're maybe five, six weeks old." Karen picked up the brown kitten and reached for a fresh towel. "They ought to be twice this size. But their sense of smell isn't good enough to encourage strong appetites, and they're so thin." She shook her head and tentatively offered the kitten to Melinda.

"What would I have to do?" Her hands trembled as she reached for the baby and its towel. The brown kitten was so light in her arms, its miniature paws so delicate.

"They'll need quite a bit of care." Doc regained some of his composure as he turned to the tasks that were needed. "First, their eyes will need to be washed twice a day, and there's a salve to put in them. Wipe their noses in the morning, at night, and when you get home from work. There's medicine to give them, too. I can mix it into a liquid that you syringe into their mouths. Like Karen said, they obviously haven't had enough to eat. We've got a high-calorie formula for you to start them on, the bottles and everything. Most of all, we need to keep them warm and keep them together, somewhere quiet they can rest."

"Will they even ... will they make it?" Melinda had to know what she was up against.

"They can." Doc nodded cautiously. "But the odds are against them. The next few days will be critical."

She looked down at the frail brown kitten in her arms, the baby's watery eyes already focused on her face. The calico that Doc still held seemed too tired to lift her head, but she purred when he petted her back with a gentle finger.

Melinda couldn't bear to study the third bundle, which Karen reverently lifted from the table before starting for the exam room's door, tears rolling down her face.

These little ones were so frail, but Melinda could sense their determination to survive. "Show me what I need to do."

Doc gave her an encouraging nod. "I'll get everything together, have it ready this afternoon. You're off at four, right? Let your car heater run a bit before you come by. We've got a spare carrier, I'll heat up some clean towels when you get here. I can't thank you enough, Melinda. No matter what happens, they get a chance because of you."

Karen returned, washed her hands and wiped her face. Doc left for a farm call, and Melinda helped Karen settle the kittens in a large crate. With their immediate needs met, the little girls curled up in a nest of fresh towels and fell asleep.

"I'll keep them in here until you get off work." Karen carefully covered most of the kennel with a soft blanket. "You don't know how relieved I am that you can take them. It's the only way. Doc rarely swears, but you should have heard him when he ran in here this morning." She reached for a notepad and started list of all the supplies that would go home with Melinda and the kittens. "It's been a few months since we've lost a patient, and it's always so hard. But that little boy kitten, he was just so sick ..." Karen's voice trailed off, thick with more tears.

"I've never seen Doc look like that." Melinda was unable to resist one more peek at the kittens before she and Karen left the room, pulling the door tightly closed. "I don't think he's a violent man, but maybe it's just as well you don't know who abandoned them."

She slowly retraced her steps to Prosper Hardware, her knit cap pulled low and her parka hood gathered tight against the rough northwest wind.

It was a bitter, gloomy day, but the walk was only two blocks and she needed the time to think. She was excited, and sad, and more than a little afraid.

What had she just agreed to? Could she save the kittens, with Doc and Karen's help? If the babies didn't make it ...

Too quickly, she was back at the emergency veterinary clinic in Minneapolis, holding an exhausted Oreo in her arms as the technician gently administered that last, final injection. Oreo hadn't been seriously ill even once in the six short years of his life, until the day she came home and found him having a seizure on the kitchen floor.

His prognosis was dire from the start, and there was nothing she could have done to save him. But these two little ones might have a chance, and she was determined to see they got one. Her mind swirled with all of Doc's instructions, the medicines and the formula and the bathing that was going to be an around-the-clock commitment.

"I just hope I can do it." She crossed Third Street and passed the post office, thankful she was only steps away from Prosper's Hardware's green awning, which would block the worst of the icy wind. "All I can do is try."

The helpless kittens consumed her thoughts all afternoon, despite a surprising rush of customers and the need to pack away the last of the store's Christmas decorations. Doc said the kittens needed to stay warm, and be somewhere quiet where they could rest. That would mean a place where Hobo couldn't disturb them.

The farmhouse's upstairs was surely too cold, despite her dogged efforts to shrink-wrap all the windows. Hobo loved to sleep on the crazy quilt in Horace's old bedroom downstairs, so the kittens couldn't roam around in there, either. But the adjacent half bath would be perfect. It had a generous floor vent, added when the bedroom's original closet was remodeled into a bathroom a few years ago. The tiny space had no windows to let in drafts. And if the kittens strayed from their nest, they couldn't get too far.

Melinda thought wistfully of Oreo's soft bed and the colorful toys she had donated to a shelter soon after he passed away. She didn't have much to offer the tiny kittens but a stack of clean towels. A plastic tote or a cardboard box, not unlike the one they arrived in at the clinic, would have to do. She braced herself for a raucous ride home, remembering the stressful November morning when she escorted Sunny and Stormy to what was surely their first-ever trip to a veterinarian. But Karen said the kittens would spend most of their time sleeping, even in the car.

"Don't expect them to have too much to say," she cautioned Melinda that afternoon as she added a heating pad, a low-sided plastic pan and bag of litter to the box of supplies on the clinic's counter. "Just try to keep their eyes and noses clear and encourage them to take a little formula. I've mixed a liquid vitamin for them, too."

One of the kittens let out a cautious "mew" when Melinda stepped out of the clinic's vestibule with the small carrier in her arms, the cold trying to slip behind the blanket wrapped around the crate and the warmed towels lining its interior. With the car's heater humming on high, she headed west out of town for the six-mile drive to the acreage.

"It's going to be OK now," she cooed to the kittens as she turned south off the blacktop, the gravel road's coating of snow thankfully muffling the road rock's usual rattle under the tires.

As Karen predicted, the crate had been silent so far. "We're almost there. Only two more miles, then over the bridge at the creek and then we'll be home."

Even on this gray January day, when the dreary sky was only a few shades darker than the dull snow that blanketed the empty pastures and fields, the charming farmhouse cheerfully beckoned from up the lane.

White clapboard siding rose up to meet the deep gables of the roof, which was wrapped in gray-green shingles. Gray trim outlined the house's generous windows, including a picture window with a leaded-glass top that gazed east toward the rolling fields beyond the gravel road. A wall of windows marked the enclosed front porch, an automatic timer ensuring the still-cheerful Christmas lights glowed merrily in time for Melinda's return each afternoon.

The red barn, trimmed in white, stood tall and proud just across the driveway from the house, and the matching machine shed and chicken coop rested beyond the garage, where the lawn met the windbreak. The rows of hardwood and evergreen trees continued around the northwest corner of the acreage and marched on to the east, sheltering the dormant garden and the north side of the house and yard.

Some days, she still couldn't believe this sweet place was her home. Even with the limbs of its oak and maple trees bared to winter's winds and the once-lush grass covered with snow, this little farm was as lovely as that day in June when she first saw it.

The acreage had been so charming that Melinda, a small-town girl who'd lived in the city for nearly twenty years, had barely blinked at the list of chores and responsibilities that came with the month-to-month lease she signed.

As she carefully turned up the gravel lane, fitting the car into the tire tracks ironed in the snow, Melinda wondered about the feeble kittens' first home. Did they even know what it was like to live indoors with people?

"Just wait until you see this place." She glanced in the rearview mirror, to where the kittens were still silent in the backseat. "It's amazing. There's all this wide oak woodwork, and built-in bookcases and a fancy buffet with glass doors, and a fireplace, too." Whatever was she doing? She didn't have to sell these kittens on the farmhouse. A warm box was all they required. That, and lots of love and care.

"Anyway, you'll see all that later, when you are feeling better. And I promise that you don't have to meet the barn kitties, Sunny and Stormy. But there's someone very special that I'm sure you'll get to know."

As the car pulled in by the garage, Hobo dashed out the doggie door at the top of the house's back steps. A second entrance inside gave him access between the enclosed back porch and the kitchen. His shaggy brown coat and white paws looked remarkably clean, which told Melinda he'd spent most of the day curled up on Horace's bed, rather than running around in the windbreak. The white tip of his tail waved in greeting as he hurried past the picnic table, which rested under the oak tree between the house and the garage.

"And here he is now," Melinda told the kittens as she waved to Hobo, who waited until the car was in park before running around to her side of the vehicle.

"Hobo!" She slipped out and shut the door quickly, trying to keep the kittens warm. "You'll never believe who I found in town today! Two more kitties! Let's get inside and get their new nest ready before we get them out of the car, OK?"

Hobo followed along as she searched for a plastic tote and put itin the small downstairs bathroom, then returned to the car for the litter pan and other supplies. Once the small bin was stacked with towels and the heating pad settled inside, she hurried to retrieve the kittens. Hobo let out one excited bark when she returned to the kitchen, then sniffed the bundled carrier and gave her a questioning look.

With the kittens settled in their nest and the bathroom door firmly closed against Hobo's curiosity, Melinda changed into her chore clothes and started her evening rounds.

"There's some new kids in town," she told Sunny and Stormy as they circled their dishes in the barn's grain room, eager to enjoy the reheated chicken gravy that Melinda poured over their usual kibble. "When it got colder, I was disappointed that you two refused to come into the house like Hobo did. But it all worked out, didn't it? You've got your heat lamp in the cubbyhole under the haymow stairs, and you're safe out here. And these little kittens will get a chance."

The sheep were lined up at their troughs on the other side of the aisle's fence, bellowing their impatience. Annie, the most demanding of the flock, glared at Melinda through the grain room's open door, jealous of Sunny and Stormy getting their supper first.

"Yes, Annie, I know," Melinda called out, waving at the sheep. "Just a minute, OK?"

She sat on the upturned wooden crate in the corner of the grain room, and Sunny's fuzzy orange face soon appeared at her knee. In a second he was in her lap, purring and requesting a tummy massage. Stormy, always the more-cautious of the two, was content to rub his gray-tabby back against the leg of her insulated coveralls. Despite their love of mysterious, cobwebbed corners and rolling in the dirt, both cats were always immaculately clean. Even this time of year, Stormy's white chest and paws were as bright as fresh snow.

"Do you remember what it's like to be so small, like the little kittens in the house?" she asked the cats. "I wonder where you two came from, what your life was like before you showed up here in Horace's barn. And then Horace joined his brother at the nursing home before you really got to know him, and then this crazy lady from the city showed up, and you didn't know what to think."

Melinda laughed, remembering all the times she had crouched, motionless, near the skeptical cats with a spoonful of chicken baby food in her hand, trying to gain their trust.

"My two boys," she whispered, holding Sunny closer. "You don't know how excited I was to discover you were here. You may not be house kitties, but you are still special."

Hobo wasn't in the yard when she left the barn, and she had to make the trek to the chicken coop alone. He wasn't waiting on the back porch when she clomped in the door, her boots caked with dirty slush. She scrubbed her hands at the kitchen sink, more vigorously than usual, then turned into the dining room and then the living room. He wasn't sprawled out on the floral rug in front of the fireplace, or lounging against either of its flanking bookcases. She didn't see him curled up on the bed in Horace's old room, and the door to the stairwell was closed.

"Hobo?" Where could he be? She entered the bedroom and walked around the iron bedstead to find him, nose on paws, lounging in front of the closed-off bathroom. A warm light spilled through the gap between the door and the floor, but there was no sound from inside. He simply wagged his tail in greeting, unwilling to leave his post.

"Yes, the babies are inside." She crouched down to stoke his fur. "Are you guarding them for me? Thank you. I need to get in there and help them, OK?"

She filled a small plastic box with all the kittens' food and medicine, then edged around Hobo to enter the bathroom. At first, there was only silence. Her heart dropped, remembering the motionless bundle on the clinic's exam table. And then, there came a weak wail from inside the tote, followed by a second. She let out a big sigh of relief.

"Scared me there for a minute, babies." She peeked inside the open tote and gently pushed back the layers of towels. "Let's get you cleaned up and try to eat some supper."

Both kittens gazed up at her with wonder, or at least, they tried to. Their eyes were partially closed, their red, swollen eyelids startling in the bright light of the bathroom.

Karen had wiped the kittens' faces a few hours ago, but both had fresh discharge around their eyes and nose. Just as Melinda gingerly lifted the brown kitten from the nest, the baby sneezed out an alarming amount of greenish discharge. Then she howled and flung her tiny white paws about in protest of being separated from her sister.

"I know, it's scary. But you won't be apart for long." Melinda grimaced as she dabbed at the kitten's delicate features.

She had to get the liquid antibiotic in them first, then try for some formula before applying the eye salve. If the healing goop wasn't blocking the kittens' vision during all this activity, maybe they wouldn't be so anxious.

She certainly was. The babies were so small, and she could feel the brown kitten's spine as she settled the baby in her lap. "Tiny paws, tiny claws, tiny tails. Whatever am I going to do with the two of you? We've got a long road ahead of us. Some of this will seem icky, I know, but I'm just trying to help."

The calico, warily watching her sister's treatments, meowed in response and Melinda laughed softly. "That's right, you have to let me help you. Let's get started."

Following Karen's instructions, she rolled hand towels around one kitten and then the other, then wiped their faces with a warm, wet washcloth. The tip of the medicine dropper barely fit in their tiny mouths, but Melinda was proud that only a bit of the antibiotic ended up on the kittens' chins. Then she offered the doll-sized bottle of formula. Each took a bit of nourishment, but neither showed interest in the water dish or the litter box.

It seemed to take forever to open the miniature tube of eye salve, and there were squeals of disgust when the goop was applied. The calico ended up with a blob on the side of her face, but Melinda wiped it away and tried again.

It was a relief to snuggle the kittens back in their nest. She checked the heating pad, washed her hands, and slipped out of the cozy bathroom.

After she ate her own meal, packed her lunch for the next day and cleaned up the kitchen, she settled on her elegant beige sofa with a triumphant sigh. With its cushions protected by a tucked-in fleece blanket and the curved back piled with additional cozy throws, the modern couch no longer seemed out of place in this slightly scruffy farmhouse.

She flipped on the television and her reading lamp, reached for a blanket, then eagerly opened the seed catalog she'd forgotten about that afternoon as her mind focused on the unexpected responsibility that had come her way.

"Well, Auggie said I needed to get a hobby," she reminded herself as she flipped through the first few pages. "Somehow, I don't think things will be dull around here now. And maybe I can get Mom to show me how to knit this winter, too." Diane had gifted her family members with hand-knitted scarves for Christmas, and even created two extras for Susan and Cassie, Melinda's longtime friends from Minneapolis.

Next Christmas, she was determined to make her own handmade gifts. She'd meant to this holiday season, but time got away from her and it never happened. Whatever this new year might bring, she was determined to slow down and enjoy it. And for the next hour or so, that meant dreaming of spring as she paged through the seed catalog.

Her first stop was the section where dozens of tomato varieties beckoned with their ruby-red fruits and lush green leaves. Melinda could almost feel the summer sun on her shoulders and the dirt on her hands, even though night had long since fallen and the garden slumbered under a blanket of snow. Next came the squash and melons. Horace had planted so many pumpkins in that far corner of the patch, and one wooden crate down in the root cellar held the promise of more pies than she could reasonably eat. But there'd been only one watermelon vine. She should do more this year. There was nothing more refreshing on a humid evening than a slice of watermelon, chilled in the refrigerator.

"Oh, the fridge." She grimaced as the antique appliance cycled on in the kitchen, its sound more a grumble than a hum. "I might have to replace it. I might have to replace the old stove, too. Well, I'll think about that later."

She turned to the next section and gazed at the perennial flowers. There were so many choices! She could plant more peonies, maybe soft pink ones that would be a pretty contrast to the established row of magenta blooms on the south side of the house. And more dahlias, and sunflowers for the birds ...

Her mind kept wandering to the kittens huddled in the bathroom. Should she check them again? Or did they just need to sleep? She would give them a look-over before bed and set an alarm for two in the morning, in case they needed anything.

It was a little lonely in the living room without Hobo taking up his half of the couch. He'd left his guard post long enough to eat supper, then returned to the floorboards outside the bathroom door. When the options for green beans and sweet corn couldn't hold enough of her attention, Melinda finally set the catalog aside and padded into the next room, reaching for an old blanket draped over the bed's iron footboard.

"Here, Hobo." She shaped the blanket into a nest next to him. "If you're going to stay on watch, you might as well be comfy." He turned her way, licked her hand, and shifted to rest his head on the blanket.

There in the bedroom, away from the chatter of the television, she could hear the whistle of the driving wind as it wrapped around this northwest corner of the house. Despite the furnace humming along in the basement, the oak floorboards were still chilly.

Tears welled up in her eyes as she thought of the helpless kittens and their now-lost brother. How many hours did they suffer in that cardboard box last night, out on the stoop of the vet clinic? Who would do such a thing?

She may never know. But it was an act of grace that the kittens found their way to Doc and Karen, and just in time. She looked at Hobo, at the way he watched the glowing gap under the bathroom door with such tenderness and concern.

He had arrived at the farm three years ago under mysterious circumstances, a puppy discovered by Horace and Wilbur under the lilac trees marking the front corner of the yard.

Hobo wasn't the first animal Melinda had loved that seemed to appear out of nowhere. She'd found Oreo as a hungry kitten hiding under the Dumpster behind her apartment building. Sunny and Stormy had turned up in Horace's barn only a few weeks before Melinda's arrival. And now, these two kittens.

"You know what it's like, don't you?" She put an arm around Hobo. "You were all alone and then Horace and Wilbur took you in, gave you a home. I don't know if these little ones will stay for long. We'll have to wait and see."

But in her heart, Melinda knew the decision had already been made.

* 3 *

She stumbled through the windbreak, wrapped in layers of thick clothing that hampered her movements but somehow wouldn't allow her to get warm. Her chore boots were missing, her bare feet raw and numb as she tripped over the twigs and tree limbs lurking under the dirt-crusted snow.

Tiny kittens were everywhere. Behind every tree, crouching in the skeleton-bare undergrowth that rattled in the howling wind. Hiding in the battered plastic carriers that appeared every time she turned around. As soon as she reached for a towel or blanket that might warm one baby, she would spot another kitten crying in distress just out of her reach. She couldn't move fast enough to gather them all. Despite their thin flanks, runny noses and crusted eyes, they vanished from the basket at her feet as soon as she placed them inside.

And that baby over there, the one beneath an ice-smothered patch of downed evergreen branches, was so very, very still. If only she could reach him in time ...

The alarm's *beep-beep-beep* startled her awake, her eyes needing a moment to adjust to the heavy darkness. Her nose was chilled, the hand that had worked out from under the thick comforter was clumsy as it fumbled to silence her phone. *It was only a dream*, she told herself, but the wail in the wind was certainly real.

She could hear it, even now, even though the farmhouse's storm windows were securely fastened and the inside wooden sashes wrapped with plastic. A mysterious chill whispered in her uncovered ear, reminding her it was impossible to keep out all the drafts on a frigid night like this one.

She knew exactly what time it was. Two in the morning, and time for her middle-of-the-night kitten check. Bracing herself for the chill of her bedroom, Melinda pushed the covers wide and rolled up and out, hurrying to shove her wool-socked feet into the slippers that waited on the rag rug next to the bed.

This house was a hundred years old, and while it was sturdy, she knew the walls were uninsulated. She warmed herself with the thought that someday, when she owned the place, maybe she could find the money to change that. Until then, she would know the winter wind's direction based on which of the farmhouse's rooms were the coldest. Tonight, it was blowing straight out of the north.

It was a cold, lonely time when nothing was stirring. Except for the mice that always seemed to find their way inside, wriggling and squeezing through any tiny gap they could find. Melinda cringed as she heard the faint staccato of miniature toenails hurrying down the hall, across the bare hardwood floors and away from her movements.

"Ugh, I need to get more traps." She pulled on her robe and entered the hall. But a few sneaky, creepy visitors would never keep her from her rounds. She didn't even bother to turn on the lights as she felt her way down the stairwell, another random draft brushing her arm as she turned past the window in the landing.

What had happened to the woman who arrived here only seven months ago, the one whose hands shook with disgust as she tracked a cheeky cricket around her bedroom in the middle of the night?

She'd become a seasoned veteran of the varmint wars, a fight that started soon after the first frost arrived in October and would drag on into spring, if not longer.

The traps lurking throughout the house and the basement were frequently set and reset, the jar of cheap peanut butter in the cabinet above the kitchen phone replenished with alarming speed. Sunny and Stormy, content with their generous rations of kibble and leftovers and known to hunt only for sport, had long ago tired of the gifts the mouse traps brought their way. Melinda now made her death marches to the windbreak, where she unceremoniously tossed the corpses into a sheltered spot just behind the largest oak on the edge of the treeline.

It occurred to her now, at this wee hour when everything was somehow startlingly clear, that maybe this new disposal method wasn't the best option. The dead mice, frozen but mostly intact, seemed to be disappearing from their burial grounds. Maybe they were just being smothered by the marginal rounds of snow that fell every few days. Or was something else going on? Was something …

There was a snuffle at the bottom of the stairs, the pitter-patter of larger paws on the other side of the closed door. Hobo had heard Melinda's descent, and was waiting for her in the much-warmer living room.

She reached down to rub his ears. "How are our little patients tonight? I hope you're sleeping on your cozy bed, Hobo, instead of the cold floor outside the bathroom door. The danger is past, you know."

For three days and nights, she had fussed over the kittens and prayed for their recovery. They were checked on every four to five hours without fail, her neighbor Mabel Bauer taking the midday shift when Melinda was at work.

"Whatever would I do without Mabel?" she asked Hobo as they turned through the living room into the downstairs bedroom. "I bet you love the chance to see your old friend every day."

Mabel and her husband, Ed, were Melinda's closest neighbors, living a half-mile north past the creek and just beyond the first crossroads between her farm and the county blacktop. Mabel was a childhood friend of Ada's, and Ed was a retired farmer with lots of time on his hands and a mind stuffed with useful information.

The kittens heard Melinda's approach and began to meow, high-pitched sounds that had shifted from weak to insistent in just the last day.

Their now-demanding calls told her all she needed to know: The babies had turned a significant corner and were gaining at last.

There had been a scary patch the other evening when the little calico's right eye had again swollen completely shut, and she refused the formula Melinda begged her to swallow.

Melinda had feared the worst and called Karen, who told her to up the kitten's medication. "Don't worry, she'll come around. She's got the will to live, they both do. I saw it in them the day they arrived."

The calico baby had bounced back quickly. Her color-blocked face popped out of the tote when Melinda eased open the door, and she gave Hobo a curious-yet-haughty stare.

"You'll have to live in here for a few more days, at least," Melinda told the kitten, who let out an indignant howl and launched her tiny paws against Melinda's fleece pants and began her usual climb. The brown kitten, her long tabby coat tousled from sleep, waited patiently for Melinda to scoop her up in her arms.

To Melinda's surprise and relief, the food dish was half empty, the mix of canned food and warm water offered at bedtime apparently sampled and found to be agreeable. The litter box had also seen more traffic.

"Are you starting to eat on your own?" she asked the brown kitten, who flexed her little white paws and began to purr. "Oh babies, good job!"

Both kittens' eyelids were still swollen, but the pus was gone and their noses were nearly clear. Melinda ran warm water over a clean washcloth, balancing the brown kitten in one arm while the calico tried for another pant-leg ascent, then settled on the floor next to the heat vent and gathered both babies in her lap.

They protested at the wet warmth rubbed over their faces, another sign of recovery, and complained when Melinda expertly applied the eye slave. Maybe, in a few days, they'd be well enough meet Hobo and even start to play and pounce. She should find them some toys. There was a sack of colorful stuffed mice under the kitchen sink. Sunny and Stormy had rejected two of those unnatural things with barely a curious sniff. But wasn't it a six pack? That would mean four were left, two per kitten ...

Melinda woke with a start, disoriented. Her back was stiff, her right arm pinched just above the elbow where it was lodged against the toilet. The kittens were asleep, nested in the towel in her lap. What time was it? There was no clock in the bathroom. She gathered up the kittens, trying not to shuffle them awake as she tucked them into their tote, then struggled to her feet.

Horace's bedroom was still blanketed in inky darkness, but that wasn't very reassuring this time of year. Hobo, who had returned to his place on the bed, raised his head and gave Melinda a questioning look as she raced past him into the living room.

The round-faced antique clock on the mantel pointed its hands at three and six. For one terrible second, Melinda thought it was six-fifteen. Then she blinked and looked closer, relieved to see it was only three-thirty. A dash up the stairwell, and she'd gain a few more hours of sleep before morning chores.

Another draft brushed her cheek, forcing her to glance around the shadowy living room. She looked over at the picture window, cloaked in its lightweight cotton curtains, then at the thick fleece throws folded on the back of the couch. Somewhere, in the back of her sleepy mind, a plan was forming. It was still there, and sharply in focus, when she arrived at Prosper Hardware the next morning.

"Fleece curtains!" she announced to the men gathered around the coffee pot. "That's what I need! That'll stop the drafts. And it comes in so many colors, you know, tan and soft green and a pretty cream." Melinda waved the window dimensions out with her hands while she waited for Auggie to top off his mug at the sideboard.

"Sounds like a big project." George eyed her with concern. "How many nights in a row have you been up with those kittens?"

"Oh, it's nothing." She shrugged and added a generous pour of peppermint-mocha powdered creamer to her coffee. It was the one holiday leftover still hanging on, and she loved its rich flavor. The Christmas cookies were gone, at last.

After the men left the other morning, she sneaked out to the gravel parking lot behind the store and, with only a twinge of guilt, dumped the last few behind the oak tree along the alley. Prosper's raccoon population would enjoy the treats, and since the vintage pop machine under the tree was out of service until spring, no human residents were likely to discover her crime.

"I'll get out my sewing machine and have them done in no time," Melinda hurried on, trying to contain her excitement. "I'm going over to Swanton tonight to have dinner with my parents, I'll stock up on fleece then. I'm thinking a nice medium gray in the living room, you know, warm-toned and pretty. It'll be a perfect complement to the blue-gray color I painted in there last summer."

Jerry nodded, trying to appear interested in her decorating plans. Auggie just gave her a level stare over the top of his glasses, then turned to Doc. "Well, anyway, how have the gravel roads been lately? Bet they're drifting some with this wind. You know, I think we're due for a heavier round of snow in a few days."

Melinda's mind was still on the curtains as she straightened the store's single aisle of groceries and household items later that morning. She yawned as she lined up the boxes of cereal. How was it only ten? She had a long day ahead of her. The coffee group's members had already scattered and the store's early-morning rush was over. Prosper Hardware was blissfully quiet, at last.

Bill was at work on a lumber order, the soft hum of the table saw in the wood shop making her long for a quick nap.

"Only a few more nights of this two a.m. feeding stuff," she reminded herself as the canned soup fell back into its usual neat rows. "The kittens are going to make it, and that's what matters."

She had moved on to the refrigerated case and was counting its selection of milk and eggs when the bell tinkled above the front door. It was Evan Kleinsbach, Auggie's son, with little Chloe in tow. They had shopped at Prosper Hardware a few times since Christmas, and the other day Evan had loaded chicken feed into Melinda's car at the co-op, but there hadn't been a chance to talk.

But then, questions such as "are you looking for a better job?" and "is your dad still speaking to you?" would be awkward at best. As for how Chloe's mom, Carrie, was faring at the opiate rehabilitation center in Madison, Melinda wondered but didn't want to nose into his personal life.

Especially if anyone else might overhear. While most of Prosper's residents seemed kind and good-natured, she knew there were too many listening ears and prying eyes in a town this small. Her sudden arrival in June had fed the local gossip mill for weeks. Evan and Carrie were separated, and Melinda was single. She wouldn't be surprised if a few people had the two of them nearly walking down the aisle.

Evan was sort of handsome, she had to admit. And they had a few things in common. He was only a few years younger than her, and she understood how hard it could be to return home under trying circumstances. But beyond that, they couldn't have been more different. Evan was trying to care for a young daughter, navigate a tentative truce with his father, and cope with the breakdown of his marriage.

"Hey, Melinda." Evan offered a warm smile as he reached for a plastic shopping basket. There were flecks of gray in his brown hair and still a trace of worry in the lines around his kind brown eyes, but he was in much better spirits than the defeated man who arrived in Prosper just before Christmas.

"Hey, Evan, it's good to see you." For a moment, she cringed at how tired she must look, her hair in a clumsy low ponytail, a few swipes of mascara the only beauty routine she had time for that morning. Then she was annoyed with herself. Why did any of that matter?

She walked around to the main aisle and leaned down to speak to Chloe, whose dark curls were barely contained by a pink knit cap. "Hi, Chloe, how is Daisy?" The little girl's tortoiseshell cat was her best friend, one of the few parts of her young life that hadn't changed in the past few months.

Chloe's brown eyes lit up at the mention of her kitty. "Daisy loves all the toys she got for Christmas! Yesterday, she played with her purple ball for hours and hours."

Evan and Chloe were staying rent-free at a vacant family home east of town, thanks to the kindness of the cousin holding the property's deed. Santa, with the help of Melinda and her neighbors, had made sure they had a wonderful holiday, complete with a Christmas tree and decorations, as well as donations of clothes and toys.

"It's pretty quiet in here today." Evan glanced around the store. "I have to say, Chloe and I wanted to get out around people as much we wanted to check off our shopping list. I guess we're not used to being way out in the country, in that big old house. It's certainly different than Madison."

"Sorry, I'm afraid you're a bit late for socializing." Melinda had to laugh as Chloe, her wide eyes taking in the dizzying array of items packing the shelves at Prosper Hardware, ran off toward the clothing area and nearly disappeared inside a rack of sweatshirts. "The big rush ended only half an hour ago. Your dad says the last few days have been busy down at the co-op, too."

Evan flinched slightly, and Melinda wished she'd made no reference to Auggie. But then he shrugged. "Yeah, I guess it has been. You know, Chloe's been looking forward to coming in here for days." He watched his daughter with a mix of pride and something else Melinda decided was the near-constant exhaustion of being the only parent of a child so young. "This store carries a little bit of everything, which is sensory overload for a four-year-old."

"We try to keep everyone entertained. You know," Melinda thought of something, "Nancy's got a preschool story hour starting up later this week over at the library. Thursday afternoons, I think. Chloe might like that."

Evan looked relieved. "That's a great idea. She's not school age yet, of course, and she loves to stay with Grandma, but it's been hard for her these last few months." His shoulders dropped and he stuffed his hands into the pockets of his parka.

Melinda was running out of breezy things to say to fill yet another awkward silence. The lack of solid sleep the last few nights wasn't helping. And besides, Evan looked like he just needed a friend.

"I'll spare you the polite chatter about the weather and such," she finally said, lowering her voice, even though Chloe was out of earshot and there were no other customers in the store. "How are you doing? I mean, really doing? You've had a tough time of it."

"Oh, you mean that whole messed-up-life thing?" Evan's smile tried to return. "Well, I'll tell you: It's horrible. You're the first person in Prosper to just come right out and ask, instead of hemming and hawing and changing the subject. Thank you for that." He reached into his pocket for his shopping list.

"People around here seem to always be of two minds at once," she told him. "On one hand, they're infinitely curious about other people's personal lives. On the other, they want to avoid emotional messes like the plague. They mean well, but it makes it hard. Especially when ... I mean ..."

"Oh, like when your estranged wife is in rehab, and you've lost your home and your job?" Evan rolled his eyes but managed to laugh. "Or maybe, when you catch your Dad watching you carefully, as if he doesn't trust you to do things right, although all you're doing is loading feed into the back of someone's truck?"

Melinda laughed, too. Evan might be going through a hard time, but he wasn't afraid to see things for what they were. That took courage.

He ducked his head. "I'm sorry, I shouldn't complain about Dad. I have a lot to be grateful for. Chloe and I have a place to stay. She's been healthy, only had a short cold there right after Christmas. I have a little work, even though it's just part-time, and the unemployment money is still coming in for another month yet."

"I suppose I should say something super-positive. Like, 'it'll all get easier' or 'things will turn out just fine.' But how about I just say that I hope things get better?"

Chloe ran back to her father, neon-pink knit gloves clutched in her hand. "Pretty, Daddy!" She waved the pair around, her eyes shining. "Can I have them?"

Evan hesitated, then checked the price tag. "They aren't very warm, but they're only a buck. Sure, why not?" Chloe gave a happy squeal and dropped the knit gloves into her father's basket.

"Living on the edge," he told Melinda as Chloe hurried away to see what other wonders Prosper Hardware had to offer. "We'll be big spenders today, once we get what's on the rest of our list."

Another customer arrived, a woman looking for a replacement hinge for a kitchen cabinet door. With Bill busy in the back, Melinda walked her over to the fasteners aisle and searched for something that matched. By the time she returned to the counter, Evan and Chloe had their basket full.

"Thanks for telling me about the story hour," Evan said as she rang up their purchases.

"What a great idea. My mom can drop Chloe off, and I'll swing by the library and pick her up when I get off work. It'll do Chloe good to make some friends."

Melinda found herself thinking about Evan later that afternoon as she drove the ten miles from the farm into Swanton. It was the county seat, her childhood home and, with nearly ten thousand residents, a metropolis compared to little Prosper. Coming home had only strengthened her already-strong ties to her parents. She couldn't imagine how difficult things had been for Evan while he was away, and how tense they still were now he was back.

His mother had remained supportive of him over the years, despite his troubles, but Auggie's concern had long ago soured into frustration and distrust. Evan and Auggie's awkward truce was thanks mostly to Chloe's presence, but how long might it last?

She felt so blessed to have hear parents nearby, especially since her sister lived in Milwaukee and her younger brother was in Austin, Texas. For nearly twenty years, time with her parents had been limited to occasional weekends and special occasions. Now, she could eat dinner with them any time she wanted, or meet her mom for an impromptu lunch or a few hours of shopping.

Melinda offered a prayer of thanks as she turned into the parking lot of Swanton's lone superstore and parked next to her mom's car. Even though they'd seen each other just three days ago, Diane gave her daughter a big hug.

"Oh, honey, it's so good to see you." She pulled the hood of her parka up against the cold. "We're free to shop for at least an hour, since your dad's handling dinner. He's baking pork chops, and there's some new salad he wants to try."

Since his retirement from the local communications company a few years ago, Roger had decided to improve his cooking skills along with his golf game. Diane, a retired teacher, was always happy to let her husband take his turn at the stove.

"I want to stock up on some things while we're here." Diane reached in her purse and pulled out a list. "I heard we might get some decent snow in a few days. But first, let's get that fleece for your curtains project. I can't wait to see what you have in mind."

Diane wasn't the only person monitoring the forecast. The next morning, George pulled a carefully folded piece of paper from the front pocket of his overalls.

"Mary's got a list here, says we need to stock up. Melinda, you're not supposed to let me leave the store without all this stuff. Toilet paper, bread, a gallon of milk, and a dozen eggs."

"Shouldn't be a problem." She poured a cup of coffee and took a tentative sip. Not too bad. Auggie was late, so she'd made the first pot. "The truck came yesterday, we're fully stocked on groceries."

"Why does everyone want those four things when it snows?" Jerry asked as he added his coat to the hall tree. "Toilet paper, I get. That's something you never want to be out of. But the rest? These days, it would take a monster blizzard to trap people at home. Besides, we're only supposed to get four inches, tops."

"Just enough, I suppose, that you won't be able to get by with the county plows making only one pass through town," George said understandingly as he filled Jerry's mug. Prosper was so small that it didn't have a public works department, and had to rely on county crews to blade the snow from its streets. That cost money, of course.

"Well, I guess we're lucky that's it's been a quiet winter so far." Jerry consoled himself with one of the cornbread muffins Melinda had brought in. The jar of homemade strawberry-rhubarb jam that came with them seemed to raise his spirits. "And George, if you and Mary get stuck at home, I guess you'll at least be able to make French toast. But really, I'm not too worried about the forecast."

"I wouldn't be so sure about that."

Auggie paused for a dramatic moment to let his announcement sink in, then wiped his work boots on the rubber mat and went straight for the coffee without bothering to remove his coat. He was so preoccupied, Melinda wondered if he forgot he was wearing one.

"I was checking online this morning. That's why I'm late." Auggie's knack for predicting storms was known all over the county. And whether it was scientific expertise, intuition or simply luck, his predictions were correct about half the time. Just good enough for people to listen.

"I think this storm is going to be a bad one." He sounded cautious, but could hardly keep the grin off his face. "Far worse than what those TV people are saying right now."

"How bad?" Doc leaned forward in his chair. He spent many of his working hours traveling the gravel roads, and was almost as obsessed with the weather as Auggie.

"Several inches of snow, coming tomorrow." Auggie had at last remembered to remove his coat, and now peered into his coffee mug as if reading tea leaves in its bottom. Melinda smothered a laugh.

"I think it'll rain a bit first, just like they say, and quickly change over to snow." He turned serious. "But I think they're wrong on that 'couple inches' thing. There's too much moisture with this system and its still gathering strength out west. My projection is eight inches, or a few more. High winds, too."

Everyone looked at Melinda. "You ready for something like that?" Jerry's concern echoed the worry on the other guys' faces.

She was already thinking through her winter-storm checklist, the one she'd drawn up in November. Auggie had predicted a blizzard right before Christmas, and it never materialized. But that meant the odds might be in his favor this time. "I'm stocked up, mostly, but the kittens might need more medicine in a few days."

"I'll get that ready for you," Doc said. "I wanted to get Karen or myself out there to check on them, I don't want you bringing them outside and to town in this damp, but we'll wait on that. Sounds like they're doing great, anyway."

George nodded proudly. "I think you've got it all under control. You'll do just fine, then, whether we get four inches or six."

"Eight." Auggie pointed at his old friend for emphasis. "I said eight inches. At least."

* 4 *

Auggie's prediction spread through town that afternoon, the debate over its accuracy spurred by both the professional forecasters' opinions and the unusually mild temperatures. By the time Melinda left Prosper Hardware shortly after four, the consensus was that nothing other than a little rain or snow was on the way.

Sunny and Stormy also believed Auggie was bluffing. She discovered both cats sprawled out, without a care, on the picnic table when she arrived home from work. Hobo also seemed unconcerned. He dashed back and forth, frolicking in the last lumps of dirty snow that stubbornly clung to the grass between the house and the garage. A brilliant sunset capped off the calm day, and Melinda grew so warm during her storm preparations that she had to remove her knit chore cap.

She carried more firewood from the machine shed and stacked it in the back porch, then went to the barn to drop more bales of hay and straw through the haymow floor's trap door. Once those were neatly stacked in the aisle, she filled a row of clean chore buckets with fresh water in case the power went out and the well pump stopped working. Extra straw was fluffed in Stormy and Sunny's hideout under the haymow stairs, and a fresh layer of bedding added to the chicken coop. She even sprayed a bit of oil on the barn's and chicken house's door latches, in case they became coated with ice.

Shovels and bags of ice melt stood at attention just inside the back porch door. There was plenty of bottled water, and the cellar and kitchen were bursting with food. The closet in Horace's old bedroom held her stash of flashlights, lanterns, batteries and just about anything else she could possibly need. The idea of a big storm was almost starting to sound like fun.

A light mist began to fall the next morning as she drove into town, humming along to the radio. The fields were blanketed with fog, but the still-warm air made it feel more like early spring than winter.

"A snow day was always something to celebrate when we were kids," she mused as the co-op's storage tower appeared on the horizon. "If I can't get into town tomorrow, I'll have time to start on those fleece curtains. But the official forecast hasn't changed much. Auggie would hate to admit it, but there's always the chance he'll be wrong."

The man of the hour had yet to arrive at Prosper Hardware, so she set out the folding chairs and made the coffee. Jerry soon wandered in, then George.

"I can't believe I'm saying this," George said as he pulled off his coat, "but it's too warm and humid out there, for this this time of year, anyway. Rain in January? I don't know, but it feels like this storm could be a big one, given how my knees ache this morning."

They had just settled in with their coffee when there was an urgent pounding on the front door. The huddled-over stranger offered a friendly wave and pointed at the handle. Melinda glanced at the clock. Prosper Hardware didn't open for twenty minutes, but she felt bad leaving the guy standing out there like that. It was raining hard now, the gloomy skies turning a heavy shade of slate, and the store's dark-green awning offered little protection from the bracing wind.

She hesitated for only a moment, then slipped the deadbolt to the side. A rush of damp air, noticeably colder than an hour ago, blasted her face as she opened the door. "Can I help you?"

"I need ice melt and some batteries," the man gasped, pushing back the hood of his parka and wiping the cold rain out of his eyes. "Thanks for opening early. I live twelve miles out, and I want to get back home as soon as I can."

Her confusion must have been obvious, as the man gave her a surprised look.

"Haven't you heard?" He shook off his heavy gloves, which were soaked through. Water dripped out of his trimmed gray beard. "Weather service just updated their forecast. We're under a winter storm warning, starting at noon. Eight inches on the way."

"Oh, sorry, I didn't know." She was about to add that Auggie, unlike the professional forecasters, had predicted that very outcome the day before. But the urgency on the man's face told her he didn't have time to chat.

"We've got some ice melt right up front here, and batteries are in the second aisle. Anything else?"

The man paused for a moment. "I better get some milk and eggs."

George, trying to fight down his laughter, gestured at the refrigerator case and then the grocery aisle. "Bread's over there, too, while you're here."

Before Melinda could ring up the man's purchases and lock the door behind him, three people rushed in. Then two more customers, then five. The counter hadn't been cleaned, and she always checked the cash register's drawer each morning, just to make sure the tally Bill left on the notepad underneath was correct.

But never mind that now. The stack of plastic hand baskets was nearly empty, and oversized snowflakes suddenly appeared outside the plate-glass windows.

She had never been so glad to see Bill hurrying up from the back, still wearing his parka. "What's going on?" He shook out his soaked cap and looked around. "There's people parking in the back lot already."

"One guy wanted in, so I opened the door," she said in a low voice so Bill could hear her over the rising din in the store. "Then, a dozen more just came out of nowhere. Word now is eight inches of snow, just like Auggie predicted. I guess we're open early today."

The phone rang. A woman wondered if the store had flashlights in stock. When Melinda said there were a few left, the woman begged her to save one back and quickly hung up.

Before she could ask Bill to grab a flashlight, two men started to argue over the last bag of ice melt by the front counter. Bill quickly stepped between them.

"We've got more, don't worry. Pull around back after you pay. It's on a pallet right inside the door."

The next call was from Auggie. "I was right!" he hooted. "It's going to be worse than they said. Dan and I are swamped down here, I won't make it over there today."

Melinda could barely keep up with the checkout line, which buzzed with a mix of worry and excitement. Jerry folded the metal chairs against the wall and elbowed through the crowd to reach the counter. "I encouraged George to head home. Doc just called me, said he's working a round of farm calls before things get too bad. He's already told Karen to reschedule tomorrow's appointments. What can I do to help?"

"Check that grocery aisle for me, will you? Bill's parceling out ice melt and shovels. There's more bread and such in the storeroom, if you can bring some down. I'm afraid the milk and eggs in the cooler are all we've got, though."

Jerry ferried supplies for nearly an hour before a phone call sent him across the street to City Hall. Then Uncle Frank arrived. Melinda was surprised but relieved, as Bill was still busy in the back.

"I couldn't stay away." Frank's defensive tone told her he'd already been chastised by Miriam, who was down with the flu. "I knew it would be crazy in here, and it's only three blocks, you know. They're dismissing school at ten, so this rush isn't going to let up anytime soon."

"Well, if you're going to stay, we could use the help. But you let Bill handle the heavy stuff, OK? No lifting. Here, you take the register and I'll check the shelves."

The eggs were nearly gone, and only two cartons of milk remained. She counted four loaves of bread and a few random boxes of cereal. The soup had been raided as well. There were more non-perishable groceries in the upstairs storeroom, but when they ran out, that was it. The truck wouldn't come again for two days.

She was bringing down packages of toilet paper when the weather radio screeched on the counter. The storm alert had been upgraded to a blizzard warning, with gusts over 45 mph, whiteout conditions and up to a foot of snow. The flakes were now falling thick and fast, City Hall and the library erased into shadows as the wind whipped down Main Street.

The toilet paper packs were snatched from her arms before she could even get them on the shelf. She hurried behind the counter to sack purchases while Uncle Frank continued to ring up orders.

Bill came up from the back, clutching his phone. "Tony just texted everyone, said the roads are getting worse and we need to be ready to head out." Bill, like Doc, was a volunteer with Prosper's emergency medical department. "He said there's already a pileup on the state highway north of here. If any more calls come in, Prosper needs to take the lead."

"There goes our last gallon of milk," Uncle Frank sighed as one woman, bundled in heavy layers but wearing a triumphant smile, hurried for the door. "If this keeps up, they'll close the interstate up by Mason City. It's been years since they've had to shut those big gates."

Melinda was trying to mop up puddles of slush from inside the front door when Esther arrived.

"You are to get out of here, Melinda, and right now." Esther rubbed her ruddy cheeks. "Miriam just called me. She'd come herself if she wasn't so sick."

"Oh, Esther, thank you so much for coming!" Melinda hugged her friend, then hurried upstairs for her coat, hat and gloves. The driving snow stung her face as she staggered out Prosper Hardware's back door. Even here, in the relative shelter behind the two-story brick building, the wind was relentless. Her car was already covered in slushy snow with an underbelly of ice, and she rushed to clear the windows and get behind the wheel. She flipped on the lights and wiper blades, but left the radio off. All of her attention had to stay on the six long miles that stood between her and home.

As Prosper's buildings and trees fell away, the view out the windshield faded to white. It was as if all the color had been erased from the sky and fields, and the blacktop was now only two tire tracks of pale gray snaking down the snow-covered road. Melinda crawled along, trying to get her bearings in the changed landscape, straining to spot the junction with the state highway.

"I'll get home just fine. I just need to go slow, that's all." She hovered over the steering wheel as she drove straight into the furious storm. "Oh, but this is bad."

Beads of ice started to stick to the wiper blades, despite the roar of the defroster. A white cloud advanced in the other lane, and she slowed to a crawl and braced for the wave of snow thrown by the plow's blade.

The junction had to be just ahead, although she was going more by memory than what was visible out the windshield. She braked tentatively, a series of gentle movements, and slush flew out of the wheel wells as the tires rolled slower, then slower yet, and miraculously came to a halt only a few feet before the stop sign.

"OK, OK." She let out a shaky laugh. "That's good. That's half the battle right there."

The state road appeared to be deserted but she looked both ways several times, searching for lights or shapes that would signal another vehicle. She said a prayer and tapped the gas. The tires spun for a second, then the car lurched through the intersection.

"Only three miles, just three more miles," she said through gritted teeth. "Then I can turn south and have the wind behind me. I just have to make it to my corner."

Melinda drove this road every day, knew every house and field drive, but she couldn't see more than a few yards past the front of the car. She was grateful for the farms huddled on the north side of the road, as their windbreaks and buildings offered short-lived relief from the driving snow. After what seemed like an hour, she spotted what had to be Will and Helen Emmerson's farm on her left. Her corner was next, almost there ...

She leaned forward, watching for any sign the road was widening into a crossroads. All of the sudden, she saw it. She instinctively hit the brake, then realized her mistake. There was a split second of weightlessness that nearly made her heart stop, then the back of the car slid away and everything began to spin. She tried to cut the wheel, but it was too late.

Under the roar of the snow hammering the car, Melinda heard the slushy rumble made by her tires as they left the road's tracks. All she could think about, all she could pray for, was that she was alone. If another vehicle was coming ...

There was a loud, icy rattle and a jarring lurch, then the car stopped. She held her breath for a terrible moment, and braced for the impact of another vehicle slamming into her car. Nothing happened. Her windows showed only a swirl of white, but she hadn't felt the car drop into a ditch.

"Oh, thank you God," she gasped. "Where am I? I have to get out of the way."

The blinding snow cleared for a moment, and Melinda discovered she was just past the intersection, her car now facing back east toward town.

She tried for a little gas. The car jerked ahead, then bumped into the snow and ice piled up on the shoulder, a barrier that must have stopped her car from leaving the road. She moved into reverse, tried to straighten her wheels, and crept back to the corner. Her hands still shaking, she took a cautious tack to the right and turned south.

She wanted to stop, to pull over and collect herself, but had to press on. The gravel road was in worse shape than the blacktop, any tracks left by the snowplow already erased by the wind. She took a deep breath, and pushed the gas pedal down. If she lost her momentum, she'd get stuck.

She didn't dare stop at her mailbox. The car skidded slightly as she turned into the lane but she barely noticed, all her energy focused on the comforting shadows hinting that her barn, house and garage were just ahead. She rolled to a stop about ten feet from the garage door, but it was close enough.

Melinda didn't care that she'd have to shovel to get her car inside, that the blinding snow was going to make her evening chores incredibly difficult. She had made it home, and that was all that mattered.

"Oh, thank God." She put her forehead on the steering wheel for a moment after she cut the engine. A seal of ice cracked loose as she shoved the car door open, the insistent wind threatening to trap her inside. Hobo didn't meet her on the back porch, but she heard his toenails tapping across the hardwood floors as she came into the kitchen. He whimpered and barked, sniffing curiously at Melinda's snow-caked jeans and parka.

"OK, we've got a new rule," she told him. "Until this blizzard stops, you can only go outside if I'm with you and you're on a leash."

She locked both doggie doors, unwound her ice-crusted layers, then noticed the answering machine blinking on the counter.

The first message was from Mabel, asking Melinda to call when she made it home. "Ed and I are trying to watch for your car, but we can barely see the road."

The other was from Horace. He wanted to know how she was "getting on," as he put it, and reminded her about the length of rope in the garage that stretched from that building's far corner to the chicken house.

Melinda sank into one of the chairs at the kitchen table, first calling her parents and Aunt Miriam, and then Mabel and Horace.

"Looks to be a bad one blowing in," Horace said. "I gotta say, I think I'll be glad to sit this one out here in my recliner. You're prepared. You'll do just fine."

There had been dozens of blizzards over the decades, and Horace had faced them all. But gazing out the kitchen windows into the yard, where the barn was barely visible and night promised to come early, Melinda wasn't sure how she was going to do the same.

The driving snow would make it nearly impossible to draw water for the chickens from the hydrant by the garden. She filled a bucket at the kitchen sink, then changed into old clothes and bundled into her chore gear.

Before she picked up the pail and her best shovel, she gave Hobo a hug to comfort him as well as herself.

"You stay here with the kittens, you're in charge. I'll be back as soon as I can."

She pocketed her phone inside her coveralls, fastened her headlamp around her knit cap, tightened her hood over the top, and pushed her way out the back porch door.

The viciousness of the wind nearly took her breath away. The snow it spat in her face was no longer wet and heavy, but had ratcheted in intensity. There was no way to know how much snow had already fallen, as none of it seemed able to find a place to rest.

She nearly stumbled down the steps, their edges no longer visible, and lowered her head to turn into the driving gale and shuffle to the garage. A drift was already forming against its rolling door, and she shoveled at a frenzied pace until the ice along the bottom cracked and she could slide the door free.

It was a small victory to get the car inside. She reached for Horace's rope and the water bucket, tied the rope to the metal eyelet on the back corner of the garage, and trudged toward the chicken house, trying to keep her balance. Nearly out of breath, she fastened the rope over the hook next to the door and used her glove-padded fist to bust the crust of slush forming on the latch.

The chickens clucked nervously and scuttled about, as if they didn't recognize Melinda under her extra layers of gear. Not wanting to open the door again to dump the birds' water pan, she instead reached for a spare bowl on the shelf and filled it full, then set out an extra-generous ration of feed.

"I know I'm early today," she called to the hens as she worked quickly, trying to comfort them over the roar of the storm outside.

"And I don't know what time tomorrow I'll get back out here. Pansy, don't look at me like that." The moody hen, who had taken many opportunities to peck Melinda when she first arrived at the farm, only offered a stare that said she doubted Melinda could fill Horace's snow boots.

"Am I glad I cleaned your coop out last fall, girls, and patched all the cracks in the floor before I loaded the straw back in. I will come back, I promise. You'll just have to soldier on until then, OK?"

The rope guided her back to the garage, then she stumbled to the house to get Stormy and Sunny's supper. The barn door faced north, and Melinda's arms were barely strong enough to wrench it open against the howling wind.

A chorus of indignant "baaas" answered the squeal of the barn door's frozen hinges. Melinda expected to find refuge from the unrelenting wind once she stepped inside, but a strange draft greeted her instead. The top of the sheep's pasture door had come undone in the gale, driving snow inside and dropping it along the wall.

"I'm coming, girls, I'll fix it." She hustled to the aisle gate, her layers slowing her down.

It was too risky to open the bottom of the exterior door and step out to reach the top's latch. Leaning as far over as she dared, she finally grasped it, and fought the wind to lock it closed.

With a gasp of triumph and relief, she marched back through the sheep's area to the gate. The anxious ewes pressed close to her for reassurance, the roar outside threatening to drown out their plaintive calls.

"I'll get you some more dry straw in a minute." She patted some of the ewes' wooly foreheads. "But first, I've got to fix that door."

She hurried to the grain room and pawed through its corners until she found a roll of wire. Snatching a set of pliers off the tool shelf, she cut off two generous lengths, then snipped two more.

Sunny, his golden eyes wide and cautious, found her as she came out into the aisle.

"Where is your brother?" She paused long enough to give Sunny a comforting pat on the head.

"I want everyone inside and safe. No one's going anywhere until this storm is over."

She twisted one wire through and around the latch on the sheep's bottom door, then locked down the top. She bent the last two lengths in half, pocketed them, and rushed to the cats' hideout under the stairs, her heart pounding. Stormy, who barely lifted his head at her approach, was curled up in his half of the bowl-sized dent in the thick bed of straw.

"Oh, thank God. Stormy, you scared me. Here, boys, I've got your supper and some to spare. I know it's early, so eat whenever."

The cats eagerly started in on the canned food while Melinda added a generous scoop of kibble to their other pan and filled their heated water dish to the brim. She loaded the sheep's troughs with double rations of hay and oats, scooped away the wet straw, then checked that the ewes' automatic waterer was still rumbling along. Her last stop was to slide the plywood cover over the small hole used by Hobo and the cats in the far wall.

Once outside, she turned her back to the screeching wind and lashed one of the wires through the barn door's latch. Then, her head bent low against the blinding snow, she found her way back to the chicken house to twist the last section through its door handle. The tracks she made only half an hour ago were already erased, slowing her stumble back to the porch steps.

Melinda was gasping with exertion by the time she returned to the comforting light and warmth of the house. Hobo met her in the kitchen and followed her into the bedroom, then waited patiently outside the bathroom door while she cared for the kittens.

Then she turned on the television and stretched out on the couch, trying to leave enough room for an eager Hobo to hop up on the far end.

Her knees were stiff from mushing through the rapidly rising drifts, and her arms sore from lugging the filled water bucket to the coop, but she'd done it. Everyone was safe and in shelter, literally locked in for the night.

Nightfall arrived before five, the wind that pushed in with the dark more ferocious than before. The farmhouse's metal storm windows began to rattle in the gale. The lights flickered once, then twice, but stayed on. She plugged her phone into its charger, then picked up the receiver of Horace's wall-mounted unit to listen to the comforting dial tone that still hummed through the line.

She had just put a frozen pizza in the oven when the Mason City television station updated its forecast: Twelve to fourteen inches of snow by sunrise, blizzard winds all night long and through most of tomorrow. Snow plows would be pulled off the region's roads within the hour, as it had become impossible for them to stay ahead of the storm. Just as Uncle Frank had predicted, emergency crews were scrambling to lock the steel gates on the entrance ramps to the interstate, fifteen miles to the north.

It was almost bedtime when Hobo gave her a meaningful look and padded out to the kitchen. Melinda bundled into her boots and coat, snapped the lead to his collar, and opened the insulated steel door.

The storm door's metal latch was frosted over, even though it was on the inside. Through the fogged-over glass, she searched for the reassuring glow of the yard light, but it couldn't be seen.

A snowdrift had appeared where the back steps used to be. Hobo dropped his tail and whimpered.

"I know how you feel. I'm scared, too. We won't go far. Don't worry, I'll help you."

The suction from the wind driving around the corner of the house threatened to pull the storm door's latch out of her clenched hand. She fumbled down the steps, Hobo almost in her arms, then tried to block him from the worst of the gale. Snow sandblasted the back of her parka and stung the side of her face.

There was a strange whistle in the wind, an uneasy sound that suddenly manifested into an eerie wail.

Under her warm layers, fear snaked down Melinda's spine. She wrapped one gloved hand over the other and tightened her grip on Hobo's lead. "I have to hold on, I just have to." The wind carried her words away.

Her heart was racing by the time they got inside. She focused on rubbing Hobo dry with a towel and checking all the door locks, then made her way upstairs. In her bedroom, up on the northwest corner and without the comforting chatter of the television, the storm was even louder. She cowered under the covers, trying to block out its roar.

Melinda tossed and turned, her mind working its way back to those terrifying moments outside with Hobo. And to this: A feeling that *someone*, or *something*, had been right behind her.

And then, more: Tonight wasn't the first time she'd sensed a threat lurking somewhere she couldn't see.

Last summer, after a tornado skirted the farm and plowed off to the northeast, leaving heavy skies and an icy wind in its wake, she had stumbled through the hail-beaten pasture to guide her sheep out of a lonely stand of trees and back to the safety of the barn. The angry wind that tried to push her back, turn her from her task, had been filled with an ominous power that left her feeling small and scared.

Once again, she felt so alone. She had wonderful neighbors, supportive friends and family, modern technology at her fingertips. But this terrifying night made her mind wander back to when she was young, and the terrible tales Grandma and Grandpa Foster told when they thought little children weren't listening.

Times when the snow was so deep that they were stranded at their farm for weeks, and recitations of older-still stories of pioneers going mad as the cold and isolation of winter crushed them in its grip.

The wind's whistle changed pitch again, the blizzard cranking into a higher gear. And then, an unmistakable sound under the roar: an icy, deliberate *tap, tap, tap* on the north window, a noise so small yet so distinctive that her heart nearly stopped.

And then the tapping manifested into a scratching, like a fingernail dragging through the skim of frost smothering the storm glass.

Melinda didn't pause to push the thin cotton curtains wide and verify her fears. She snatched her phone, the battery lantern and her comforter and raced for the hallway, stubbing her toes on the rag rug by her bed. Thank goodness she'd left the door at the bottom of the stairwell ajar, and the corner lamp glowing in the living room.

She flung herself down the steps and rounded the landing as if someone was following her. At last she was out into the living room, the door slammed shut at her back. If only she had another length of wire to lock it down, too.

Hobo raised his head, Melinda's fear mirrored in his eyes, when she dodged around the corner and into Horace's old room. She sank down next to him on the crazy quilt and wrapped her arms around him. Hobo licked her hand in sympathy.

"It's just a branch, you know, there's nothing to be afraid of." Her words were hollow, a gentle lie to get through this wild night. No trees brushed the north side of the house, only a few evergreen bushes and two rows of insulating straw bales, and they huddled against the foundation.

She pulled back the bed's quilt and underlying blankets, punched up the rarely used pillow beneath. Her comforter went on top, the layers arranged so Hobo's nest wouldn't be disturbed. The warm glow of the living room's lamp was just outside the open door.

All the commotion brought a round of calls from inside the bathroom, the kittens' high-pitched meows barely audible over the roar of the storm. She got up one last time and opened the door.

"My little babies." She reached for one of the warmed towels in the tote and scooped the kittens into her arms. "Just for tonight, you are coming with me."

She left bathroom door open and the light on, then curled up on her side, her back to the storm. With the kittens tucked into their towel and snuggled in the sheltering crook of her arm, Melinda pulled the covers over her head and waited anxiously for sleep to come.

* 5 *

The snow was so heavy, and there was so much of it, that it took over twenty minutes of spine-jarring shoveling before Melinda could get close enough to the mailbox to crack the ice off its face and tug down its door. There were only a few circulars in the box, but her spirits still soared as she reached inside. The junk mail was a comforting reminder that the rest of the world hadn't slowed to a stop during the past forty-eight hours, even though hers had.

The mail carrier must have made it this far Wednesday morning, before the storm hit. And after her white-knuckle drive home that afternoon, she hadn't stopped to check the box. Yesterday, of course, there was no mail. And no snowplow, either, until just after dark, when she glanced out the dining-room windows and saw the silvery spark of emergency lights as the county's rig churned up the road from the south. She'd let out a celebratory whoop that startled the kittens, who were dozing in the nest of fleece scraps from the sewing project spread out on the table.

Sensing her elation, Hobo had barked and raced for the back door. She hesitated but let him out, urging him to stay close to the house. But really, he couldn't get far. The drifts west and north of the garage were at least three feet deep, a rolling sea of white that had obliterated the garden and nearly erased the snow fence behind it.

Nathan arrived this morning long before it became light, his snow blade anchored to the front of his pickup. He cleared the lane and made a circular pass through the main yard, busting down the drifts between the garage and the barn. The truck's horn sounded its greeting as Melinda came out the back door, ready to start chores, and he chugged away to clean Ed and Mabel's drive. She had shoveled a haphazard path to the chicken house, trying to follow the gaps between the drifts, then rushed down to the mailbox as soon as the eastern horizon eased toward sunrise.

The sky was now a brilliant blue, the surface of the ice-crusted snow sparkling with a diamond-like sheen in the faint light. She clutched her thin stack of mail, a much-needed lifeline to the rest of the world, as she trudged up the drive. There'd be more today, and tomorrow, and life would get back to normal. After a day trapped at home, the camaraderie around the Prosper Hardware coffee pot and the sea of customers that would surely flood the store pushed her to start for town as soon as possible.

Unlike Hobo, Stormy and Sunny were in no hurry to explore the blizzard's aftermath. They came out of their hideout long enough to get some attention and eat breakfast, but were snoozing under the heat lamp by the time she finished feeding the sheep. The ewes were restless after being locked inside for two days. Melinda explained how the sun had to melt away at least some of the snow, but Annie still stomped over to the pasture door and gave her a nasty look.

"Annie! Get over here and eat your grain before the other girls get it gone. It's the middle of January, you can't run around outside every day. What do you expect?"

Just as Melinda finished her rant, she heard the skittering of paws above her head, rushing across the haymow floor. There was no need to clomp up the stairs and investigate this visitor. Yesterday morning, when the storm was still howling outside, a masked bandit had leaped out from behind the sheep's metal feed barrels just as Melinda was about to pry off their lids.

She had screamed, and the raccoon hadn't, but the terrified critter bolted for the haymow and the safety of its stacks of hay and straw.

"I'm opening the cats' door," she announced now, stepping to the foot of the stairs to be sure her proclamation would be heard. "You know where it is. Blizzard's over, Ricky. I want you out of here by tonight."

The snow covering her gravel road was packed thick and tight, thanks to another pass made by the county plow that morning. But the ditches were level-full and drifted even higher, the fields and pastures so smothered with snow that only the fences' top sections were visible.

She crawled along, braking long before both country intersections between her farm and the highway, unable to confirm she was alone until the last minute thanks to the mounds of snow everywhere. The cherry-filled coffeecake she baked yesterday, riding along in the passenger seat, would hopefully lift her friends' spirits.

The Main Street painting on the town's welcome sign was partially obscured by the blobs of snow clinging to its surface, but "Prosper: The Great Little Town That Didn't" still stubbornly greeted visitors from along the bottom.

"Oh, it's good to be back in civilization! Even if not all of it is visible."

Several trucks were already at the co-op, haphazardly parked around the lot's mountains of cleared-away snow. Several people were trying to find their sidewalks, one man alternating between making a path and collecting the downed tree branches exposed by his shovel.

Her yard would also be littered with branches once the snow melted. There would be a mess to clean up, but maybe there was a silver lining: A tossed twig or two might have caused the eerie noises outside her bedroom window during one of the wildest hours of the blizzard. But then, the tapping and clawing had been so ... lifelike, yet not ...

Melinda pushed those uneasy thoughts away. Yesterday morning, with Hobo serving as Watson to her Sherlock, she'd marched upstairs and pushed wide the curtains that protected her bedroom's north-facing window. The outside storm glass was frosted over, as she expected, but the icy film was unmarked and undisturbed.

She had chastised herself for letting fear and loneliness get the best of her, straightened her tossed-about bed, and went downstairs to turn on the coffeepot so the comforting aroma would greet her when she returned from chores.

There were three trucks parked as close as they could get to Prosper Hardware's curb, which was invisible under the barrier of snow lining both sides of Main Street. Auggie was already inside, as were Doc and Jerry.

The store's back lot was plowed, but barely. She eased in by the vintage pop machine, which had most of its face wrapped in a scarf of drifted snow, and kicked down the leftover drift by the building's back entrance to get inside. Auggie's crowing reached her ears before she even got the pass-through door open.

"Fifteen inches! That was a real, old-fashioned blizzard, wasn't it? Can you believe it? It's been sixty-eight years since we got that much snow in twenty-hour hours. One for the record books, for sure!"

He was grinning ear to ear, his snow-dusted wool cap still askew on head. His coat, at least, had been haphazardly tossed on the hall tree by the front window. For a second, Melinda didn't see a man just over sixty. She saw a little boy thrilled to receive what he'd asked Santa to bring him for Christmas, and then some. The fact that Auggie received his historic storm nearly a month late didn't seem to matter.

"Why, we had over six inches the other night before I left the co-op," he went on breathlessly, "then eight more in just ten hours." He paused long enough to take a hearty gulp of his coffee and trail Melinda to the sideboard, where she was about to cut into the cherry coffeecake.

The exhaustion lines around Jerry's eyes matched those etched on Doc's face. "Well, I hope we don't get a storm like that for another sixty-eight years." Jerry rubbed his cheek, as if trying to wake himself up. "The plows couldn't keep up, and there were accidents all over the place. Thank God we didn't lose more of the power grid than we did. Melinda, how are things out your way?"

"I nearly wiped out getting home the other day, but I made it. Got all the animals locked in, then huddled down in the house to ride it out." She thought of her panic and terror and almost said something, but stopped. Today, with the sun shining and the roads opened, it all seemed a little silly.

Despite Auggie's hovering, she handed the first piece of coffeecake to Jerry, and the second to Doc.

"I knew you'd be able to handle things," Doc said as he gratefully accepted his slice of cake. "How are the kittens?"

"Improving every day. I was able to cut back on their meds, just like you suggested. You should have seen them yesterday, jumping and playing. I had the sewing machine out, making those fleece curtains, and they got right in the middle of everything. Hobo watches over them like a proud papa. Maybe by this weekend, I'll be ready to give them the full run of the house."

"Glad to hear it. That's two patients I don't have to worry about." Doc's shoulders sagged with fatigue. "You should see the list of farm calls I need to make today. Got the tire chains on the truck last night. But if the wind stays calm and the roads get cleared, maybe I won't need them for long."

"That wind was something else." Jerry shook his head as he filled his coffee mug. "Even here in town, you couldn't see but a few feet. Total whiteout in the country. Auggie, what was the highest gust you recorded?"

Auggie paused dramatically before answering. "We got several gusts up to fifty, but the worst was a fifty-six. Fifty-six miles an hour! Gauges clocked that one just after eleven Wednesday night."

Melinda shivered. That was around the time she heard the wind change and the unearthly tapping on her window.

"But that wasn't the highest one around here," Auggie continued, a bit let down.

"Over at Elm Springs, they clocked a fifty-seven." But then he perked up. "We did tie, though, with Charles City for the highest recorded snowfall for yesterday's date. By the way, Melinda, George called. He's staying home."

Bill soon came in, toting a plate of blueberry muffins. "I see my wife wasn't the only one in a baking mood. We've about got a buffet going. I'm sure it'll be crazy in here today, so we should be able to unload it all, no problem."

"How are things at the co-op?" Jerry asked Auggie. "Bet you'll be busy, too, being closed yesterday and all."

"First day in about twenty years that we haven't been open because of the weather. The rural roads are still rough, and it'll take people time to plow out, but I expect the place will be hoppin' by noon. Have to say I'm glad Evan's still here to give us a hand."

Before Melinda could ask how Evan and Chloe had fared during the blizzard, Auggie continued.

"Evan's doing a good job." He shrugged, as if he didn't want to raise his hopes too much. "He shows up to work on time, does what I ask him to do. I think he's really trying, this time. And Chloe," his brown eyes lit up, "she's wonderful. Jane loves watching her while Evan's at the co-op. They're having tea parties and such. But he's going to have to find something else. Part-time at my shop doesn't pay much and honestly, it's slow this time of year, anyway."

"Well, you're doing what you can to help out," Jerry offered. "I'm sure Evan appreciates it."

Auggie didn't respond at first. "Yes," was all he said, then changed the subject.

"Bill and Melinda, do you have much dog and cat food in stock? I'm about out, and no feed truck coming until Monday. If you do, I'll send people your way."

"Appreciate it." Bill went behind the counter. "It's not the brands you carry, of course, but there's still some bags in the back. It's the bread and milk we're desperate for. It's all gone. I hope our truck can get here tomorrow."

"What are you doing?" Jerry turned in his chair.

"Making a sign." Bill reached for a notepad and a marker. "Better that people know what the deal is. It'll save a lot of questions today."

The store wasn't as busy as Melinda expected, a steady stream of customers rather than the madhouse it was as the blizzard bore down on the area. But it was the necessities that everyone wanted.

"Are you sure you're out of milk?" one woman whispered to Melinda as she swiped her credit card. "I hear the crowds are terrible over in Swanton, at both the superstore and the grocery store." The lady paused, then offered a secretive smile. "I'm not fussy about the price, you know."

"I'm sorry, we really don't have any," Melinda said gently, fighting back her laughter.

A thought flashed through her mind, a long-forgotten rumor about her great-grandfather selling something stronger than milk from the back room during Prohibition. "But tell you what," she leaned over the counter and lowered her voice. "The truck arrives at nine tomorrow, as long as the roads don't get worse overnight."

Uncle Frank called, wondering if Melinda and Bill needed his help. "Miriam's not quite over the flu, but I'm just fine. I can head over there. I'm sure you're busy."

"You take it easy today, make sure you don't come down with it next," Melinda told him. "We might need your help tomorrow, to run the register while Bill and I unload the truck." That seemed to appease Frank.

"And Uncle Frank, please don't try to shovel. You let your neighbor handle it, that's what you're paying him for."

At lunch, Melinda warmed up a serving of the chicken and noodles she'd made yesterday, and then slid across Main Street to the library, anxious for a friendly chat with Nancy and to select another novel from last week's shipment.

Nancy glanced over her black-framed reading glasses as Melinda shook the snow off her shoes. She was in her mid-fifties, with a few sophisticated gray streaks in her dark, bobbed hair. Her thick-cabled turtleneck was a flattering shade of dark blue, and a surprisingly stylish pair of winter boots steamed on the rubber mat by the floor register.

"Am I glad to see you!" Nancy gave Melinda a warm smile and pointed with her pen at the cased opening that joined the two city buildings. "You're the first patron of the day, and not one person's come in at City Hall. With school still closed, it's been pretty quiet. How are things over there?"

"Fairly busy, but we're running low on the stuff people really want." Melinda plopped her canvas tote on the library's counter and pulled out a hefty hardcover book. "Finished it last night, after I got all those fleece curtains hemmed and hung up. It's amazing how much you can get done when you can't leave the house."

"I bet those curtains look great, from what you said about the colors you picked out." Nancy slid the novel over the desk's scanner, then added it to a nearby shelf. "So, what did you think? There's three people waiting for it who'll be glad you finished it so quickly."

"It was good, although I think I liked his last novel better. The plot felt a little thin this time around, like he's running out of new ideas."

"You always know what you're going to get with that guy, for better or worse." Nancy rolled her eyes. "But it doesn't matter. When he's got a new book out, I just have to read it." She paused, then leaned over the desk.

"I've got an idea, something I've been kicking around. It's been so dull around here since the holidays. Everybody's just trudging along; the cold and snow don't help. What do you say to us starting a book club here at the library?"

Melinda's eyes widened with excitement. "Nancy, that's a wonderful idea! When I was trapped at home yesterday, I was thinking that I need to get out more, meet some new people. Seems like all I do is get to work and back, and to my parents' in Swanton."

Nancy grinned and rubbed her hands together, unable to contain her enthusiasm. "Even if there's just a few of us every month, I think our little club could be great fun! And I want to get more adults into the library. Our children's events are well-attended, but so many parents just drop off their kids and pick them up. I want to remind everyone how much this library has to offer."

"So, what do we do to get things started?" Spring was so far away, and Melinda needed something to look forward to.

She hoped to get together with Cassie and Susan for Susan's birthday later in the month, but who knew what the weather would be like?

The only big thing on her calendar was lambing season, which wouldn't happen until late February. And she wasn't sure if she was more excited, or afraid, about how that might go. Based on their thickening frames, she guessed four of her ewes were pregnant, all thanks to a random hook-up with the ram living in the pasture across the road last summer.

Doc and Karen would be on call, and several neighbors had already promised to lend a hand, but Melinda still felt woefully unprepared.

"Well, I think we won't hold the first meeting until late March, at least. That'll give me time to spread the word, pick the first book, order more copies and let people get a chance to read it. Tuesday nights should be a safe bet. How about I get something on the city's website and out on social media? Do you think the Swanton newspaper might run something?"

"I'm sure they would." Melinda drummed her fingers on the desk, thinking of the possibilities. "I wish we could start it sooner, but you're right, we need time to promote it."

"I know how you feel." Nancy sighed as she reached for a stack of books that needed to be returned to the shelves. "It's that whole cabin-fever thing. We all need something to look forward to, I guess. I get to my kids' activities, and then church and work, and that's about it."

"Well, this will be a good thing, for both of us. And some others as well. It's the New Year, after all. This just makes my day! That, and picking out some more books while I'm here."

What a difference one day can make, Melinda thought as she drove home that evening, a brilliant set of sun dogs keeping watch in the western sky. These early weeks of the year were a time for reflection and looking ahead. And she had been doing plenty of both lately.

After all those months of upheaval and change, she was where she wanted to be. But as content as she was with her choice, that wasn't going to be enough in the long run.

What did she really want to *do*, beyond working at the store and caring for her animals? Melinda had no idea. Making some new friends would be a good first step.

* 6 *

Melinda was so busy watching her feet, trying not to slip on the roughly shoveled path while balancing the sloshing water bucket in one hand, that she almost missed the fresh tracks peppering the snow on the north side of the chicken house.

It was the iced-over door latch that brought her up short, caused her to set down the pail and reach for the screwdriver she now carried in one of her pockets for this very task. She was chipping away with her makeshift ice pick, the beam of her headlamp the only useful light at this hour before sunrise, when the screwdriver slipped from her clumsy, thick-gloved hands and dropped into the slush banked by the door. Hindered by the bulk of her warm layers, she crouched down and started to search. Just as she reached for the screwdriver, she glanced up and saw the definitive march of paw prints skirting the far edge of the garden, lurking dangerously close to the chicken house, then wandering off into the windbreak.

Had those tracks been there yesterday? She couldn't be sure, as both rounds of chores had been completed in either low light or outright darkness for nearly two months. It hadn't snowed for three days, making the crust of the blizzard's leftover drifts an increasingly crowded canvas for all the wildlife making Melinda's farm their home. From the wealth of tracks she saw every day, her place was teeming with life, even during this coldest time of year.

Snowy prints crisscrossed the sleeping garden, slipped around the outbuildings and dashed through the open space between the garage and the barn. And with the help of the internet, she had become an expert at reading the footprints she found: the dash-dash-hops of the rabbits; the raccoons' claw-heavy, angled marks, which unfortunately sometimes led to Sunny and Stormy's barn access; and the delicate impressions made by the deer as they tiptoed from the windbreak to the birdfeeders, then down the driveway to the fields beyond.

But these new prints, challenging her from behind the chicken house, made her pulse race.

They were wider, deeper, set apart at a noteworthy distance that told of a larger animal. And they made their own way, confidently breaking off from the usual routes the other animals followed.

She left the water bucket by the chicken house, made sure the door latch was still securely fastened, and gripped her screwdriver as if it were a knife. The eastern horizon showed only a faint stripe of gray, full dawn still several minutes' away, but she had to discover where, or to what, these tracks might lead.

They were no kind of match to Hobo's feet. She thought of Sunny and Stormy's curved paw pads, of the sure-footed way her barn cats stalked across the snow during those rare times they bothered to leave their heated house under the haymow stairs.

The shape of these prints was very similar, but much larger. Suddenly, she remembered Horace's seemingly exaggerated tales of cougars and bobcats roaming the township's snow-covered pastures, and her heart froze.

Then her feet were moving, and fast. Melinda had to get to work, but she had to see what she could see, before the melting sun or other animals' wanderings might obscure or distort these tracks. She fell in step with the prints until they reached the windbreak, then lost them in the snow-dusted branches and dead leaves littering the floor of the timber.

She glanced to her left and saw another solitary trail that aimed for the machine shed's corner and made a careful path along its frozen-down rolling door. The tracks gave a wide berth to the searching beam of the yard light, then nosed along the side of the barn. They paused in a jumble of trampled prints by the cats' entrance, then doubled back past the garage and returned to the grove.

And then, something else: As she passed the machine shed from a new direction, she spotted a different set of large tracks, more angular this time, slipping around the back of the building and into the windbreak.

Melinda removed her gloves and, with her fingers shaking from cold and fear, reached inside her coveralls for her phone and snapped the best photos she could in the early-morning gloom.

"Even if Hobo made the dog-like ones behind the shed, I can't explain all of these other, rounder ones away," she told Doc later that morning as she passed him her phone.

Doc set his coffee mug on the store's sideboard to free his hands for a closer look, then gave a low whistle and shook his head. "How big, you say?"

"Maybe three inches across? Or maybe, not quite that large," she quickly added, unnerved by the surprise and concern on his face.

"I didn't have any way of measuring them, you know. And maybe they had been there a while. If they had, the sun could have melted them a bit yesterday, making them bigger." Her wavering voice trailed off in the coffee group's stunned silence as the photos made their way around the circle.

Doc didn't seem convinced. "They look really fresh, the edges are still nice and sharp."

"These tracks went right along the outbuildings," she said anxiously, "like whatever it was, it was looking for a way in." *Or an easy meal.*

"Well, you never know, I guess. Maybe the prints weren't this big to start with." Doc searched for something comforting to say. "Either way, I'd keep those chickens locked in for a while, even during the day, even if it's nice out. The good news is, if you're seeing rabbit tracks and such, there's plenty of other prey for, well, anything that's hungry enough to chase it down."

Jerry, who had just arrived, hastily removed his coat and hurried over to study the pictures. "Man, look at those. Do you think it could be a cougar? A bobcat?" He turned to Doc and Auggie. "Are there coyotes around?"

"Oh, there's coyotes for sure," Auggie answered. Melinda usually appreciated his forthright manner, but this was one time she wished he didn't sound so sure of himself.

"Guy came into the co-op just yesterday, said there's a pack out his way, over northeast of town, down in some set-aside pasture edged in timber." Auggie paused only long enough to add a hearty sift of powdered creamer to his mug. "He says those coyotes are bold, they've got the run of the place since there's no cows in that field this time of the year. Says he hears them sometimes at night, calling back and forth down by the creek."

Melinda shivered. "Well, I haven't heard anything like that. And I would think Hobo would bark if he sensed anything roaming around outside. Like I said, he sticks close to the house, even when he does go out."

Doc seemed to be considering something. "You said the one set of prints went right to the front of the barn, then veered off. How big's that opening Horace put in for Hobo and the cats?"

Melinda tipped her head, thinking. "Not sure, exactly. Maybe nine, ten inches wide? And it's a little taller than that. Hobo can just make it through, I've seen him do it. There's a plywood piece on a track inside, it slides over to close the hole. Unless the weather's bad, I leave it open since Sunny and Stormy use it all the time."

Doc looked at Auggie and Jerry. Auggie raised an eyebrow at Melinda.

"Sounds like those cats need to stay in at night until things settle down. How handy are you with a hammer?"

It was nearly dark when she arrived home that evening, and a biting wind was cranking up by the time she changed into her chore gear and stashed her supplies in a plastic sack.

"Six inches? How is this going to be big enough?" she muttered as she knelt in front of the barn, the knees of her coveralls sinking into the icy slush. She tried to position her back to the wind, then pushed the plywood scraps Bill cut that afternoon against the barn wall and transferred their corners with a black marker. "Stormy and Sunny better not get too fat this winter, or they won't be able to slip through."

Because Hobo spent most of the winter in the house, he only entered the barn when accompanying Melinda on her chore rounds. That meant the entrance could be made smaller until spring. There had been much debate among the guys about just how wide the opening should be to let the cats in but keep predators out. Just before Auggie and Jerry's discussion escalated into a shouting match, Doc settled things with a quick search on his phone.

"Six inches wide, six inches tall," Doc had announced. "Apparently that's standard door dimensions for those little houses people build for feral-cat colonies. If it's good enough for them, it'll work for Sunny and Stormy. Once they're inside for the night, lock them in until morning."

As she huddled next to the barn, failing miserably at grasping a plywood scrap, nail and hammer in her gloved hands, Melinda would have laughed if she hadn't been so cold and frustrated. When she decided to rent this farm, she imagined herself waltzing from one fun creative project to another. She never thought her limited carpentry skills would be used in a desperate bid to keep some wild animal away from her beloved cats.

She swore again, adjusted her headlight, and finally tossed the gloves to the ground. The hammer's wooden handle was icy to the touch, but the nails were worse. Her stiffening fingers were clumsy, and it took several more tries to get the first two nails started, the ones that would hold the plywood pieces steady while she finished her work.

There was movement around the corner of the barn. Her pulse picked up, and then she saw Stormy watching through the fence.

"What are you doing out here? Why aren't you inside? Pretty soon, I'm going to make you go in the barn and stay there. I don't know what's roaming around out here, and I don't want either of you to find out the hard way."

She shivered again, remembering the ominous tracks she'd discovered that morning, and pounded the final nail flush with three urgent swings of her hammer. "It's not fancy, but it will do."

Stormy sniffed curiously at the fresh-cut plywood, hesitated for only a second, then leaped through the smaller opening with ease. He turned and popped his head out the hatch, watching Melinda gather her supplies with what was a smug look if she'd ever seen one.

"So you like it, huh?" She paused long enough to give him a loving pat. "Outdoor access will only be available from sunrise to sunset, until further notice."

She glanced around the farmyard, where the shadows were deepening as the last of the day's light disappeared from the horizon. It was already dark inside the windbreak, the rows of sheltering trees quickly morphing into a foreboding place full of secrets. There was no sound or movement other than the whistle of the wind in the bare branches.

Melinda gathered her courage and her tools, scrambled to her feet, and hurried toward the comforting lights beckoning from the back porch. She still had to do chores. And the sooner everyone was locked in for the night, the better.

* 7 *

"I spy some of Miriam's famous cinnamon rolls!" George exclaimed as he shuffled into Prosper Hardware, his snow-crusted gloves tucked under the arm of his parka. "That means there's something going on. What's up?"

"I start my new job today." Frank beamed as he pulled the rolls apart and placed them on napkins. Doc and Jerry were already in their chairs, coffee cups in hand.

"New job?" George frowned as he shook off his coat. "Miriam banned you from working here, except during emergencies. Who in town is even hiring these days? And aren't you supposed to take it easy?"

"I am," Frank said sarcastically, rolling his eyes. "Except when I'm supposed to be *exercising*." Frank, at Miriam's insistence, began walking half an hour every day once his cardiologist cleared him for activity. When the weather turned colder, he thought he was off the hook. But then a delivery truck arrived at their Victorian on Cherry Street with a treadmill in the back.

"And anyway, George," Frank added as he helped himself to what seemed to be the largest roll in the pan, "Miriam didn't ban me from Prosper Hardware. I just cut my hours back, is all."

Melinda wasn't about to correct her uncle. Other than the store's holiday celebration, it had been months since she'd seen him this excited. The gooey cinnamon rolls, spackled with cream-cheese frosting and studded with pecans, weren't exactly on his approved food list, but she was tired enough to let that go, as well.

Since she discovered the foreboding animal tracks four days ago, Melinda had been on high alert as she crisscrossed the farmyard.

Yesterday, just as the cloudy skies deepened into twilight, she was almost sure she saw movement in the windbreak behind the chicken house. It was so fast, and so subtle, that she tried to tell herself she'd imagined it.

The fresh snow around the coop was blank and smooth this morning, but it was too late.

She'd tossed and turned for too long last night, worries mounting in her mind, before finally falling into a restless sleep.

"As for my new gig, George, I'm the first person to ever hold this position." Uncle Frank gestured grandly with his cinnamon roll as he took his usual chair.

"I'm the city's newest employee. Starting today, I'm the Archive Coordinator, according to the resolution passed by the council just a few weeks ago."

Auggie's skeptical expression was full of comments and questions. Before he could start in, Jerry raised a hand.

"It's a volunteer position," he told Auggie. "Frank's just going to sort through some of the records and stuff packed upstairs at City Hall."

"I can sit in a chair over there as easily as I can plop down in my recliner at home," Frank went on. "Remember back before the holidays, when Melinda helped me get the city's Christmas decorations down from storage? There's file cabinets up there stuffed full of old papers and documents and such. Nancy's going to have me sort through everything, find some way to organize it."

"Oh, that's right, that little project you were talking about." Auggie took a hearty bite from his roll to keep from laughing.

"It's an important job." Frank cut Auggie off with a look. "Stuff's been filed away up there for decades. I'm going to unpack it all, log the contents into the city's computer system, and help Nancy and Jerry assess the condition of the artifacts. Then we'll come up with the best way to preserve all the documents, and I'll scan them into digital files, too."

Later that afternoon, Melinda heard the unmistakable screech that signaled someone was trying to send a fax to the printer in the store's office. It was a supply confirmation that needed a signature from either Frank or Miriam.

Aunt Miriam was at home, probably enjoying the peace and quiet of an afternoon without Frank blasting the television. Melinda knew he was still across the street at City Hall, and jumped at the chance to run out for a few minutes. Prosper Hardware was slow that day, just a few customers here and there, and Melinda had already mopped the slush from inside the entrance and tidied the shelves. The seed catalog stashed under the front counter could wait a few minutes' longer.

She grabbed her coat, told Bill she'd be back in a bit, and stepped out into the fresh air.

Along with a change of scenery, she was curious to discover exactly what Frank was up to over at City Hall. She loved history and wanted to learn more about this project. Who knew what he might find?

There was a small collection of old photographs on display at the library, along with a few musty county history titles and one too-short shelf of vintage high school yearbooks. But surely, there had to be more.

City Hall's upstairs had once been the town's gathering place, and the now-silent stage on one end told tales of the dances and community activities held there long ago. Now it was a stuffy, dreary space, packed with dusty boxes, dented file cabinets and rejected office furniture. The perfect place for mysteries to hide.

Nancy was at her other desk this afternoon, the modern one in the front of City Hall. The cozy silence that welcomed

Melinda as she stomped the slush off her boots told her Nancy and Frank were the only ones around.

"Hey." Nancy looked up from her monitor. "What's up?"

"Not too much. But I've got something Frank needs to sign for the store."

"He's set up in that cubbyhole across from Jerry's desk." Nancy pointed behind her. "And don't worry, Jerry brought all those boxes down from storage. The heaviest thing I'm letting Frank lift is an old book or two."

Prosper City Hall was housed in what was once the grandest building on Main Street, a golden-brick structure with high ceilings and heavy moldings. The city took it over decades ago when the previous owner fell on hard times. Officials got the building for just a dollar, but it wasn't the bargain it first appeared to be.

The structure needed serious upgrades to its mechanical systems, and several windows had to be replaced. Now it was sectioned off into small offices and storage rooms, a tired kitchen, and a modest council chambers furnished with metal tables and folding chairs. The back section, as well as the metal shed out on the alley, housed the volunteer emergency department's gear.

Melinda passed the binders and folders tossed about on Jerry's unorganized mayoral desk, then heard the rustling of paper nearby.

She took a quick right into a sudden, short hallway, and then a left. There was Uncle Frank's balding head, barely visible behind a stack of cardboard boxes.

"Well, howdy." He looked up over his reading glasses at the sound of her shoes squeaking on the scuffed wood floor. "What brings you over here?"

"Purchase order to sign." She rummaged in her parka pocket and pulled out the form. "It came by fax. Doesn't everyone email this stuff nowadays?"

Frank laughed as he reached for a pen. "Not this place. Their accounting department is old-school." He handed her the form, then gestured at the mess around him.

"Looks like a lot, doesn't it? But Jerry says this load barely makes a dent in what's upstairs. This'll keep me busy for months, I bet."

Melinda never could have imagined Frank happy at a desk job. For four decades, he'd been as much of a fixture at Prosper Hardware as the pressed-tin ceiling and the oak checkout counter. But his circumstances had changed, and he seemed to be adapting just fine. He'd needed a new purpose, and something came along to fill the void. She knew that feeling, too.

"This is the perfect gig for you, Uncle Frank." She couldn't resist thumbing through a stack of city council agendas that looked to be forty years old. They'd been drafted on an old typewriter, the kind with an ink ribbon and metal keys. "You've lived in this area your entire life. You know just about everyone in town, if not the whole county. And I can't wait to see what treasures you find."

Frank laughed. "Well, I've been at it maybe four hours and I'm already finding some good stuff." He reached for a worn, leather-bound ledger and carefully opened the cover.

"Census records!" Melinda leaned over for a closer look. "From ... what's the date, 1910? These were just stuffed in a box upstairs?"

Frank shook his head. "Can't believe it myself. These would be the city's copies, of course, from the federal count." He closed the ledger and gently set it on the corner of the desk.

"I'm starting a special pile of things that need to be preserved and added to the library. That, or they need to go to the county historical society in Swanton."

Melinda peeked in another box, fascinated by the dusty pages inside. "This one looks like maps of some sort, maybe." She forced herself to step back. "I wish I could stay and play Nancy Drew, but I'd better get back to the store."

"Oh, here, you might like this." Frank reached into another box behind his chair and handed her a small, yellowed book.

"Farmer's almanac from sometime in the 1920s. It's not anything of use to the city, not sure how it got stuffed in here. Probably some clerk had it on their desk or something. Might make for some fun reading."

Melinda felt a thrill in her fingertips as she cradled the fragile artifact in her hands. It had only a paper cover and the edges were a bit crumbled, but the book was still intact. She gently turned a few pages.

"Moon phases, weather forecasts, planting guides ... Uncle Frank, this is perfect! It won't be long before I can start planning my garden for this year. Who knows what I might learn from this?"

"Well, enjoy." He reached for another stack of file folders. "I'm determined to get through this pile before three. Then it'll be time to head home for my nap."

Melinda clutched the almanac close as she stepped from the warmth of City Hall into the dreary, sleepy afternoon. She couldn't wait to pore over the book's faded pages. The almanac made her think about the future, all the possibilities that would come to the farm when spring arrived.

"Only two months. Two months until the first day of spring." Melinda knew as well as anyone that winter could linger long past March 20, but that didn't matter. She was grinning by the time she opened the front door of Prosper Hardware, so thrilled with her new treasure she nearly forgot about the purchase order in her coat pocket.

She refused to look at the almanac during gaps between customers the rest of the afternoon, afraid the delicate book might get ripped or have something spilled on it. As soon as she got home from work, she set the almanac on top of the fireplace's right-side bookcase, out of reach of Hobo's curious nose and the kittens' playful paws.

Once the supper dishes were washed, she lit a fire in the hearth, reached for her lavender throw blanket, and settled in her reading chair. The new fleece curtains wrapped across the windows buffeted much of the draft, but it still felt good to be by the fire and under the floor lamp.

She glanced around the cheerful living room, at Hobo and the kittens snuggled on the couch and the flames in the fireplace, and listened to the soothing quiet of a cozy farmhouse on a bitter January night.

"Let's see what's in here. I've been waiting all afternoon to take a better look."

As she slowly turned the almanac's fragile pages, absorbing its weather predictions for 1923 and planting dates that followed the moon's phases, Melinda felt the present slipping away.

Horace's scuffed leather recliner had been parked in this very spot, and the pattern of wear on the oak floorboards indicated the room's layout probably hadn't changed for decades. She imagined a young Horace sitting right here, enjoying a detective or Western novel after his chores and schoolwork were finished. Or his father, or maybe his mother, resting before the fire.

This sitting room would have been comfortably crowded on cold winter nights, even if only some of the eight Schermann siblings were gathered around the fireplace. She tried to remember what Ada had said about the history of the house; it seemed as if Horace's grandparents built it, so they would have enjoyed this cozy spot, too. They surely turned the pages of an almanac, maybe even one similar to this, and took encouragement from its promises of spring.

She turned in her chair to take a closer look at the almost-forgotten titles lined up on the shelves of the bookcase just behind her. The cabinet on the other side of the fireplace held Horace's significant stash of Westerns and thrillers, along with the treasured books she brought to the farm. But these nearby volumes were older, their covers dark and worn. She didn't see anything that appeared to be an almanac, but long ago, there might have been one resting on that very shelf. Or hanging on a nail in the kitchen, probably by the back door.

Melinda felt the weight of the farmhouse's history on her shoulders. The place was going to pass out of the Schermann family, but she was more than eager to carry it forward.

She was studying a list of planting dates when a tiny pair of white-capped paws appeared on the armrest.

The brown kitten didn't hesitate for long, gathering her strength and pulling herself across the small gap between the couch and Melinda's chair. Her fluffy tail up with confidence, she nudged the almanac to the side and purred as she kneaded the soft fleece blanket, her miniature claws working out, then in.

"Look at you!" Melinda rubbed the kitten under her chin. "Always looking for the best spot, huh? You keep this up, and you and your sister over there are going to need names."

She had been holding off on that decision, telling herself there were just too many to pick from and besides, the kittens' permanent families would probably give them new ones. With their time of danger finally past, the kittens' sweet faces had been posted on the vet clinic's social media pages as well as the office bulletin board for a week already.

Melinda kept expecting to hear from Doc or Karen, a request for her to bring one or both of the babies in so they could meet a potential adopter. But so far, nothing. Doc came by the other day to look them over, and Melinda had tried not to laugh at the sight of tall, gangly Doc trying to squeeze into the tiny downstairs bathroom to collect stool samples from the litter box.

"Everyone wanted the two of you to make it, and now we know that you will," she told the brown kitten, then looked over at where the calico baby, her eyes lovingly focused on Melinda's face, lounged against Hobo's side.

The kittens' previous life was surely a hazy memory at most for two so young. Did they remember their mama? Their brother, who didn't survive? What about being left on the stoop of the vet clinic in that cardboard box?

"That would seem long ago, I would think, when you're now only eight weeks old, huh?" she whispered to the brown kitten. "My other life feels like a long time ago, too."

It had been so rewarding to help the frail little ones, once she gained the knowledge and confidence to meet their medical needs. Their circle had slowly expanded, and they now enjoyed free run of the downstairs when Melinda was home. They were allowed to roam in Horace's bedroom when she was away, and many evenings she returned to find Hobo stationed on the living-room side of the closed door.

The kittens were so playful, and surprisingly trusting of people considering how they came to be a part of Melinda's life. But sometimes they did something, or looked at her in a certain way, that made her heart hurt.

Hadn't Oreo's face lit up like that when he saw a bird out the window? Wasn't that same corner of the couch his favorite napping spot?

Melinda loved Stormy and Sunny, couldn't imagine what her farm would be like without them.

But there was something different about having kittens in the house. These little ones and their antics, at times, were a too-fresh reminder of her beloved Oreo.

"Do you see that kitty up on the mantel?" she asked the brown kitten and pointed to Oreo's photo. "That's my Oreo. He was my kitty before I came here, before you arrived." The baby's gaze followed Melinda's finger, then she nudged Melinda's hand with her fuzzy head, and began to purr.

It was time to start over, and Melinda knew it. It might be hard some days to see the little ones gallop across the floors in search of their toys, or snuggle on her bed the way Oreo used to do.

But then, the thought of them going away, of anyone else adopting the kittens ... *her* kittens ... nearly broke her heart. Hobo was attached to them, too, always allowing their playful swats at his tail or requests to rest their chins on his paws. It was as if Hobo knew they needed special attention, needed all the love he had to give.

"So you'll stay, then." She gently petted the brown kitten's ringed tail and looked over at the calico, who stretched a paw in Melinda's direction as if agreeing with this plan. "We'll decide on names another day. For tonight, let's see what interesting things we can find in this book, OK?"

Some of the home remedies seemed ridiculous, and a few brought a grimace based on their ingredients of garlic and mustard or even turpentine. "I think I'd rather suffer than use these methods to get better," Melinda groaned. She flipped to the monthly lists of notable days, then suddenly stopped reading.

"You guys!" She gasped and looked at Hobo and the kittens in turn. "Do you know what January seventeenth is? It's a special day that honors St. Anthony, one of the patron saints of animals. People get their animals blessed then, for extra luck. And that's only a few days from now."

Her home church in Swanton had hosted blessing ceremonies when she was a child. The family even took their Lab, Casey, to one year's celebration. She was sure that was in the fall, however, not January. She carefully set the yellowed almanac aside and turned to a modern research method.

"Oh, I see." She scrolled down her phone's screen. "There's actually a second chance to do this, when St. Francis is honored in October."

She looked again at the young kittens, who were just starting to thrive. She thought of her sheep out in the barn, especially the ewes growing wider every week with unborn lambs. She remembered the mysterious tracks marking the snow around the chicken house.

Melinda had already taken advantage of one tradition to protect her sheep.

On Christmas morning, she fed them bundles of hay left out the night before to collect what Horace believed was a special frost. He had asked her to carry on the Schermann family's custom, and she'd been happy to comply.

"I think we can use all the help we can get," Melinda told the kittens. "Do you believe in signs? I think I do. No, actually, I know that I do. This almanac arrived just in time. But I don't think I can do this on my own. Maybe we need to get someone with a little more, well, influence to help us out."

But who would perform such a blessing, and at this time of year? The closest clergy member was Pastor Paul Westberg at the Lutheran church just down the road. But he and his wife, Amy, and their kids lived in Prosper, six miles away. Besides, Melinda wasn't a member of the congregation, although she had considered going to services there. With the winter weather so unpredictable, she might not always be able to attend church in Swanton with her parents.

"And I doubt Pastor Paul makes house calls, at least for this sort of thing," she told Hobo, who had sensed her excitement and was now fully awake, watching for hints about what might happen next. "I guess it will have to be me."

Then she had an idea, and reached for her phone again. "But I could use some help. And I think I've got just the right person in mind."

✳ 8 ✳

The unmistakable aroma of oatmeal-chocolate chip cookies filled the kitchen as soon as she pulled the pan from Horace's old electric range. Just in time, she sidestepped the kitten pouncing on the laces of her sneakers.

"Grace!" Melinda balanced the hot cookie sheet in her padded hand as she swiftly closed the oven door, barring its interior from the calico kitten's curious paws. "I almost didn't see you there! You can't sneak up on me like that when I'm at the stove, OK?"

Grace flattened her ears for only a second, the mostly-orange one a beat ahead of the black one, then narrowed her intelligent green eyes at Melinda. Grace had appointed herself the boss of the house as soon as she received full access, quick to choose the spot on the sofa that was most to her liking and demanding the kittens' canned food be offered on a set schedule. Even Hobo let Grace have her way, patiently waiting his turn for some of Melinda's affection when the regal calico had already claimed her lap.

Hazel evaluated the situation from the dining room's doorway, her nose working at the smell of the cookies and her golden eyes wide with curiosity. Her brown-tabby fur was even longer and thicker than her outgoing sister's mane. The short-bristled brush Melinda found months ago in the back porch closet, her best chance at keeping Hobo's coat clear of weed seeds and dirt, wasn't going to be good enough for these two lovely ladies. Neither was the plastic comb she had just used to smooth the worst of the play-induced tangles from the kittens' fur.

"Today's a special day," she told the kittens as she filled another tray with scoops of cookie dough. "Now that you both have names, we're having company this afternoon. Someone wonderful is coming to give you a blessing, you and Hobo and all the animals outside, including Sunny and Stormy."

She reached down to give Hazel a pet, as the kitten had been unable to resist the sight of her sister romping with a toy mouse by the kitchen sink and had decided to join the fun. "And it's just as well you haven't met them yet. They're big boys, and used to having this farm to themselves. We'll keep it that way, at least for now."

The cookies' aroma wasn't interesting enough to rouse Hobo from his nap on Horace's old bed, but he sensed the car rumbling up the driveway before Melinda caught sight of it out the kitchen windows. He dashed past her and slipped out his doggie doors before she could get her coat on, as eager as she was to have visitors this calm-if-cold Sunday afternoon.

"They're here!" she told Grace and Hazel, almost laughing at how excited she was. Other than her parents occasionally coming to the farm for supper, Melinda hadn't hosted company since her family's Christmas celebration. The cozy kitchen was bright and clean, the table cleared of its usual clutter of magazines and mail, and Horace's old coffeemaker was already gurgling away.

Angie adjusted a gray knit cap over her auburn curls as she exited the car, then waved energetically from where she'd parked next to the garage. Emma and Allison tumbled out of the back seat and were met by Hobo, who was eager for pets and attention.

Melinda wanted to rush out to greet her friend, but took her time on the back steps. She carefully shoveled and salted them every day, but they were always in danger of growing a sudden crust of ice.

"It's been forever!" Angie exclaimed as she gave Melinda a hug. "Probably only, what, four weeks? But it seems like longer than that."

"I'm so glad you could help. Thanks for not thinking I'm a crazy woman. Not everyone would go along with this idea."

"I'm honored to use my status as a leader of the church to aid in this community outreach event." Angie made a grand, sweeping gesture with her arm.

"Who knew being a member of the Sunday school board carried so much clout? Nathan said I should go online and fill out one of those ordination forms, make it official." She motioned for her girls to start for the house. Allison, who was five, reached for little Emma's mittened hand and guided her across the snowy yard. Hobo stayed close to the girls, his tongue hanging out with happiness.

"We'll make the rounds at home, too." Angie added her coat to the row of hooks inside the back porch door, then helped her daughters out of their parkas. "Emma and Allison insisted on it. I figured, why not?"

"We're going to go around and tell all of our animals that we love them," Allison said.

Melinda looked at Hobo, who had followed them inside and was dancing back and forth between the girls and Angie to get as much attention as possible. *I'm the one here who's really blessed*, she thought, swallowing the sudden lump in her throat.

"I'm sure they will like that," she told Allison, then hurried to pull the last pan of cookies from the oven. "And thanks for coming to help me today. We'll have cookies and cocoa when we're done. Maybe you can hand out the treats as we go along, OK?" That made both girls' eyes light up with excitement.

"As for the blessing itself, I hope what I found online is good enough," she told Angie as she added the cookies to a cooling rack on the counter. "It's over there on the table."

Angie picked up the sheet of paper, and began to nod as she scanned its contents.

"Looks good to me. Simple, direct, loving. Perfect. Mind if I get some more use out of it this afternoon?"

"Might as well. This can be like a dress rehearsal for your own ceremony later. Well, are we ready to head out? I think we'll start in the chicken house. Allison, can you pick up the bucket of carrots there on the back porch?"

Eager to have an important role in the proceedings, Allison hurried out of the kitchen, Hobo at her heels. Emma, who was barely three, was now engrossed in sliding the toy mouse across the linoleum for Grace and Hazel.

"The kittens will still be here when we get back." Angie ruffled her youngest daughter's blond hair. "How about we go see all of Melinda's other animals? She has chickens just like we do."

Melinda's appearance in the chicken house in the middle of the afternoon caused ruffled feathers, curious clucks, and more than one irritated glare from Pansy. The three strangers in tow didn't help ease the hens' suspicions. Emma wanted to pet all the chickens, an idea they quickly rebuffed.

In the end, Angie simply stood in front of the unused brick chimney, the only possible focal point in the space, and intoned the blessing in a sort-of-shouted prayer that could barely be heard over all the wing-flapping and squawking. The chaos was far from the soothing, comforting event Melinda had imagined, but it would have to do. The carrot slices were a hit, however, and the hens began to settle down once the treats were spread out in their pans.

Things went much smoother in the barn, where the atmosphere was more relaxed.

The winter sun was already dipping toward the western horizon, flooding the feeding areas and stalls with pools of warm light. For once, there was no wind rushing past the barn's sturdy corners or seeping around its four-paned windows, only a gentle silence and the comforting rustle of the sheep shifting about in the straw.

Stormy, to Melinda's shock and delight, did not refuse Allison's request to hold him while Angie placed a gentle palm on his gray fur. Sunny leaped into Melinda's lap the moment she sat on the wooden crate in the grain room, and was content to stay there as the blessing was repeated.

"You're getting really good at that," she told Angie. "You should hire out as an animal blessing ... specialist? I don't know what else to call it. But you've got a knack for it."

"Well, Nathan and I are looking to expand our operation." Angie laughed. "We were thinking more along the lines of organic certification and such, but maybe we need to think outside the box." She turned more serious.

"I'm glad you called. I think I needed this reminder that I can't control everything that happens. I worry too much. I'm always sending up good thoughts for our animals, even when everyone is well and happy. And when something goes wrong? I keep God busy with my requests, I think."

"I know what you mean." Melinda gently pushed Sunny out of her lap and followed Angie and the girls into the main aisle of the barn. "If I'm not praying for them all to stay safe, then I'm praying for it not to be too cold or, well, it's always one thing or another."

The peaceful stillness came to an abrupt end, however, when they approached the gate into the sheep's run. The ewes called back and forth to each other and began to pace, curiosity and nervousness reflected in their dark eyes. Some of the ewes pushed toward the troughs along the fence, anticipating an early supper, and the shyer ones darted away from their visitors.

Annie eyed Angie warily, let out a bellow of suspicion, then hoofed over to a far corner where she could better study the situation. Melinda wondered if Annie remembered the foggy October morning when Angie and Nathan had arrived at the farm with their trailer, expecting to transport the sheep to the sale barn in Eagle River. That was the morning Melinda realized she couldn't leave this farm, and she couldn't let the sheep go, either.

"And look at all of you now," she told the ewes as she and Angie came through the gate, this time with a very different plan in mind. "All twelve of you are doing great, and a few of you are going to be mamas soon."

Allison and Emma stayed in the aisle, stepping up on the lowest boards of the fence to watch the proceedings from a safe distance. Melinda and Angie walked among the ewes, rubbing backs and handing out the larger carrot pieces from the bucket, as Angie again recited the prayer.

"Well, that went well," Angie said as they returned to the aisle. "I had to give the blessing several times over, but everyone got in on it, that way. And I think you're right, Melinda. I would say four of the ewes are pregnant."

Allison gasped. "Are you going to have baby lambs?"

"Yes, I sure am! In maybe a month or so. You can come see the babies when they are born." This brought shrieks of excitement from the girls, who apparently had a secret they could no longer keep.

"Mommy's having a baby, too!" Emma shouted as she bounced on the fence, startling the ewes. "We're getting a brother or sister!"

"Angie!" Melinda gasped and hugged her friend. "This is wonderful news! When?"

"In July." Angie beamed. "Oh, we're so excited! We told the girls after my last doctor's appointment, on Friday. We were going to wait a bit to tell people outside the family, but I guess this is too much of a secret for these big sisters."

Angie instinctively touched her stomach, then rolled her eyes. "Just look how big those ewes are getting. I'll be waddling around myself, toward the end. And it'll be during the hottest part of the year, which won't be pleasant. But it's so worth it." She turned to her daughters with a raised eyebrow. "Girls, let's see what you think. Can you pick out which of the sheep are going to have a baby?"

Allison and Emma fell silent, engrossed in their task.

Melinda couldn't hold back her laughter. "Farmers in the making, those two. Look how they're sizing up the ewes."

Allison quickly pointed out two of the sheep who were noticeably wider than the rest.

"Very good, honey," Angie said. "Anyone else?"

"Is Annie going to have a baby?" Emma pointed to the corner where Annie hung back from the group, still watching Angie. But when she heard her name, Annie circled the flock and barged in to where Allison and Emma waited at the fence. Annie was the little girls' favorite, and she knew it.

"No, not this time." Melinda sighed gratefully as Annie soaked up all the attention. "I'll have my hands full as it is. She would probably expect me to fluff her lambing pen's straw every hour and bring her all the carrots I have. The other sheep I think are having babies, by the way, are Number 18, the one closest to the gate; and Number 7, over there by the pole."

"Everyone looks healthy," Angie said as she pocketed the blessing. "You're working wonders with them."

"I'm trying to stay on top of things. Lambing time will be here before I know it. Part of me wishes it was over with, part of me wishes I had more time to get ready."

"Well, preparation is half the battle." Angie motioned for the girls to step down from the fence and start for the door. "When we get to the house, I'll look through Horace's sheep supplies and see what might be expired or missing. What Auggie doesn't have at the co-op, you can get from Doc and Karen."

Hobo was waiting for them outside. Allison and Emma ran ahead with him to the house, eager to spend more time with the kittens. Melinda and Angie took their time, enjoying the last of the sun's gentle warmth as they crossed the yard.

"The girls have been full of questions about Grace and Hazel," Angie said. "I showed them the kittens' pictures on my phone, the ones you sent me once they were doing better. They wanted to know where the kittens came from. I just told them you were helping Doc and Karen, and we had to wait until the kittens were big enough before we could visit them. I love their names, by the way."

"Hazel has the sweetest golden eyes, and all that honey-brown fur. And Grace, well, it just seemed to fit. She's quite the princess already." Melinda held the porch door for Angie. "And as I realized that first night, it was an act of grace that brought them here."

The girls settled on the couch, Allison holding a squirming Grace and little Emma cradling a sleepy Hazel. Melinda was next to them in her reading chair by the fireplace, Hobo at her side, as Angie repeated the blessing three more times.

The words of comfort and protection were now so familiar that they flowed through Melinda's mind before Angie could recite them. She watched her friend place a gentle hand first on Hazel, then Grace, and then Hobo, and felt a special peace fill her heart.

She had caring friends and family, a cozy home, and a new outlook on life. The last one was something she never could have imagined, but somehow, it felt right. And now, there was Angie's wonderful news to celebrate. She silently rejoiced for her friend, and wondered what other blessings the new year might bring.

✳ 9 ✳

Melinda was stumped. The man just stared at her, frustration in his gravelly voice.

"It's batting, you know," he tried again. "Thick stuff, with plastic on the back. Comes in a roll. If you don't carry it, where can I get it?"

She glanced out Prosper Hardware's wide windows, trying to buy some time while she figured out what this guy wanted. There was a brittle edge to the sunshine, the clear skies an icy shade of blue.

The only "batting" she was familiar with was used to sew quilts, and she doubted this burly man wanted to rush home to finish a craft project. "Do you mean insulation? Like fiberglass?"

"Yes!" He slapped the oak counter for emphasis. "Need to wrap my water pipes, and do it today. We just bought an old house south of town. Can't be too careful in this cold. Supposed to get to twenty-five below tonight."

The harried man rolled his eyes when she broke the bad news: Prosper Hardware didn't carry insulation, and it wasn't something Auggie sold at the co-op. Maybe he could try the superstore over in Swanton?

"They only had a few rolls," he grumbled. "I already called. They sold out last night. Looks like I gotta drive up to Mason City, then."

"Sorry we don't carry what you need." She understood the man's frustration. Mason City was thirty-five miles away. "You're right about the cold snap, I'm afraid. Auggie said it might get to thirty below by tomorrow night."

"Let me guess, he made his prediction with a grin on his mug, right?"

Before she could admit he was correct, the guy shook his head. "Auggie brings nothing but bad karma to this town with his hopes for mayhem and destruction, and all just so he can write it down in that weather log of his."

He paused long enough to pull his navy knit cap down past his receding hairline.

"Never met anyone so opinionated and full of himself. Thinks he's better than everyone else, but he's just a stubborn ass. I refuse to step foot in that co-op, I'd rather drive over to Swanton than give him any of my business."

The man made a dismissive gesture with his hand and zipped up his coat, then turned back toward Melinda. "Well, don't freeze to death tonight. I better get on the road." A blast of icy air rushed in as the man stomped out.

"What was that all about?" Bill came up the main aisle. "I could hear him all the way in the back. Everything OK?"

"Here's the recap: We don't carry insulation. That makes him mad. Auggie's an ass. And he brings this town bad luck."

The grumpy customer's rant made her uneasy, but not because he was rude. While most shoppers were patient, she'd dealt with a number of unhappy people in the past seven months. A smile and an understanding tone went a long way with most of them.

It was the talk of brutal, sub-zero cold that had her worried. The farmhouse's basement pipes were insulated, but there was still the risk of the acreage's lines freezing up and leaving her and the animals without water. Ed had mentioned such a possibility before Christmas, when he gave the sheep's automatic waterer a cautiously optimistic evaluation.

"I haven't had any trouble with my water lines yet this winter," she told Bill, "and I hope I never do. But I don't like the sound of the forecast. When I get home tonight, I've got to turn some of my faucets to a steady drip. Then I guess I'll hope for the best. I don't know what else to do."

"That's the important thing, keep the water moving. And open the cabinets under the kitchen and bathroom sinks, let the warm air get to the pipes where you can." Then he smirked. "Do you have any five-gallon buckets?"

"I sure do." She already had a plan. "I'm going to use one of them out in the barn, so I can let that inside hydrant drip, too. Whatever it takes to keep the lines open."

"Well, of course." Bill was laughing now. "But make sure you have a spare, one that's clean enough to bring in the house. A toilet seat fits nicely on the top, and those buckets are just about the right height, too."

Melinda rolled her eyes.

"I mean it." Bill turned serious. "If you lose your water, you lose your sewer. I know Horace isn't the most forward-thinking guy, but I bet he still tore down the old outhouse years ago, right?"

"This could be a long week," she groaned. "I got through that blizzard with barely a scratch. I thought it couldn't get worse than that."

"Oh, but it can," Bill said cheerily, gesturing for her to hand him a snack-size bag of chips from the oak counter's display case. He reached around for his wallet. "Forgot part of my lunch. But yeah, a deep freeze will bring things to a halt around here. The Methodist Church already canceled their soup supper for tomorrow night."

"So I heard." She counted Bill's change, trying to keep the disappointment out of her voice.

The congregation had moved the event up to the last Thursday in January, trying to fit it in before renovations began in the building's basement. Now, the dinner wouldn't happen until spring.

"I was looking forward to that, believe it or not. It sounds like their soup supper is the biggest date on Prosper's social calendar this time of year."

"It is," Bill said mischievously. "But you've still got a big night out coming up, don't you?"

"Don't say it," she warned him.

"What?" Bill snickered.

"Bill." She glared at him. "Evan's just being nice by asking me to dinner. And I'm just being nice by going. Actually, it was all Chloe's idea. She remembers how much I like her cat, that's all."

Evan and Chloe had come into the store yesterday after story hour. Chloe was in high spirits, excited to show off her Valentine's Day craft and tell Melinda about her new friends. She wanted to stay at the counter while her father shopped, and by the time he returned with his purchases, the little girl was asking Melinda to visit Daisy, her cat.

"No one comes to our house." Chloe had looked so sad. "Except for Grandma and Grandpa that one time."

Touched by his daughter's enthusiasm, Evan had suddenly insisted Melinda join them for dinner. Afraid to disappoint a lonely little girl, Melinda had blurted out she would be happy to accept his invitation. Unfortunately, Bill had witnessed everything.

"It's just a friendly visit," she reminded Bill now. "You should have seen Chloe's face, she was so excited."

"Uh-huh." Bill crossed his arms. "Look, my wife and I started dating junior year at Iowa State. So it's been ..." He looked up at the pressed-tin ceiling, calculating. "Fourteen years? Fourteen years since I've asked someone out on a date. So yeah, I'm out of practice. But I have to say, Evan seemed pretty thrilled when you said yes."

"Bill. Let it go. He's married."

"*Separated*. I heard he's already filed for divorce."

Melinda felt her cheeks start to burn. She didn't like the direction this conversation was going. Why did Bill have to make such a big deal out of all this?

"Mabel is right, you guys are the worst gossips around." She busied herself with closing the cash register's drawer and tidying the counter.

"Far worse than any group of women. And as for what you heard, how do you know it's even true?"

Bill raised an eyebrow and was about to say more. She waved him off. "Oh, never mind."

"Well, maybe I'm jumping to conclusions," he admitted. "But you could do worse."

"With who?" She threw up her arms. "How many single men over the age of, what, thirty-five are in this county?"

"My point exactly." Bill rattled his bag of chips at Melinda. "I'm not even sure who else is around for you and Karen to fight over. Well, I'm going on break. I'll be upstairs."

Driving home that evening, her mind went back to Evan and Chloe's invitation.

Bill was right, Evan had seemed genuinely delighted when she agreed to come for dinner. The way he smiled at her, the way his kind brown eyes lit up with ... what?

"Forget it." She slowed the car for its turn on to the gravel road, whose built-in traction had long ago disappeared under the slick, packed-down snow. "I've got bigger things to worry about right now."

It was so cold that Hobo didn't rush out to meet her car when she pulled into the yard. Instead, he was waiting for her in the kitchen, where the kittens were playing hide-and-seek under the table.

"Am I glad Horace has that garage," she told him. "And that the car's gas tank is nearly full. If I'm lucky, it'll start in the morning."

She bundled into her chore gear, adding a second knit hat and stuffing another pair of gloves under her warmest ones, then peered out the back porch's frosted windows to where the iron hydrant stood next to the snow-covered garden. The thought of trying to work the pump's heavy handle in this bitter cold made her shiver, then pick up a clean, empty bucket and double back to the kitchen's deep sink. Hobo made no move to follow her outside.

Instead, he stretched out on the porch floor as if to say, *I'll wait right here.*

"Good boy." Melinda rubbed his ears. "I'll be back as soon as I can."

The icy air whooshed up her nose and made her gasp. She paused on the back steps long enough to wrap her scarf one last turn. It was nearly twilight, deep shadows reaching across the silent yard as the sun set in a misleading haze of red and orange. The water pail threatened to pull her off balance and soak her coveralls as she toddled, chin tucked low and one boot in front of the other, down the roughly shoveled path to the chicken coop.

She hurried back to the house and heated some leftover gravy in the microwave, then poured it into the cats' food bucket and snapped the lid tight.

The creak of the barn door's hinges caused Stormy to poke his head out of the cats' cozy hideout under the stairs, but he and Sunny weren't willing to leave the glow of their cave's heat lamp. Even for chicken gravy.

"I don't blame you," Melinda pulled her scarf away long enough to say. "You two stay in there. I'll bring your stuff over here." She fluffed the deep straw in the cubbyhole, then fit the cats' gravy dish and bowl of kibble in one corner. Their heated water bowl was brought out of the grain room and plugged in right outside their nest's entrance.

Between their thick, wooly coats and the snug, sturdy barn, the sheep didn't seem fazed by the cold. She set out the ewes' grain and hay, then hurried through the gate to check the automatic waterer was still working. She slid the cover over the cats' barn entrance, barely pausing to wonder what other, wilder critters she might have locked in for the night, then set a five-gallon bucket under the hydrant next to the sheep's feed bins. Bill was right; a pail that size would make a passable toilet in an emergency.

"I hope I don't need this, but just in case." She reached for another bucket, the one that looked the cleanest, and set it over by the exit.

The water gushed out of the hydrant, and she throttled it back to a tiny trickle. How much would it take for the bucket to overflow overnight, turning her barn's concrete floor into an ice rink? She had better trudge out here again, just before bedtime, and swap this bucket for an empty one.

After she washed the supper dishes, she left the kitchen faucet dripping and opened the cabinets under the sink.

The mysterious creak of the painted-over doors was enough to bring Hazel and Grace padding in from the living room, where they had been curled up with Hobo in front of the fireplace.

"What's all this?" she asked the kittens, who paused only long enough for wide-eyed peeks into the deep shadows under the sink, then dived in with a bravery far bigger than themselves. Hazel instantly reached out to investigate the rusting canister of some long-forgotten cleanser.

"Oh no, you don't. It's not safe. Guess I need to clean under here first."

Hazel didn't protest when Melinda scooped her up, but Grace howled with frustration when she was set away from the sink and the cabinet doors snapped shut. Two cardboard boxes stuffed with junk and thirty minutes later, the kittens were released from their temporary bathroom jail. The kitchen sink's open base was now pet-proofed, its interior warmed by the heat rising from the nearby floor register.

Melinda repeated the process in both bathrooms, then filled several buckets and jugs with water and stored them in the basement, away from three sets of prying paws. The thermometer outside the kitchen windows already showed fifteen below. She'd done all she could. All that was left was to hope, and pray, that the farm's lines didn't freeze overnight.

Hobo was sprawled across the couch, apparently unfazed by the plummeting temperatures outside. As she snuggled into her reading chair with the kittens, Melinda found herself soothed by the faint *drip, drip, drip* that echoed under the hum of the television.

But she felt a bit overwhelmed, too. Her rush to purge the clutter under the sinks had turned into a reminder of just how much stuff was, well, stuffed inside this century-old house.

"I don't think Horace and Wilbur ever threw anything away," she told Hobo, who only gave a contented sigh and rolled over. "Yeah, it's not your problem, is it? But someday soon, it's going to be mine."

Just before bed, she dashed out to the barn to swap the hydrant's buckets. She would have paid good money (even though she didn't have much to spare) to avoid that chore, but there was no one else to do it.

Everything was on her. Curled up in bed, the covers pulled so high that there was just a sliver of space between their hems and the pillow, Melinda felt the weight of what she was doing, of what she'd promised Horace.

Last fall, when the skies were a brilliant blue and the acreage's trees blazed with red and orange leaves, it had been so easy to tell Horace she wanted to stay. The holidays were filled with merriment and family and friends, the first snows mere nuisances easily managed with a little extra grit and a lot of extra work. But then came the blizzard, which smothered the yard with snowdrifts several feet deep. And now this, a night so bitter cold and still that it seemed as if the entire world would turn to ice. Out there, in the dark, it was getting colder by the minute and there was nothing she could do to stop it. She drifted off at last, lulled to sleep by the steady drip of the bathroom faucet down the hall.

Melinda sat up suddenly, startled awake by something she couldn't name. It was just after three. In an instant, she knew what was missing. Not bothering with her slippers, she threw off the covers and rushed into the hall. Sliding on the slick hardwood floors in her sock-covered feet, she rushed into the bathroom.

There was only the faintest trace of water in the sink. Too many seconds passed before she spied one glittering, hesitant drop clinging to the bottom of the faucet. She flipped the hot water tap, then twisted the cold one wider. A feeble trickle appeared, then it was gone.

She reached across to the bathtub and cranked the handle. Nothing. Finally there came a gurgle, a gush of air, and an angry splash of icy water from the faucet. She huddled there on the bath mat, tears of despair and gratitude mingling on her face, and watched the thin rope of water stream into the tub's drain. The coldest hours were just coming on, as Auggie always said they did, and the temperature wouldn't bottom out until just after sunrise. If the pipes froze and the weather stayed bitterly cold, it could be days before her water would flow again.

Melinda considered her options, wiped her tears, and got to her feet. Hobo met her at the bottom of the stairs, sniffing curiously at the electric space heater she had pulled out of her bedroom closet. The one that used to warm her living room on frigid nights in Minneapolis. "I maybe shouldn't do this," she told Hobo, who whimpered at this strange activity in the middle of the night and the quaver in Melinda's voice. "But we don't have a choice."

The downstairs bathroom was tiny and windowless, her best bet. The heater was parked in front of the open sink cabinet and pointed toward the water pipes. She checked the safety valve, flipped the switch and cranked the dial, and the heater roared to life.

With the kittens' litter box brought out into Horace's old bedroom, she latched the bathroom door behind her. Grace and Hazel, still cuddled in a pile of blankets on the bed, watched her with wondering eyes.

"Sorry, girls. No privacy for you until this cold snap ends. I can't risk anyone getting in there around that heater."

She hurried to the basement for the rest of the clean water pails, slowed her steps long enough to collect the five-gallon bucket waiting on the back porch, and marched upstairs, Hobo falling in behind her. She set the big bucket next to the toilet with a defiant thud, then filled every last pail from the struggling bathtub faucet before dialing it back to a trickle.

"It's all we can do, Hobo," Melinda whispered as she ushered him out of the bathroom and closed the door. She was exhausted, but knew the promise of checking the lines again would be the only way she could fall back asleep.

The taps were still dripping at four-thirty, the downstairs bathroom as warm as a sauna. At six, she was relieved to find nothing had changed, despite the thermometer's mercury huddled down at twenty-eight below.

The barn's hydrant dribbled on, its pipes buried deep under the concrete floor and not more than ten feet from the farm's well. Melinda cracked the cats' outside passage just wide enough to allow any trapped wildlife to escape, deciding the portal was small enough, and far enough away from her animals' bedding areas, that it wouldn't cause a draft inside the barn. The cats' and chickens' heated water bowls, as well as the sheep's metal contraption, were cold to the touch but still humming along and unfrozen.

Melinda hated to turn off the space heater in the downstairs bathroom, but was too afraid of fire to leave it on while she was at work. After protesting twice, her car finally mumbled to life.

Prosper Hardware's phone was already ringing when she came in from the back, a man calling to see if the store had plastic buckets in stock (yes) and if it carried space heaters (sorry, no). George had left a voicemail, saying it was too cold for him to venture out. Auggie and Doc were also no-shows.

"I wouldn't trade places with Doc for a million bucks, making the rounds in weather like this," Jerry said as he bundled up to trudge over to City Hall. "If I didn't have that paperwork waiting across the street, I'd be at home. It's like that joke I saw online yesterday. 'Iowa: Come for the culture. Stay because your car won't start.'"

The phone rang all morning, people desperate for anything that might help thaw their water lines. She patched most of them back to Bill, who tried to give advice and referred them to plumbers in the area.

The thermometer bumped up to a heat wave of two above zero by noon, but at least one more night of near-record cold was still to come. As she fielded the frantic calls, Melinda made a decision: She'd get up every two hours that night, every hour if she had to, and check her taps. Her wee-hours desperation had saved her water supply, and she wasn't about to lose it now.

She yawned as she fumbled with her keys on the farmhouse's back steps, unwilling to remove her thick gloves. As she clicked the lock, a commotion started up inside, a cacophony of scratching, tumbling noises. She instinctively glanced down at the doggie door, then across the yard to the barely-open hatch in the barn wall. What if some wild animal had traded one shelter for another?

She cringed and turned the doorknob slowly, the creak of the latch answered by more frantic movements inside. Closing her eyes and tightening her grip, Melinda pushed through the door to find two pairs of eyes glowing with fear.

"Sunny and Stormy!" she gasped, then lowered her voice as the cats dashed for the safe space under the porch bench.

"Hey," she tried again, this time barely above a whisper. She gently latched the back door and set her purse and tote on the bench's padded seat. "What are you doing in here? Did you come in the doggie door, just like Hobo?"

Sunny let out a tentative howl. Stormy only cowered down, attempting to disappear between Sunny's fluffy orange back and the wall.

Melinda had to laugh as she lowered herself to the chilled floorboards. Her dear barn kitties had done on their own the very thing she once tried to force them to do.

"Last fall, I attempted to bring you two into the house, or at least into this porch. But you refused." She pointed at the arm of her coat. "And I had the scratches to prove it. Did you just decide it was time? Desperate times, desperate measures, and all that?"

She stretched a tentative hand toward the cats. Sunny seemed to regain his confidence, and slowly slid out from under the bench to rub his cheek against her palm.

Stormy inched forward, but still hesitated to give up the safety of his post.

Melinda glanced at the pet door that opened into the kitchen, then back at the wide-eyed cats.

"It's not a question of whether you want to come all the way inside. I don't think that's even been considered."

There was the sound of large padded feet on the other side of the pet door, then Hobo popped his head through and let out a happy whine.

"Is this your doing?" She slid across the floor and wrapped her arms around Hobo, who was wriggling in delight. "Did you tell Stormy and Sunny that it's better in here, show them how to get in?"

At the mention of his name, and seeing the attention lavished on Hobo, Stormy at last crawled out from under the bench and placed a tentative front paw on Melinda's jeans. "Sorry I startled you, Stormy." She gave him a gentle pat on the head. "If you stay in here, you'll find we have lots of strange sounds and activity at different times of the day."

Grace and Hazel hadn't shown any interest in following Hobo through the flap that took him from the kitchen to the back porch, but Melinda knew that could soon change. She might need to arrange a supervised introduction, and keep the kittens safe in Horace's bedroom when she was at work, just in case.

How long would Sunny and Stormy stay? She had no idea. Every time she thought she had them figured out, tried to anticipate their habits and moods, they showed her something new.

It took a few extra trips to the barn, but she soon had a cardboard box stuffed with clean straw settled in one corner of the porch. The cats' heat lamp was hooked a safe distance above it, and their food bowl and water dish waited nearby. Another cut-down box was filled with fresh litter and set by the boot caddy. Only a crazy cat would venture out on a night that was going to be this bitterly cold, and Sunny and Stormy had proven again just how smart they were.

"So if you're not house cats, and you're not my barn babies right now," she told them before she went into the kitchen, "I guess you're my porch kitties. As for how long this will last, I'll leave that up to you."

❊ 10 ❊

The bare-limbed trees crowded closer to the road once she turned off the county highway southeast of Prosper. It was already dark, even though it was just before six. Her car's headlights caught the slight swerve in the snow-dusted gravel, then the angles of the iron river bridge just ahead.

"Almost there." Melinda took a deep breath and turned down the rock radio station she'd hoped would raise her energy and calm her nerves. The cold snap had broken three days ago, and while she no longer got up overnight to check her water lines, she was still catching up on her sleep.

Her back porch had also returned to normal. The first day temperatures moderated, Sunny and Stormy followed her to the barn at evening chore time, padded into the grain room, and sprawled out on the concrete floor in the exact spot where their dishes usually sat. Melinda took the hint, and put all of their belongings back in their rightful places.

If only tonight could be that easy, she thought as she turned left on the gravel road that wound along the east bank of the river. Why had she ever agreed to have dinner with Evan and Chloe? She could be at home, curled up in her reading chair with a good book, the kittens in her lap and Hobo sprawled out on the couch, not worrying if her hair looked right or if the faded lavender sweater she'd snatched off the closet shelf was too slouchy.

"It was the only clean one that didn't have cat hair on it."
She reflexively brushed at her nicest pair of jeans with one
hand as she steered with the other. Hobo had jumped on her
at the last minute, his nose working overtime at the salad and
garlic bread stuffed inside her canvas tote.

Evan had texted that afternoon to say spaghetti and
meatballs were on the menu, along with brownies. Melinda
wished she had a few more details to go on, like if he was
excited she was coming over, or if this was only a good-
hearted attempt to make his young daughter happy. Or how
she really felt about seeing him again.

There was some sort of movement in the brush up ahead,
to the left where the land sloped to the river bottoms. She
snapped her thoughts back to the road, hoping a deer wasn't
about to leap in front of her car. Just last week, Karen had
nearly wrecked her work truck responding to a night call at a
farm not far from here. The poor animal had collided with the
front of her vehicle, then ran off into the woods.

If she hadn't been going so slow, Karen told Melinda, the
deer might have rolled up the hood of her truck and came
right through the windshield. After a moment to compose
herself, Karen had continued on, determined to reach the
distressed cow waiting for her down the road. She came out of
the barn to find the farmer had banged out the worst of the
dents in her dangling bumper, and lashed it to the truck's
frame with lengths of wire. Karen had offered to scrap the
veterinary bill for his help, but he'd refused. "Can't have you
driving these snowy roads with a banged-up truck." The man
had shrugged away her suggestion. "With Doc home with the
flu, I don't know what I would've done if you weren't here."

Melinda smiled as she made the last turn, which led up a
steep hill and away from the river. That's what people did out
here, they helped each other. "I'm just helping, too. Evan and
Chloe are lonely. I'm trying to make them feel welcome, like
so many people did for me when I first came back."

The battered mailbox at the crest of the hill was the only
sign she'd reached the old Benniger farm, as the stately brick

house was far down the lane and shrouded by both darkness and a thick stand of trees. As she bumped down the rutted drive, which had recently been bladed sort-of-clear of snow, Melinda wondered how long Evan intended to live there.

His cousin, the owner, said Evan and Chloe were welcome to stay as long as they needed. The brick house was stately and impressive, with heavy white cornices crowning all of its windows and a dark slate roof. But while the Christmas decorations Melinda and her neighbors brought over during the holidays had chased some of the gloom away, she sensed the once-grand estate was too large and dreary to make a permanent home for such a small family.

Melinda angled her car in next to Evan's, which was huddled near the expansive front porch. The faint glow from the yard light softened the veranda's peeling paint and slipping angles, but the hulking shapes of the tumbledown barn and sheds across the clearing still made her shiver. She gathered her purse, her tote and her courage, and rapped loudly on one of the ornately carved front doors. The grand vestibule buffeted the living room from the porch, and she hoped Evan had noticed her headlights coming up the drive. She didn't want to stand out here, on this windswept ridge, longer than necessary.

The oak door, right on cue, let out a melancholy creak. "Good evening," Evan drawled in a mock-sinister voice as he beckoned Melinda inside. They both laughed heartily, breaking the tension. "What brings you to this abandoned castle on such a dark and dreary night?"

"The promise of fabulous spaghetti. It smells wonderful. I hope you haven't been slaving in the kitchen all day."

He beamed and shrugged, his brown eyes dancing with humor. "I opened a few jars about a half an hour ago. However," he raised a finger, "I did roll the meatballs myself."

The few flecks of gray in Evan's dark hair stood out in the harsh light of the vintage chandelier that glared down from the vestibule's high ceiling. But she could tell he'd recently shaved, and his pullover seemed a bit nicer than usual.

"Well, I have a confession, too. I only had to get out a knife to prep the salad and the bread. Seriously, though, this place feels a bit strange at night. I bet you and Chloe stick to these front rooms."

"Absolutely." He took her tote bag as they entered the living room. "But I'm relieved to say, I haven't had any strange experiences yet, if you know what I mean. As for Daisy, you'd have to ask her." The tortoiseshell cat, curled up on the faded couch pulled close to the fireplace, opened her green eyes when she heard her name. Daisy offered Melinda a casual "meow" and rolled over.

There was the echo of running feet in the hallway, then Chloe appeared. The little girl bounced into the room, wearing a dark pink sweater Melinda recognized as a hand-me-down from Angie's daughter, Allison.

"Melinda, come see my doll house! Santa brought it for Christmas." The miniature two-story structure sat in the corner by the television, its wallpaper tired and faded. But it was filled with a haphazard collection of small-scale furniture and tiny people, even a little dog.

"Thrift store," Evan told Melinda in a low voice under Chloe's exclamations. "Chloe," he said loud enough for his daughter to hear, "we're about to eat. You can show Melinda your doll house after dinner, OK?"

"My people are having a party, too," Chloe called over her shoulder. "I have to help them get ready."

Melinda followed Evan into the kitchen, unsure what to do with her coat. Or herself, for that matter. He pointed to some wall hooks above a rubber mat, but gestured for her to leave her shoes on.

"Cold floors around here, no matter how high I crank the furnace. And I try not to. I've never lived in the country before. I had no idea how expensive propane is these days."

"I know what you mean. Old houses are hard to keep warm this time of year. You should have seen the look on my face when my propane delivery guy filled my tank just before Christmas."

Evan laughed, then looked around the kitchen, which was neat and clean, if a little bare. "It's been a learning experience for me, too. Sorry I haven't had time to set the table."

Grateful to have something to do, she reached into the upper cabinet next to the sink. Mabel's secondhand dishes were still there, along with a few glasses Helen Emmerson added from her kitchen.

Helen's bright tablecloth remained on the table, its holly berries now a step behind the season but still cheerful. The scatter rugs Mabel had pulled out of storage warmed the tired linoleum in front of the sink and the stove.

The spaghetti was delicious, and Melinda was pleasantly surprised Chloe didn't turn her nose up at the salad's vegetables. The little girl's chatter about Daisy and her new story-hour friends kept any awkward silences at bay, and Melinda relaxed and begin to enjoy herself. Evan's former career in information technology had, by his own honest assessment, made him completely unprepared for the quirky customers that frequented Auggie's co-op, and he soon had her laughing at his fish-out-of-water stories.

"It's the same at Prosper Hardware. I learned quickly that every bit of local gossip runs through that store. Maybe there's something about helping people that makes them feel they can open up to you. I guess when you're ringing up someone's toilet paper, all those barriers just fall away."

Evan promised Chloe they would enjoy the brownies once the dishes were done. Without being reminded by her father, she took her empty plate and cup to the sink before hurrying back to her doll house in the next room.

"She seems to be adjusting well," Melinda said as they cleared the table.

"I hope so. Everything's been really hard for her." He suddenly turned quiet, and a bit of the former despair appeared on his face. Melinda wanted to say something to encourage him, but wasn't sure what that might be.

"I can't imagine what this has been like for you, Evan," was all she said, then reached for the comfortingly familiar dishtowels stacked on the counter. They used to be Mabel's. "Tell you what. You wash, I'll dry."

His smile returned. "I appreciate the help. By the way, Chloe loves story hour at the library. Thanks for suggesting that. It's really helped her adjust to living here."

"No problem, I thought she would like it." Melinda wanted to ask Evan how he was adjusting, but wasn't sure if she should. Chloe was a safe topic of conversation, but they'd just about covered all those bases already. Maybe he would offer that other information on his own. She busied herself drying a glass he handed her way, and waited.

A heavy silence settled between them and refused to leave, despite the cheerful hum of the television in the next room and Chloe's chatter as she set up the dinner party in her doll house.

Melinda decided if she and Evan were going to stand at the sink like this, shoulder to shoulder, she would have to get more personal.

"So, do you plan to stay here, then, at least for a while?"

"Well, I really don't know." Evan was quick to answer, as if he'd also been struggling for something to say. "I've got a month until my unemployment benefits stop. That, and part-time at the co-op, has kept us afloat. I'm grateful for what we have, really I am, but it's not going to be enough. I have to find a better job."

He paused only long enough to hand her a plate. "And while I'm glad David let us stay here for free like this, I don't want to take advantage longer than I have to. Besides, this mansion's way too big for us. Chloe still sees it like we're camping, but she'll get tired of it eventually. We need a real home. And then, she misses her mother, and ..." His voice trailed off as he added more dish soap to the dissolving suds in the sink.

"I'm sorry," he said at last. "I shouldn't burden you with all this. Let's see, I think you simply asked if we were going to keep living in this house, and I guess the answer is yes for now, but no for later. I have no idea what to do."

What Evan decided wasn't any of Melinda's business. But as he talked about his uncertain future, she found herself hoping he would stay in Prosper. She pushed those feelings aside and focused on wiping the silverware.

"I remember what that's like." She tried to keep her tone understanding but neutral. "But you'll find your way through this, somehow."

Evan stared out the window over the sink, as if trying to see through the thick darkness outside its panes. The sheer brown curtains, dusty with age, were barely wide enough to cover the tired wooden frame and were no match for the gusts rattling the metal storm window. Melinda felt a chill as an icy draft seeped into the kitchen.

"I wish I was as settled as you are now," he finally said. "I have to say, I really admire what you've accomplished. You've found a whole new career, a little farm, all your animals. And it sounds like you're really becoming a part of things in this town. Dad says you ought to run for mayor."

Melinda snorted and nearly dropped the still-slick glass in her hand. "Oh, come on, he can't be serious. Besides, I don't live in the city limits; I can't get on the ballot. I'll stick to planning holiday festivals. But he's kind to say such things."

Evan didn't respond, and she saw the tension in his jaw as he focused on scrubbing the pasta pot. She shouldn't have said that. Unfortunately, Auggie's interactions with his son could not always be considered "kind."

"I think your Dad just hates to admit he's wrong," she said gently. "And just so you know, when I came back, I was a total wreck. I'm sure I looked like the best niece ever, giving up my whole life to rush home and save my family's business. But coming home was an escape for me, the easy way out. And I knew it."

"I hated to have to come back here," Evan said suddenly, lowering his voice and glancing into the living room. Chloe was still busy with her doll house, describing its occupants to Daisy. "I stayed away all those years because that's what I wanted to do, to build my own life. But now, I've got Chloe to think of. She deserves the best life I can give her. She should have two parents." He hung his head, and Melinda could see the tears in his eyes.

"But you know, Carrie's doing so much better." He tried for a smile, and Melinda was struck by the hope and admiration she heard in his voice. "She's so strong, she really wants to put this all behind her. And while we've had our troubles, she's an amazing mother."

Melinda tried to mirror his smile, and reinforce it with what she hoped was an encouraging nod. She had to be careful how she reacted, what she said. In his usual forthright way, Auggie had already told her all about Evan and Carrie's troubles, sparing none of the unflattering details.

She couldn't let on about what she knew. Or at least, what she'd heard. All she could do was dry another plate, add it to the stack on the counter, and wait for Evan to say more.

"I just hope I can fix things." He lifted the sink's stopper and let the dirty suds drift down the drain. Then he reached for a clean sponge and started on the counter, carefully wiping away all the stray soap and water. "I just want to make everything better." He glanced in to where Chloe was playing, then suddenly turned to Melinda with a grin. "It's never too late for a fresh start, right?"

The way he looked at her, with so much ... admiration, she guessed it to be. But was that all? She didn't know, and couldn't risk trying to guess.

"Everything will fall into place somehow." She handed him the last dry glass to store back on the cabinet shelf. "It will just take time."

For a second, their hands touched. Melinda felt a not-unpleasant twinge run up her arm. She tried to move her hand away, but not too quickly. Evan was still smiling at her. Was he about to say something? Did she want to hear it?

"I brought some toy mice for Daisy." She busied herself with shaking out the damp dishtowel and draping it over the oven door's handle. "Hazel and Grace have more than they can play with, my mom brings them new toys constantly."

Evan turned away and gave the counter one last swipe with the sponge. It was as if that moment never happened.

"Daisy will love them, I'm sure. That sparkly purple ball you gave her at Christmas is her favorite, though. She carries it everywhere."

They drifted into the living room. The Christmas tree on loan from the Emmersons had been taken down, of course, but the high-ceilinged room remained softer and warmer for all the cozy touches brought in during the holidays. Helen's thick-knotted afghan was draped over the back of the lumpy brown chair, and the bright throw pillows still rested on the faded green couch. Evan thankfully took the chair, which meant Melinda didn't have to decide where she should sit.

Between the police procedural on television, the surprisingly good brownies from a boxed mix, and Chloe's eagerness to show off her doll house, Melinda once again felt her unease lift away. An hour passed quickly, the conversation focused on the quirky people she and Evan knew in Prosper and safe topics such as the weather. Despite his quiet tendencies, Evan had a razor-sharp sense of humor and was a quick study of everyone he'd met in town.

One round of laughter was interrupted by the deep chime of a clock from somewhere behind a set of pocket doors, and Melinda jumped.

Evan gestured over his shoulder. "There's a grandfather clock in the dining room. I couldn't resist setting it when we moved in." He turned to Chloe. "You know what that means. Time for bed."

"Daddy, no! Melinda is here."

"I should get going." She was enjoying herself, but hadn't been sure how, or when, to duck out gracefully. "My dog and my kittens will be waiting for me to tuck them in," she told Chloe. "It's their bedtime, just like it is yours." That made the little girl smile.

"Do they sleep on your bed? Daisy sleeps with me."

"They have their very own bed, one that they share. They curl up together, all on one blanket."

"I want to meet them!" Chloe gasped. "Daddy ..."

"Maybe some time." Evan's tone was noncommittal, and he gave Melinda a questioning look. She nodded, deciding she might like that, very much.

"But for now," he tousled Chloe's dark curls, "it's time to brush your teeth. Can you tell Melinda good night, first?"

"'Bye, Melinda!" Chloe landed on the couch and almost climbed into Melinda's lap, giving her an unexpected hug. "Thank you for coming to see us."

She was touched by Chloe's big heart and enthusiasm. "Thank you for asking me to visit you. I'll see you again sometime, OK?"

Chloe grinned and nodded, then ran down the hall toward the bathroom.

"She's so sweet, Evan." Melinda started for the kitchen to gather her dishes and her purse, and fetch her coat. "And she has wonderful manners for such a little girl."

"Well, we worked on those before you came," he admitted. "Just because we're isolated out here, I don't want her to forget how to act around people, you know?" He reached for his parka. "Here, I'll walk you out. I need to spread some more ice melt on those front steps, they have been really nasty since the last snow."

It was even colder than it had been two hours ago, the northwest wind whipping through the bare trees that tried to shelter the farmyard. Melinda pulled up her coat's hood, glad her car was so close to the porch.

"Your windshield's pretty frosted over." Evan dropped the ice melt bucket on the weathered porch floor and doubled back to the front door. "Go ahead and start the car. I've got a spare scraper inside, I'll help you clear it off."

They worked in comfortable silence over the hum of the car's engine. "Thanks for helping me," Melinda said when they finished. "I can't wait until spring, when we don't have to do that anymore. And thanks for having me over, too."

"I had a good time." Evan came around from the other side of the car to meet her by the driver's door.

"Chloe did, too. And Daisy," he added with a small laugh. "And you know how important it is that Daisy is happy."

"Of course. Grace and Hazel already run my house. Even Hobo lets them get their way."

"It was fun to have company, for a change. Maybe ... maybe we could meet for lunch someday, when I'm in town?"

"I'd like that." She meant it. "Just give me a call sometime, OK?"

Before her mind could register what was happening, Evan stepped in closer. His hug was a kind gesture, not exactly romantic given their bulky layers. He started to pull away, then hesitated. For one terrible moment, Melinda was afraid he might try to kiss her. And that she might feel like kissing him back.

"It's freezing out here." She shook her shoulders and took the smallest step backward. "I'd better get going. I'm glad your driveway's been plowed. It's quite aways down to the road."

"That's for sure." Evan laughed easily, and Melinda wondered if she was making too much of things. She snapped her door shut, then put the car into reverse with a mixture of relief and wistfulness and oh, she didn't even know what else. She didn't know what to feel, or what to think. She waved to Evan as her car looped the circular drive. He grinned and waved back, then turned for the porch.

"What. Was. That?" she gasped as she drove down the lane. "Oh, my God, *what was that*?" She started to laugh, and was still smiling by the time the car reached the road.

* 11 *

"I want to hear all about it," Karen whispered and leaned over the table in Prosper Hardware's office. "Once Bill leaves."

Bill snorted as he pulled his lunch out of the refrigerator. "Oooh, Melinda," he teased in a sing-song voice. "What if I want to hear all about your date, too? That Evan, he's just so cute."

"Enough!" Melinda pointed at him. "I've told you several times that it wasn't a date. We're just friends, OK?"

"Oh, so there's a 'we' now?" He raised his eyebrows, still smirking. Melinda waved him away with her hand. Anything she might say, any defense she could offer, would just throw gasoline on the fire. The sooner Bill left, the better.

Nothing had happened, anyway. But it almost had, and …

"Well, I'll leave you ladies to your gossip," he called over his shoulder as he started for the stairs.

"But Melinda, remember what I said the other day. You could do much worse."

Karen rolled her eyes as his footsteps faded away. "Bill's a nice guy, but I don't know if I'd take advice from him about my love life, such as it is. And it's not much." She turned back to her leftovers and the topic at hand. "So, sounds like things got a little interesting last night. Give me the details."

Melinda shared the highlights while she picked at her chili. It tasted so good two days ago. But she was tired of it now. Almost as tired as she was of turning last night's events over and over in her mind.

"I didn't see that coming," Karen said at the end. "Hmmm. It was a hug only, he didn't actually kiss you. But sounds like he might have been thinking about it. I'd say all that matters is, what do *you* think? What do you really think about Evan?"

"Well, I don't know." Melinda hesitated. "He's sort-of good looking, I guess. But he's more than that. He's ... smart. And funny. And, well, we seem to have a lot in common."

"That is true." Karen thought for a moment, then shrugged. "Who knows where this might lead? It sounds like you really hit it off. You've both been through a lot of change. You're both from this area, originally, and then moved back. And he's, what, only two years younger than you?"

"Closer to three. But that's not what's giving me pause."

It had been some time since Melinda had met a man that caught her interest, or one who seemed genuinely interested in her. That all seemed so long ago, back in her old life. Sometimes, she could hardly remember what that was like. What any of that was like.

"Well, he's ... messy," she finally added. "Complicated."

"Oh, you mean the whole ex-wife-in-rehab thing?" Karen said gently. "Or maybe, the single-dad thing? Or is it the doesn't-have-a-steady-job thing? But then, I guess we've all got our baggage."

Melinda tapped her spoon on the side of her plastic bowl. "I liked spending time with him, and Chloe, too. But at the same time, something's not right." She dropped her spoon on the table. "Oh, why are we even having this conversation! Nothing happened, it doesn't matter, we're just friends."

Karen waited, then measured her words carefully. "Maybe today you're just friends, but what if it becomes more than that?"

"I don't know. He mentioned Carrie several times. Of course, why wouldn't she come up in conversation? But it wasn't just that, it was the way he talked about her. He kept saying how strong she is, and how she's getting herself together. He seemed to think all her problems were just a bump in the road."

Karen stopped with her can of soda almost to her face. "Wait a minute. I thought he'd already filed for divorce."

"That's what Bill said." Melinda gritted her teeth. "But after last night, I don't know that it's true. I wouldn't be surprised if he's ... if he's not over her yet."

"OK, that's it." Karen shook her head. "Melinda, I don't want to tell you what to do but, well, I guess I'm going to tell you what to do. Be friends with him if you want, but don't even go there."

Melinda rubbed her face. "You're right. Thank you, Karen, I guess I was thinking that myself. I just needed someone else to verify it."

"He's not very stable, from what it sounds like, no matter how nice he is. And you've had so many ups and downs for so long, you're just now getting to where things have calmed down. You don't want to get caught up in his drama."

"And I think there's plenty of that." Melinda sat back in her chair, relieved. Whatever would she do without Karen? She hadn't even told Susan and Cassie yet. Evan's invitation came out of nowhere, and they didn't know him. Bill, despite his good-natured teasing, had kept his promise to say nothing to Frank and Miriam or anyone else. She didn't have to make a big thing out of this. Still, was there a part of her that was a bit disappointed, a little let down?

"Maybe he'll end up being a good friend. And I could use a few more of those my age around here. No offense."

"None taken. I know how you feel." Karen started laughing. "I love what Bill told you about Evan, how there's hardly any other decent single guys in the whole county for you and me to fight over. I do believe he's right."

Karen fell silent, and slowly stirred her soup.

"I'm glad you're not mad at me for butting in," she finally said, "suggesting you be cautious. We're not in college anymore, far from it. Used to be, the drama was part of the fun. I don't know about you, but somewhere along the way I got tired of it."

"Me, too." Melinda rolled her eyes. "Even though it wasn't really a date, I almost didn't go. I had to think about what to wear, if I should do my hair. What he might think of me, what I might think of him. Ugh, I haven't missed any of that."

"But still, wouldn't it be nice if someone really great did come along?" Karen said wistfully, then shrugged. "You know, Evan can't be all bad. Any guy that scrapes your car's windshield might be worth investing in as a friend."

* * *

The farmhouse seemed especially quiet that night. Once chores were done, Melinda didn't feel like cooking, or doing much else, either. She slid a frozen pizza in the oven and scooped out leftover salad from the night before. As she sat at the kitchen table, the newspaper spread ahead of her plate but unread, a wave of loneliness washed over her.

She wasn't really alone, of course. Hobo was snoozing on the couch, and Hazel and Grace were chasing each other across the dining room's hardwood floor, their tiny claws rapping out a playful rhythm.

But the three other chairs around the small kitchen table were empty. There was only a thick darkness outside the double windows, the yard light's feeble beam making little headway through the gloom. She sighed, and rose from her chair to pull the fleece curtains and block the dreary view as well as the cold.

Would it always be like this? Would most of her meals be only a table for one? Melinda had thought she was fine with that. But now, she wasn't so sure.

She loved her independence, being on her own, no one else coloring her decisions. After she called off her engagement to Craig three years ago, after they dropped their contract on that charming bungalow only a few blocks from her Minneapolis apartment, Melinda had decided she would never again twist herself sideways to make a relationship last.

"It has to be right on its own," she said now, to no one. "I can't change myself to make something work. And Karen's right, we're getting too old for playing games."

There had been a few guys since Craig, but none of them terribly serious and only a couple that stayed around very long. Sometimes Melinda had ended it, sometimes she hadn't. But given the path she found herself on this past year, it had all been for the best. Her life in the city seemed so far away and long ago. She actually had to think for a moment. Who was the last guy she'd dated?

"Jeff." She nodded and reached for another slice of pizza. "Some friend of Cassie's. That's right, we went to that French bistro in Uptown, the one that closed only months later. I wore that navy dress, the one that was too tight when I sat down. The food was OK. What happened with him?"

Then she grimaced. "Oh, that's right. He called me. Every day. For a week. And that was the end of Jeff."

Even so, maybe she wasn't ready to give up on love. Not yet. But Melinda had to admit, her odds of meeting someone special around Prosper weren't very promising. She'd moved here on a whim, then followed her heart and decided to stay. There had been so much going on, so much to learn and so many changes to adapt to, she hadn't given her romantic prospects much thought.

She wouldn't trade the life she had now for anything, could never see herself back in the city. But as she sat there alone in the sleepy kitchen, Melinda wondered if the decision that had opened so many doors inadvertently closed one for good. She had never thought about this before, but now she wondered: Had Horace and Wilbur ever sat here, at this table, and felt the weight of the years pressing on them as she did right now?

Neither had married. Ada said Wilbur's girlfriend jilted him while he was overseas during World War II, and Horace had always been shy. They had lived here their entire lives, one day blurring into the next, while the decades, as well as their youth, slipped away.

They focused on caring for this farm, then their aging parents and, at last, each other. Had it been enough, in the end? Or did they have any regrets? Wilbur's dementia made it impossible to ask him. And Horace didn't seem like the sort of person who'd eagerly share his deepest feelings.

Melinda kicked her feet up, her wool socks sliding over the scuffed rungs of the empty chair across the table, and stared at the calendar tacked up by the refrigerator. She wouldn't fear the weeks and months to come. She was getting older, and living in a rural area, and maybe the odds of her meeting the right guy were tipping out of her favor.

But she wouldn't dwell on it. And, more importantly, she wouldn't settle.

But then she looked over at the sink, and remembered how nice it felt the night before to stand shoulder-to-shoulder with Evan, talking, working together, despite the shabby desolation of the Benniger house. How he'd looked at her with ... what? Admiration? Affection?

And then she remembered. Something he'd said had caused her to pause, and had been lurking in the back of her mind ever since. *I just hope I can fix things. I just want to make everything better.*

What did that mean? That he really wanted to move on from Carrie, build a better life for himself and Chloe without her? Or that he just wanted to wave all his problems way, get his life back to what it used to be?

"That's not possible. And you can't fix people." Melinda took her plate to the sink and dumped it in. "You can't go back, only forward. I learned that long ago. But maybe Evan hasn't figured that out yet. It's a hard lesson to learn."

Maybe she was lonely sometimes, but she didn't need to get caught up in Evan's troubles, no matter how much she liked him and felt sorry for him. And something about Evan seemed a little weak, she had to admit, and it wasn't just because he was struggling right now. It was as if he was looking for someone to step in and push him this way or that, tell him what to do, so he didn't have to decide.

She couldn't be that person. If she had learned anything in the last year, it was that people had to make their own choices, on their own terms. As for finding love, well, that might have to wait.

The gentle pressure of a tiny paw on her foot made her look down, reminded her there are many kinds of love. It was Hazel, her golden eyes shining with pride as she dropped a stuffed felt mouse on the rug.

"Did you catch that one on your own?" Melinda picked up Hazel and held her close. The kitten tapped Melinda's cheek and meowed.

"You did? That's a really big mouse, Hazel. I bet Grace is jealous. Let's go see what she's up to."

Just before bedtime, Hobo went to the front door and whimpered. When Melinda only glanced up from her book, he moved to the window overlooking the front porch and pushed his nose between the fleece curtains, his white-tipped tail whipping back and forth. Before she could ask him what was going on, he hustled back to her reading chair and whined again.

"What is it? Do you have to go outside? But why the front porch? You know where your doggie doors are."

Hobo gave an excited bark and ran again to the front door, then pushed his nose against its oak panels. She hesitated, then reached for one of the fleece throws folded on the back of the couch and wrapped it around her shoulders. She rarely used the front door this time of year, as everyone came around to the back.

The iron knob stuck for a moment, then the hinges screeched in protest. A puff of icy air drifted in as she and Hobo slipped out, leaving Grace and Hazel dozing in a ball of fluff on the couch. Hobo went straight to the wall of storm windows, his gaze alert but his posture cautious. The moon was thin and pale, its weak beams throwing hardly any light across the snow-blanketed yard.

"Look at that," Melinda whispered as she pulled the blanket tighter and lowered herself to the chilled slats of the porch swing. "It's really beautiful, in a stark way. See how the moon makes the snow glow a little? Too bad it isn't brighter, we'd be able to see so much more."

But it soon became clear that Hobo saw, or sensed, something she didn't. His shadowy ears flattened, and he whimpered again. And then Melinda noticed them, too. Three dark shapes emerged from the windbreak, then crossed the yard with a sure-and-steady gait that took them to the birdfeeders suspended in the maple tree in front of the house.

"Look, Hobo, the deer are here!" She joined him at the windows and patted his head, trying to ease his excitement and keep him still. "We see their tracks all the time, but we don't often see them. Don't bark, OK? I hope they won't get spooked and run off."

Another deer ambled around the corner of the house, passing within a few feet of the windows. Two more appeared out of the stand of bare-branched lilac trees down where the yard ended and the ditch began. Melinda gasped in awe at the regal crown of antlers on the largest deer's head.

"He'll shed those very soon. We're lucky to see him now, when he still has them. I'm so glad you brought us out here. He's majestic, isn't he?"

The buck moved slowly, casually, following the rest of the herd to the birdfeeders. They sauntered about, feasting on the leftover seeds and empty hulls tossed down by the finicky blue jays and cardinals that gathered in the maple tree during the day. Melinda crouched next to Hobo, soothed by the peaceful scene, and decided she might want to join Ed and Mabel in setting out ear corn for the deer during these harshest months of the year. They seemed so relaxed, so reassured by the food and safety they found in her yard.

The buck's antlers lifted suddenly. His graceful legs didn't move, but she sensed he was listening and alert. The other deer froze where they were, the buffet of scattered seed all but forgotten. Did the buck see Melinda and Hobo watching through the windows? She held her breath, her hand on Hobo's collar.

No, there was something else. Because suddenly, Hobo saw it, too.

He whimpered again, this time more from fear than excitement, and edged closer to Melinda. In the gloomy darkness of the porch, she could see he was no longer watching the deer. He was looking far to the left, out to the deep shadows where the windbreak met the yard.

"What is it?" she whispered, a spark of fear wriggling down her spine. "What do you see?"

Hobo answered with a short warning bark. The deer were gone before she could blink, disappearing so fast she couldn't be sure which way they went.

Melinda shivered. It was cold on the unheated porch, but that wasn't all. Hobo was still on alert, tugging instinctively toward the windows as she tried to hold him still. Whatever Hobo saw, the buck had seen it, too. What else might be out there in the shadows? She thought about the mysterious, deliberate tracks around the chicken house, the ones she thankfully hadn't seen in weeks.

"Come on," she whispered, the silence of frigid night pressing in on them through the frosted windows. "Let's get back inside."

* 12 *

Grace batted at the ruffled cuff on Melinda's black cashmere sweater, the one she never had a chance to wear anymore.
"You might not believe it, but I used to wear stuff like this all the time." She reached for the much-used lint roller waiting on the antique dresser, then gently set Grace next to Hazel, who was more interested in napping on the tufted comforter.

"Well, I rarely wore head-to-toe black. But I did wear a lot of it, back in the day." She rose to inspect her reflection in the dresser's silvered mirror. "It's elegant, sophisticated. Perfect for the corporate world. Or a funeral."

She did look chic, Melinda had to admit. Very chic, and very tired. Her black skirt had just the right bit of flare in its hem, and her brown waves were rolled back into a simple bun. But the carefully applied makeup couldn't quite erase the worry lines around her green eyes, and her pale skin was as dull as the dreary skies on this early-February afternoon. She was tired of the snow and the cold, and worn out from two nights of frantic cleaning after Kevin called to say a member of the Schermann family had passed away.

"Thank God it's not Horace." She pawed through her jewelry box to find her silver filigree necklace.

"Or Wilbur. Or Ada, either. My heart about stopped, you know. Turns out it's some nephew, a guy from Chicago. He loved to spend his summers here, at the farm, when he was young. And now, he's coming back one last time. He's going to be buried at the little church cemetery down the road."

Hazel and Grace were unfazed by this bit of Schermann family news. They were only interested in the glinting silver chain, and focused on it with the wide-eyed obsession all three-month-old kittens have for anything shiny.

Melinda knelt next to the bed, then lifted the necklace out of the kittens' reach and offered them both apologetic cheek rubs. "You might not like this, but after the funeral, everyone's coming here, to our house, for a sort-of reunion. We're going to have lots of company in a few hours. You girls can stay up here with Hobo, away from the commotion."

Hazel gave a tentative mew, and Melinda kissed her brown-tabby forehead.

"I know," she said softly, "we like to keep things quiet around here. Kevin hated to ask, I could tell, but I wasn't going to let him down. He and Ada and Horace have done so much for me. But people are coming from far away, and many of them want to stop at the farm, for old time's sake."

She leaned over to hug Grace. "You're too young to understand, but it's something called 'nostalgia.' That's when you long for how things used to be."

Melinda's steps faltered just a bit as she started for the closet. Maybe these far-flung Schermann relatives weren't the only ones feeling a bit wistful these days. She'd spent a recent weekend with Susan and Cassie, meeting at the southern Minnesota lake house owned by the family of Cassie's soon-to-be ex-husband. "One more bash at the lake before the divorce is settled," Cassie had said. "I don't care if it's snowing. I can't think of a better reason to use my key one more time than to celebrate Susan's fortieth."

The getaway had been on Melinda's radar for weeks, a bright spot in the dreary stretch of days between the holidays and spring. But things weren't quite the same, and Melinda knew she was the one who had changed.

Cassie and Susan got together every week, their lives in Minneapolis still so intertwined. Both called and texted

Melinda faithfully, and she did her part to stay in touch. Kept toasty by the lake house's rumbling furnace, a blazing fireplace and lots of mulled wine, the three friends had a great time reconnecting. Cassie and Susan had promised to come to Melinda's for her fortieth birthday in March. But she knew rough weather and bad roads could ruin their plans.

When they locked up the lake house and Susan and Cassie drove away together, the tears started before Melinda made it to the main road. She rarely missed the city anymore, and couldn't wait to get back to her farm. But the hole left by her two best friends had been hard to fill, even with all the wonderful new people in her life.

Melinda wasn't quite sure where Evan fit into all this. She had run into him twice in the past week. Both times, she'd been ridiculously happy to see him, and probably grinned like a fool when he smiled at her.

The first time, when he loaded a bag of oats into her car at the co-op, she'd had an easy escape route. The second time was worse or better, depending on how she thought of it. When Evan came into Prosper Hardware the other day with Chloe, he had nearly hugged her in greeting. Melinda found herself secretly pleased but managed to gracefully duck away just in time. There were other customers in the store, and they all got an eyeful.

She had to be careful, for so many reasons. She found herself thinking about Evan, more often than she probably should. Valentine's Day was coming up soon, but it would only be an excuse to bake something and share it with the store's coffee group. Nothing more.

All the more reason to make the most of this afternoon, she decided while rummaging for her newer black pumps, the ones whose heels weren't so high. It was a sad occasion, of course, but it would be a chance to catch up with the Schermanns she already knew and meet more of the family.

Even better, Angie had asked her to help serve the funeral lunch at the church. Mabel and Ed were members of a different congregation, but Mabel had also volunteered to help. And it had been weeks since the farmhouse had been this spotless. She might as well enjoy it while it lasted.

She found her shoes just in time. The west window of her bedroom was bordered in frost, but the rest was clear enough for her to spot a familiar car pulling up in front of the garage.

"Ada and Kevin are here! Looks like Horace, too. I'm so glad he braved this weather to come." She wasn't surprised that Wilbur didn't appear to be along. At ninety-two, he struggled to get around, even inside the nursing home over in Elm Springs.

She gave each of the kittens another hug. "Babies, I'll be back as soon as I can."

How many other funerals had this farmhouse seen? Melinda wondered as she made the turn on the stairway landing, Hobo's excited barking echoing from below. It soon faded away, and she knew he was already through his doggie doors and rushing out to greet their guests.

Of course, there would have been weddings, too, and holidays and reunions and so many other, happier times. Melinda was often too busy to reflect on it, but on days like today, the farm's history nearly overwhelmed her. The eight months she had lived here were but a footnote to the decades the Schermanns spent under this roof. Even so, this farm already held a special place in her heart.

The deceased apparently felt the same. George Bradford had only spent his childhood summers and holidays here, but the pull of the place was so strong that he had insisted on being buried in the little cemetery down the road, much to the disgust of his sophisticated wife.

George was the only son of Lydia Schermann Bradford, who had been third in line behind Wilbur and Horace and the oldest girl among the eight siblings. Lydia married an insurance salesman and moved to Chicago, where the Bradfords' multiplying wealth and social standing opened many doors for George and his sister, Elaine.

Despite their upper-class upbringing, the children loved to spend weeks with Grandpa Henry and Grandma Anna and their bachelor uncles, taking the train to Iowa whenever they had a break from school.

George's law career was a successful one, and he enjoyed several years as lead partner in a Chicago firm before he collapsed at his desk on Friday, the victim of a heart attack at sixty-three. The saddest part, Kevin told Melinda, was that George was just two weeks away from a lavish retirement celebration and the chance to fully enjoy the wealth he had accumulated.

"We're having a different kind of party for him now," Melinda said with a sigh as she passed through the living room, pausing to brush a few stray pet hairs off the arm of the couch.

Hobo met her in the kitchen, panting with excitement and his brown fur cool to the touch.

"Have you been to see Horace? I can tell that you have." Hobo's white feet were coated with a fresh layer of crusty snow. "He's out in the car, isn't he?"

"Hello there!" Kevin came through the back door, his arms loaded with plastic containers. Kevin was only a few years' older than Melinda, and had a strong resemblance to Horace, sharing his uncle's lanky frame and blue eyes.

"Mom baked cookies, and there's cheese and crackers. A few snacks to keep everyone happy. We brought some pop, too, and napkins and cups." He set everything on the kitchen counter and wiped the fog off his glasses. "I'm so glad you agreed to play hostess. I suggested to several people that we just stay at the church, but they really wanted to come here."

Melinda shrugged. "This is the Schermann homeplace, after all. My Grandma and Grandpa Foster's farm was the same for our family."

Ada rushed in just as Hobo hurried back out. "You should have seen him, Melinda. Hobo nearly knocked us over, he was so excited to see us. I told Horace to stay in the car, not to chance it on all this ice and snow. Hobo just barked and barked, and nearly climbed inside. I thought he was going to plant himself in Horace's lap." Through the kitchen windows,

Melinda could see the open car door and Horace turned outward in his seat, his arms around Hobo.

"He ran right up, before Mom could even cut the engine," Kevin added. "He knew exactly who was in the front."

"I need my hug, now." Ada turned toward Melinda. "Haven't seen you since before Christmas." Ada's short white hair was smoothed into a polished style, but her kind eyes were clouded with grief.

Melinda reached for her wool dress coat, which was folded over the back of one of the kitchen chairs. "I'm so glad Horace could come at least, even though it's so bitter cold. Too bad Wilbur couldn't make it."

"Wilbur's having a tough day," Ada admitted. "He's got a chest cold. Nothing too serious, thankfully, but we didn't want to risk bringing him out. And besides, I don't think he remembers George at all, not anymore. I don't even know if he recognized us." Ada wiped her eyes with one hand. As the baby of the family, she had watched from the sidelines for years as her older brothers and sisters gradually declined.

Melinda squeezed her friend's hand in sympathy, and searched for something that might raise Ada's spirits. "I'm so sorry, Ada. Did you know Mabel will be at the church?"

"Oh, I'm so glad she can come. We talk on the phone, but don't get together often enough." Ada and Kevin both lived in Mason City. "And Melinda, I can't wait to meet those kittens when we get back. Well, I think this is everything I wanted to bring in from the car. We'd better get going."

Horace and Hobo were still lost in conversation as Melinda, Kevin and Ada came down the freshly scraped back steps. But Horace was now out of the car, one steadying hand pressed against its side.

"Horace!" Ada admonished her brother. "I told you to stay in there, with no one out here to help you. What if you'd fallen on the ice?" She clicked her tongue and shook her head. "I know what's going on. You were about to start for the barn, weren't you? You want to see the sheep, but not now. We're running late as it is."

"We've got plenty of time. I don't think George will mind if we fall behind schedule," Horace protested even as he climbed back in the passenger seat. Before Ada could respond, he turned to Melinda.

"There's the sheep farmer!" He gripped her hand with surprising strength for someone his age. "Glad you're coming with us. Hobo looks good. How are those ewes?"

Melinda tried not to laugh, as she and Horace had talked on the phone only a few days ago. With lambing season now only weeks away, she knew he would be calling more often, eager to hear all the latest.

Ada drove the two miles to the church at a careful speed, yet navigated the snow-packed gravel road with the ease of someone who knew her way. As they rolled along, she offered Melinda a "who's who" of the Schermanns, past and present.

George's parents were already gone, leaving Elaine and her kids and grandkids the only living members of that branch of the family. "Lydia was a really classy lady, you know. I looked up to her so much, she was the oldest of us girls. She's been gone for about ten years now. Our brother Carl passed last year, and Emma, oh, let's see, five years ago."

"Six years ago," Horace interrupted. "Emma had cancer."

"Yes, that right. Walter's still alive, but he's in a nursing home out in Montana. Now Edith, she's managed to stay in her own home, she lives pretty close, over in Hampton." Ada glanced in the rearview mirror at Kevin, who was in the back with Melinda. "Jen called last night to say she's bringing her grandma today. Did you say Dave's coming?"

"Yeah, he texted me." Kevin turned to Melinda. "Edith is Jen and Dave's grandma, if you're keeping score. You know Dave, of course. Jen is Dave's sister, she was at the farm last summer to help with the storm cleanup. She also came to the fall chili feed, which you were kind enough to let us host like we always used to do."

Melinda's mind swarmed with names and connections.

"I don't know if I remember Jen. I hope I can keep everyone straight."

They rode in silence for a moment. Horace, who was usually quiet unless he was telling one of his stories, suddenly spoke up.

"I remember George as this little shaver, wanting to help milk the cows and playing down at the creek." He shook his head, staring out at the bleak winter landscape. "He was only sixty-three. He made all that money, but I don't think it mattered one bit in the end."

Ada slowed for the last crossroads before the church. "That's the truth. You can't take it with you. Maybe if he hadn't pushed so hard, he'd still be around to enjoy it all."

She seemed to consider something, then continued. "George was a sweet boy when he was little. I don't know, but I'm not sure Lydia's marriage was all that solid, despite how successful her husband was. I guess we shouldn't be surprised George wanted to be buried back here. Maybe this is where he was the happiest."

The small Lutheran church rested next to the road, the cemetery behind it sheltered by a thick band of evergreen trees. A black tent was already set up in the cemetery, the flaps on its north and west sides lashed tight against the cold. The hearse was pulled up to the church's side door. Only a few cars were parked out front.

"See, we're not late," Horace told Ada. "Services don't start for another hour. I see Elaine's already here, though."

He pointed out a burgundy-colored luxury car with Minnesota plates, the only vehicle whose undercarriage wasn't smothered with gravel mud and dirty snow, and turned to address Melinda.

"She lives in Minneapolis, you know. Her husband, he's some kind of developer. New businesses and such."

"Elaine Ainsworth moves among the elite." Ada rolled her eyes as she put the car in park. "Don't think I've seen her back here in, oh, at least five years. The rest of us are just common folk, as you know. But you'll be able to spot Elaine by that silly rock on her finger."

Kevin snorted. "Mom, really."

"Well, I'm just saying." Ada tossed up her hands. "That's how Elaine is, always has been. She's my niece, but I'm not going to sugarcoat it. Her brother's death has hit her hard, of course, so she might be more temperamental than usual."

"What Ada is trying to say," Horace put in, "is Elaine's going to be cranky."

"Got it." Melinda shivered as she pushed open the car door, a damp, icy draft making her wish she'd worn pants instead of a skirt. "I'll keep that in mind."

"Uncle Horace, don't forget this." Kevin handed a cane between the seats. "It's icy out there. And it took me a whole ten minutes to get that toothy clamp thing on the bottom."

Horace seemed about to protest, then didn't. "Well, if it makes you feel better, fine." He took a few steps, then offered Melinda his other arm. "How about I escort you in?"

"I would like that." She hid her smile inside her scarf. Horace obviously wanted the extra stability, but wasn't going to ask for help.

"There's Elaine over there," Kevin whispered to Melinda as he hung up their coats.

Only a top-notch stylist could create such a natural-looking hair color on a sixty-year-old woman, Melinda decided. Elaine's sleek bob was an elegant shade of blonde, threaded with champagne highlights. Her charcoal dress was perfectly tailored, the black cashmere cardigan as simple as it was expensive. And the ring ... well, Ada was right.

"She could cut glass with that thing," Melinda whispered to Kevin. "My friend Cassie married into an old-money Minneapolis family, and her heirloom ring looks like it's from a carnival game by comparison. Is that her husband?"

"Yep, that's Edward. Look at his suit, I've never seen anything like it. Custom, I'm sure." Kevin tried to smother a smirk. "If we really wanted to have some fun, I could introduce you as my girlfriend. You could be the wayward city woman who finds herself in the country, then falls in love with the landowner's nephew. Isn't that how the story's supposed to go?"

Holding back her laughter made Melinda's eyes water. "Kevin, stop it! And I don't think Jack would find that funny." Jack was Kevin's boyfriend. "On second thought, he probably would. But please, I don't want to embarrass myself. I'm tired, and it's been a long week. So I'm begging you, don't say anything smart the rest of the day, OK?"

"You're right." Kevin got ahold of himself. "It's a funeral, I shouldn't be saying such things. Well, better go extend the olive branch. Let me introduce you, for real."

Elaine's brown eyes were swollen with tears, her grief so obvious despite her artfully applied makeup that Melinda felt sorry for her. Elaine's parents were gone, and now her brother had passed so suddenly. Melinda thought of her own family, of how blessed she was, and returned Elaine's unexpected hug with genuine warmth.

"I'm so glad you decided to rent the farm, Melinda." Elaine dabbed at her powdered cheeks with a tissue. "We couldn't have convinced Uncle Horace to go to the nursing home otherwise. He's just so feeble, you know? How we worried about him! I can't imagine why he'd want to stay out there like that, alone. But then, that farm means so much to all of us. It's been in our family for more than a hundred-and-twenty-five years."

Melinda saw Kevin force a smile. She followed his lead, but was taken aback by Elaine's comments. Horace was fairly independent for someone his age. And Elaine, from what Melinda knew, had never much concerned herself with Horace or Wilbur's welfare.

"That's amazing the Schermanns have owned the land for so long," was all she said, reaching for a conversational turn that might ease the mounting tension between Elaine and Kevin. "You all must be so proud. Isn't there a special program to honor century farms?"

"Oh, Horace and Wilbur never wanted to fuss with a sign," Kevin cut in, his tone a little too bright. "They always said they were too busy running the farm to mess with the paperwork."

Elaine just stared at him, and he started to steer Melinda away. "Well, we need to make sure Mom and Uncle Horace are getting settled."

"She's got some nerve," Melinda whispered once Elaine's attention was diverted to another relative. "Acting like she's always been there for Horace and Wilbur. It's you and Ada who do so much for them."

Kevin tried to shrug it all away. "Well, I guess you see what my mom meant, then. Tell Mabel I say hello, just in case I don't run into her during lunch."

The church basement was already filled with metal tables and chairs, the kitchen visible behind a counter-height partition in the back. The concrete-block walls were painted a soothing white, and an industrial-grade tan carpet covered the floor. Melinda waved to Angie, who was already bustling around the kitchen with a few other women, then stopped to examine the memorial display set up on a nearby table.

The heavyset man smiling in the newer photographs had to be George Bradford. There he was on a sailboat, with his wife; Melinda had caught a glimpse of her inside the church vestibule. Then came George in a smartly tailored suit, gripping another man's hand, marking a career milestone.

The next photos were still in color, but their hues were faded: George on his wedding day, much slimmer then. George grinning with pride as he balanced a toddler-aged son in each arm.

The older photos, some of them sepia-toned with age, were the most interesting. There was a little boy who looked ready to ditch his itchy wool suit. Next was a well-dressed family, not smiling, in front of an ornate iron fence with an impressive Tudor-style home in the background.

But it was the casual black-and-white shots, which took up over a third of the display, that hit Melinda right in the heart. The porch in one photo was open between its turned banisters, but she recognized it instantly. Was that really a much-younger Horace and Wilbur, in the prime of life, standing next to their father?

George, maybe five at the most, had a wide grin and a tight grip on Horace's hand. His tiny overalls and cotton button-down shirt nearly matched those of his uncles and grandfather. A little girl in a gingham dress, barely more than a baby, sat proudly in her grandma's lap, laughing and stretching her hands toward the camera.

And more: Elaine and George, a bit older and at the farmhouse's kitchen table, sprinkling sugar on cookies; George, under the maple tree in the front yard, his face streaked with dirt and a fishing pole in his hand; both children, bundled in winter coats, crouched in front of the barn, their arms wrapped around a slightly blurry black-and-white dog.

"Great memories, aren't they?"

Mabel's short white curls were tidy as usual, but she had traded her jeans and sweatshirt for a black-and-white print dress. "Elaine and George spent a lot of time with their grandparents growing up. In the summer, they'd stay for a month, at least." She reached out to reverently touch one of the farm photos. "I've never seen most of these. George surely had a few of them, but Elaine must have kept the rest, all these years."

Melinda swallowed a twinge of guilt. "Sounds like she hasn't been around much as an adult. But maybe she cares more than I give her credit for."

"She can be quite the diva, I'll say." Mabel patted her on the arm. "But who knows, maybe she's more sentimental these days. Losing a family member will do that to you."

The other volunteers were warm and welcoming. Melinda soon discovered she was having a great time, despite the cause for the gathering. It felt good to get out, meet some friendly faces, and work together as a team. Once the leftovers were boxed up, the serving dishes washed and the kitchen cleared, she caught a ride back to the farm with Mabel.

Nathan had bladed a wider circle than usual through yesterday's snow, and several cars were already parked in the cleared space between the garage and the barn.

Melinda smiled when she spotted Horace's new winter coat hanging on a peg inside the back door, next to her chore gear. "I told Ada everyone could put their things in the downstairs bedroom," she said to Mabel. "But I guess old habits die hard."

The farmhouse buzzed with conversation and even a bit of laughter. Schermann relatives occupied the carved chairs around the antique dining-room table, and the couch was packed full. Others stood in clusters, leaning against the walls and clutching cups of coffee or punch.

Kevin clomped up the basement steps with metal folding chairs under both arms, Ada right behind.

"We got the coffeemaker going." He almost shouted to be heard over the din. "And we've already gone through a pot. Standing in a cemetery on a day like today will chill you straight through."

Melinda looked around, unsure what to do or where to sit. There were so many strange-if-kind faces, and a few of them were rummaging through her kitchen cabinets. One lady wanted to borrow a cake server for the dessert she'd brought. Melinda found one, and was about to make her way into the dining room when she felt a hand on her arm.

"You must be Melinda." The petite woman had a lined face and iron-gray curls. "I'm Edith, Ada and Horace's sister. Can I trouble you for a real plate, honey? I'm afraid I'll drop one of those paper ones, my grip's not so good these days."

"Edith! You live in Hampton, right? Certainly, let me get you one." Melinda reached into a cabinet, relieved to have something to do. "Do you have a place to sit? Can I help you get some coffee?"

"Oh, that would be wonderful!" Edith's blue eyes sparkled. "I love what you've done with the place. Horace and Wilbur tried their best but, my Lord! You should have seen how it was after Mother died." She passed a veined hand over her face and groaned.

"What an infernal mess! Newspapers everywhere, muddy boot prints all over. I don't think either one of them knew what a dust cloth was for. I tried to tidy up when I visited. My Alvin, he used to tell me to let it go, but I couldn't. Mother must have been rolling in her grave."

Melinda smothered a laugh. Edith appeared a bit frail, but clearly still had her mind. And strong opinions.

She filled a coffee cup and was about to guide Edith to the dining room table, then turned to find the older woman had already started to push through the crowd. Melinda had to make a few quick turns to keep up.

"I'm glad you approve, you don't know what that means to me. I've tried to spruce things up a bit, but keep the home's history intact."

"You're the best thing to happen to this place in years, Melinda." With a sturdy ceramic plate in hand, Edith loaded it up from the spread of crackers and cheese and desserts. "Oh, I just love Ada's oatmeal cookies."

Melinda looked around to see if anyone else needed anything. George's wife and their two sons, exhausted and probably feeling out of place, had gently declined Ada's invitation and returned to their hotel in Swanton. That left Elaine to hold court with Edward in one corner of the living room. Melinda was about to approach them when she saw Jen clasp Elaine's hand and offer to refresh her coffee.

Horace was making his way toward the living room, his progress slowed by all the relatives wanting to say hello and ask about Wilbur. Melinda suspected Horace was aiming for her overstuffed reading chair in front of the fireplace, the spot where his old recliner had sat for years. The young man occupying the seat quickly got to his feet when Horace approached, and he settled in with a noticeable sigh. Hobo, who had been collecting pets and praise from the extended family, hustled over to sit at Horace's side.

Hazel and Grace had also appeared downstairs, the mysterious voices and the aromas of summer sausage and cheese too tempting to be ignored. Hazel had draped herself over the back of Melinda's sofa, in front of the picture window, where she could study the room with minimal distractions. Grace was snuggled in Ada's lap on the far end of the couch. Melinda watched Ada and Horace, both of them lost in conversation with their animal friends. For just a moment, she could imagine away their wrinkles and gray hairs, see them as children sharing moments with their treasured pets.

And then, Horace was staring through the open door into what used to be his bedroom, where a tangled heap of coats, caps and scarves littered the crazy quilt and smothered the iron bed frame. He seemed to sink further back into the padded chair, so alone despite the chatter circling around him. Every few moments, he reached over to stroke Hobo's soft brown fur.

Melinda knew Horace hated crowds, and he suddenly seemed exhausted and withdrawn. He wasn't crying, was he?

She pushed through the crowd and put a gentle hand on his shoulder. "Can I get you something, Horace?"

"I'm fine." He looked down again, then away, blinking rapidly but trying to hide it. "Hobo, now, that's a different story. He's had plenty of cheese and sausage. I didn't give him any, but he's been begging around, that rascal. There might be trouble later on."

"Thanks for warning me. I'll keep an eye out for that." She tried again. "Are you sure you don't need anything? Maybe some coffee?"

He shook his head. But then, he sat up straighter.

"Well, there is something. Get me the heck out of here, huh? I'm tired of all these people and their yakkety-yak. Let's go see the sheep."

Ada looked up when she saw her brother start for the kitchen. "Horace, I can get you a plate if you want."

"No need, Ada. We're off to the barn."

Ada was about to protest, then gave up. "Melinda, I know you'll look after him on that snow and ice. Just make him take that cane. It won't do me any good to tell him not to go."

"That's for sure." Horace turned to Melinda. "Run ahead and find my chore boots in the porch closet."

✳ 13 ✳

Melinda fussed with her gloves and hat so as not to hover while Horace slowly swapped his clean sneakers for his old rubber boots. Then he pointed out a ratty brown knit cap on the closet shelf. "Don't want to get that fancy one dirty."

She fetched it for him, then planted the cane firmly in his hand. At last they made it outside, away from the crush of relatives in the too-warm house.

The yard was silent except for the plodding crunch of their boots across the packed-down snow. Horace's gait was steady, if slow. Melinda, who was usually in a hurry to get to work or wrap up her evening chores before sunset, had to check her stride to match his leisurely pace.

They walked in companionable silence, but she knew his mind was far from idle.

Horace's sharp blue eyes slid back and forth, evaluating everything. Following his gaze, she could almost read his thoughts: Was the barn's red paint becoming too faded? How are the patched shingles on the machine shed holding up? Is that pasture fence starting to sag? He was back home, if only for a few hours, and soaking in every moment.

"I see you've been able to keep a clear path to the chicken coop, even though the drifts are pretty high this year," he finally said as they reached the concrete stoop in front of the barn door. "Things look good."

Melinda beamed, knowing that for Horace, that was the best compliment of all. "Well, it's been tough some days, but I'm hanging on. You were right. Winter is hard out here. Thanks for giving me some extra months to know for sure that I want to buy the place, for not forcing me to make a decision last fall."

"Not a problem. I knew you could do it. You just had to see that for yourself."

Before she could show him her trick to get the frosted door latch to slide easy, he already had it pushed clear. As always, the familiar sound brought a chorus of "baaas" from the sheep inside.

"You take your time," he went on. "It's a good life, but it's not for everybody. My brother Walter, now, he hated it here. Took off for California as soon as he got out of school. Myself, I just wanted to stay."

Melinda hoped to hear more, but Horace dropped his cane inside the door and quickly turned his focus to the sheep. The ewes were crowding and shoving at the troughs before he could reach the aisle fence. One broke rank and hurried behind the line, then wedged in right in front of Horace, and let out an indignant bellow. Melinda didn't have to check the sheep's ear tag to know who it was.

"Annie, it's about time you got over here." Horace leaned over and rubbed her ears. She put her front hoofs up on the trough to get as close to her friend as possible, as if he might offer her a bottle of formula as he'd done a few years ago when she was the runt of a set of triplets.

"Now, don't think I don't know what you've been up to, running the show," Horace told Annie. "Melinda keeps me in the loop." He tipped his head this way and that, studying Annie's frame.

"Looks like you were smart enough to outsmart that neighbor buck last fall." Horace chuckled. "No lambs for you, little Annie girl."

"And I can't tell you how relieved I am about that." Melinda joined Horace at the fence, reaching over to rub the ewes' noses. "I'll have my hands full as it is, without having to put up with Annie's diva demands in my maternity ward."

Horace carefully bent over and broke a slab of hay off the bale near his feet, then shook it over the fence.

"Once we get these chores done, we'll go around to the back and look things over."

Melinda hadn't expected Horace to help feed the ewes their supper, or to evaluate the lambing pens in the south section of the barn, but his intentions were very clear. And she couldn't be more thrilled.

The lambs could start arriving in about two weeks. Her limited free time was now filled with studying the birthing process, both online and from a practical guide Nancy pulled from the library's shelves. Melinda found the procedures fascinating, when she wasn't repulsed by descriptions of bodily fluids or shuddering over all the discussions about what could go wrong, and how to possibly make them right.

"Looks like there's four carrying lambs." Horace pointed them out.

"So you think Number 7 is pregnant? I thought that, too, even though I wasn't sure until just a few weeks ago. She's really starting to fill out, though."

"Yep, those are the four."

There was the *thump* of padded feet on the bare haymow stairs, and Sunny and Stormy appeared. They hadn't seen Horace in months, but even shy Stormy rushed past Melinda and ran right toward his old friend.

"Just look at you!" Horace gently patted Stormy on the head, then straightened up to greet Sunny, who posed on top of the grain barrel and meowed his greeting. "Staying warm, are you? I heard about your house under the stairs, and your time on the back porch. You boys are smart, aren't you?"

Melinda was about to reach for the grain scoop, but stepped back and leaned against the fence, letting Horace take the lead and enjoying the sheer joy she saw on his weathered face. The move to the nursing home had been the right choice for Horace. He seemed more cheerful, less shy than the June day she and her dad first visited the farm. His clothes were newer and neater, and the hearty meals served in the dining hall had added a few pounds to his lanky frame.

But being back at the farm energized him in some way. He slipped into the groove of evening chores like it was the steps to a dance he'd never forgotten.

The lambing pens needed more work, but Melinda was proud of what she'd accomplished so far. The eight stalls, four on each side of a wooden partition, opened into the U-shaped promenade that bordered the south section of the barn. It had taken hours of dirty work and a respirator to scoop out the old straw that padded the pens, and she'd been glad to only have to clean four of them.

The thin, dusty extension cords laced through the cobwebs just under the ceiling had given her pause, as did the dented, rusted heat lamps tossed on a shelf in the grain room. She used her Prosper Hardware discount to stock up on new, insulated drop cords and took advantage of a sale at the co-op to purchase shiny new heat lamps and fresh bulbs.

"Looks like you've been busy." Horace nodded his approval. "I'd say get five stalls ready, use the last one to keep hay and straw close by. Do that soon. You never know how fast the lambs will come."

Her eyes must have widened with worry, as he gave a gentle chuckle.

"It's not likely they'll all give birth on the same day. You'll just get busy, that's all. Be ready for anything, that's the way to do it."

Horace and Wilbur sold their last buck three years ago, but Horace's decades of experience were still fresh in his mind. He sighed as he studied the fence panels leaned against the wall, the ones that would serve as gates for the pens.

"That one on the far end? It's no good. Needs those slats fixed, I never got around to it. But the rest will do."

"Sounds good." She wanted to pretend everything was under control, but that was far from the truth. "Horace, I've been reading up on all this, but I have no idea what I'm doing.

How will I even know for sure if one of the ewes is going into labor, or needs help? I don't want something to go wrong."

He explained exactly what to look for. Much of it mirrored her research, but it was comforting to hear it first-hand from a seasoned veteran.

"As soon as you notice one starting, get the halter on her and get her into her own pen." He shook a finger at Melinda, his eyes bright with knowledge and memory. "That's important. It should take them a while to drop the lambs, but you never know what'll happen when. That way, if it's the middle of the night or when you're at work, she's already separated from the flock. And the others won't be in the way if you need to get in there and help her."

Melinda swallowed hard, nervous about what "help her" might entail. If it was anything like the drawings she'd seen, she wasn't sure she could.

Horace patted the arm of her coat. "They all know what to do, it's instinct. Keep the mamas clean and warm and fed, give them their space, and they should handle everything just fine. Besides, 21 and 33 have lambed before. I don't recall them having any trouble, but check our sheep book."

"The sheep book?"

"Yep, it's upstairs, in the roll-top desk there in the office. Records going way back." He thought for a moment. "You get trouble, and can't get Doc or Karen, you call John Olson. He's had sheep for years, and he'll come right over. If he's not home, Ed can help, so can Angie and Nathan."

"So what you're saying is," Melinda tried to smile as they started for the front of the barn, "I don't have to go it alone."

"Heck, call me, and I'll try to walk you through it." He paused to open the barn door, and his tone turned wistful. "Wish I could be here."

"I know. I'll do my best to make you proud."

He adjusted his grip on the cane as they stepped into the icy yard. "Can't believe I have to use one of these things. How's Pansy treating you these days? I'd like to get out to the coop, but I bet we don't have time."

The yard was still packed with vehicles, so there was no reason to rush back to the house. But she could see Horace was becoming tired, he wasn't used to so much physical activity.

He never would have made it through another winter out here, she decided. And she was sure he knew it, too.

"Pansy's queen bee, as always. I can handle the chickens after everyone leaves, when I feed Sunny and Stormy." He looked so sad; she searched for something that might cheer him up.

"Tell you what. I'll take some pictures of the chickens and send them to you. Let's get inside and see if there's any coffee on. And Mabel brought some of her chocolate-caramel bars. I bet there's a few left."

"Sounds good to me." Horace turned quiet again, and Melinda let him be. They were almost across the yard when he stopped abruptly.

"Oh, one other thing with the sheep. The first milk the ewes have is rich with vitamins and such. The lambs should start nursing quick, but if they don't, there can be trouble."

"What can I do?"

"Well, if they won't drink, you gotta get it for them. Use a clean container with a tight seal. You'll refrigerate what they don't drink at first, then warm it up and ..."

"Wait a minute." Melinda help up a gloved hand. "Are you saying I need to *milk the sheep?*"

Horace shrugged. "Like milking a cow, you know."

She just stared at him.

"Oh, that's right. You haven't. Well, it's easy." Horace made a quick gesture with his free hand, then continued toward the house.

Melinda had no choice but to follow, her mind spinning. *Milk the sheep?* She was still wondering how to get a stubborn ewe, grunting with labor pains, ushered from one part of the barn to the other. The sheep were generally an easygoing bunch. But when they got ready to give birth, surely they'd be less accommodating.

"There's some lambing bottles in the basement," Horace went on. "Or a clean plastic pop bottle works good. Single serving size," he added.

There was a flash of movement inside the back door's window. Mabel popped out on the top step without her coat, despite the cold, damp air. "There you are! I thought you'd never come back!"

Melinda was alarmed by the worry on her neighbor's face. "What is it?" She ran ahead, not waiting for Horace. "What's happened? Is someone hurt?"

"Not yet," Mabel said dryly. "But give it time. Those Schermann relatives are about to help themselves to anything not nailed down."

Melinda stood to the side to give Horace full use of the steps and the handrail. He was moving a bit faster now, but didn't seem too concerned.

As they came into the back porch, she could hear some sort of commotion inside, the charged hum of several people talking at once. And arguing. "Whatever is going on in there?"

Mabel glanced over her shoulder to make sure the kitchen door was latched tight. "First, it was just some reminiscing about old times, how the family always gathered here at the holidays." She threw up her hands in frustration.

"Then some of the ladies got teary-eyed, which I can understand. But Horace, Lillian started it all. She insisted your mother told her long ago she could have that flower vase with the roses etched on it. You know, the one with the scalloped edge that was your grandmother's?"

Horace, who had yet to say a word, only shrugged and carefully lowered himself to the bench, then started to remove his snow-crusted boots. Mabel rolled her eyes and turned to Melinda. "Maybe you know what I'm talking about?"

She did. "It's a lovely piece. I've never seen one like it." She peeked through the kitchen door's window, trying to get a glimpse of the action in the dining room.

Some woman was pointing at the china cabinet, tears running down her face.

Melinda pulled back, hesitant to go inside. They'd only been gone, what, forty minutes? How had everything gotten so out of control?

"Anyway, Lillian had her heart set on it." Mabel huffed as she hung up Horace's coat. "She wanted to know, did anyone mind if she took it home today?"

"I don't care if Lillian takes it." Horace's resignation was as strong as Mabel's indignation. "Got no use for it."

"Well, that was just the start of it." Mabel reached for the door knob. "Now everybody's got sticky fingers, you see, saying they like this picture, or that candy dish or clock or whatever."

"The mantel clock?" Melinda caught herself. She loved that clock. But it wasn't hers to give away, or to keep.

"The very one." Mabel's expression was grim. "Ada's trying to keep the peace, but I'm afraid she's losing ground. You'd better get in there, both of you."

✻ 14 ✻

Melinda felt the tension as soon as she opened the door. The conversation from the dining room had lowered a pitch or two, but was still insistent.

"If no one else wants that sugar bowl, I think my daughter would like it."

"There used to be a pheasants painting in the living room, right over Grandpa's chair. I loved it, could stare at it for hours when I was a kid. Wonder where it went? He always smoked his pipe, right after he came in from chores."

"See the pink vase in the cabinet, next to that stack of teacups? Grandma let me get it out when I spent the night, I'd fill it with dandelions. She said when I got married, I could have it."

"You didn't."

"Well, yeah, but shouldn't I get it anyway? I mean ..."

The charged debates trailed off when Horace appeared. He scanned every face as he made his way back to Melinda's chair by the fireplace, as if seeing each relative for the first time. Some offered him an apologetic smile, but others wouldn't meet his gaze. It quickly became clear to Melinda, hanging back in the kitchen doorway with Mabel, which Schermanns were stirring up all the trouble.

There was a younger woman in Melinda's reading chair this time, and she jumped up before Horace even got halfway through the crowd. He settled in with a quiet sigh.

"What's all this?" Horace asked gently. "Are we having an auction today?"

For a moment, no one answered. Ada, her lips pursed in frustration and the color rising in her neck, was still on the couch, next to Jen. Kevin was across the way in a folding chair, his blue eyes hard and angry.

"We were just talking," one of the women finally said, glancing around the group for support.

"Uncle Horace, you're getting on in years, and Uncle Wilbur, too," one man started. "We were thinking, maybe it's time to sort through a few things. Since we're all here ..."

"Not everyone is here." Edith dropped her fork to her plate with a clatter that caused more than one set of shoulders to flinch.

"There were eight of us kids, and dozens of grandkids and on down. And that's not all. Why, Father alone had five brothers and sisters. Just because you showed up today, doesn't mean you can steal whatever catches your fancy."

The man just looked at his lap.

"It's not up to us," another woman spoke up. Melinda couldn't remember her name, but was sure she'd helped clean up the farm after the tornado. "This is Uncle Horace's house now. His, and Uncle Wilbur's. He can do as he likes."

Nods and murmurs of agreement bounced around the group, but a few people crossed their arms. Everyone turned to Horace, and waited.

Melinda had no claim on anything Horace and Wilbur left behind in this house. She had known this day would come, one way or another, but the tension in the room made her cringe. And there was plenty to fight over.

The china cabinet was overflowing, the largest upstairs bedroom stuffed with antiques and knickknacks and who knew what else. Boxes and crates lined the basement shelves. The back porch closet was so crammed with gear that

Melinda braced herself when she opened its doors, always expecting something to hit her on the head. More items littered the garage, and the machine shed. What would she ever do with it all, even after the Schermanns took the things they loved the most?

Finally, Horace shrugged. "Well, I don't mind so much about those dishes. Never used them myself. As for the rest, Wilbur and I have everything we need at the nursing home. I don't care what you all decide to do."

"Thank you, Uncle Horace." One middle-aged woman rose from her chair, tears of gratitude in her eyes, and opened the china cabinet.

"You don't know what this will mean to my girl."

"Now, wait just a minute!" Another woman jumped up. "What if someone else wants that sugar bowl, Ruby? Someone not here today?"

"Well, I guess it's finders keepers, Catherine." Ruby's tone was cold and harsh. "Don't tell me you want it. You were hardly ever here, even at the holidays. I can't believe ..."

"Stop it!"

Edith was on her feet. She wobbled for a second, but pushed away the steadying hand offered by the man next to her at the table.

"Stop this, right now!" Edith hissed. "Mother and Father would be disgusted by this display of greed. Fighting over scraps, like a bunch of pigs."

"But, Aunt Edith," Ruby wailed. "Grandma told me ..."

"OK, that's enough, everyone." A man by the front door stood and made a calming gesture with his hands. "Let's all take a step back here."

Melinda guessed him to be in his fifties, with neatly trimmed gray hair and distinguished glasses. "Let's calm down. There has to be a better way to settle this." There were a few groans, but everyone gave him their full attention.

"Ron's a Realtor up in Mason City," Mabel whispered to Melinda. "He's smart. The voice of reason. I hope they listen to what he has to say."

Ron clasped his hands and looked from one end of the group to the other.

"You all know that a decade ago, when Uncle Horace and Uncle Wilbur officially retired from farming, the fields were sold off and the money split six ways. The proceeds were equally divided among the siblings that had children, just as Grandma and Grandpa outlined in their will. Horace and Wilbur retained these two acres, the house and the outbuildings, so they would always have a home. This parcel is theirs to do with as they see fit."

He paused, then spoke more slowly and gently, in a paternal tone that surely had soothed more than one anxious or angry client.

"Now, we all know Uncle Wilbur has dementia, and because of that, Uncle Horace has full power of attorney. This is his decision. As Grandma and Grandpa wished, everyone else received their fair share long ago."

"I wouldn't say the split was even." One man crushed his empty plastic cup with a furious motion. "Not for you, Ron. I noticed that when you handled the settlement, you took a hefty commission for yourself."

The grumbling started again. Edith put a hand over her gray curls and sat down, shaking her head.

"Good lord," Mabel muttered. "Every man's entitled to get paid for his work. I can't believe this."

One young woman stood up. She forced a smile, but there was a hint of frustration in her voice. "Ron is right. And we're all adults here. How about we go around and say what we want? I'll start a list. Then talk to your kids and grandkids, and let me know. If two people want the same thing, we'll deal with that later."

"I think that's a good idea," one man nodded. "This is a funeral, for God's sake. We don't have to settle this today."

Before anyone could protest, Ada got to her feet. "Melinda, where can we get some paper?"

Two dozen people swiveled to stare at her, some of them looking like they had forgotten she was there. She brushed past Mabel to grab the notepad waiting on the counter by the phone. The young woman thankfully met her at the opening into the dining room, so she didn't have to wade into the fray.

Ruby went first. She was still guarding the china cabinet, the prized sugar bowl clutched in her hands.

"You know what I want," she snapped, then reluctantly set the dish back on the shelf.

"I'd like a few of Grandpa's tools, if there's any around," a man said shyly and looked down toward Horace. He nodded.

"As I said earlier ..." One woman hesitated, then seemed to gather her courage. "I really love that clock on the mantel." Another cousin looked like he was about to say something, then only shrugged. The woman beamed.

"I'll ask my kids to be sure," the next woman said. "I don't know if there's anything we want from the house. But Melinda, those kittens are so sweet. I hear you're fostering them, and when they're ready to be adopted I'd ..."

"Forget it, Hillary." Kevin spoke in a sharp tone Melinda had never heard before. "You can't be serious. Melinda's keeping Hazel and Grace. They're not up for grabs."

"And neither is Hobo." Horace spoke up suddenly. "He's Melinda's dog now." Horace turned in her direction, his unexpected smile reaching across to where she huddled in the kitchen doorway with Mabel.

"I doubt the chickens or sheep are available, either. But if you want those, you'll have to ask Melinda later."

One man furrowed his brow, confused. "Uncle Horace, what do you mean? Not that I have room for them, but they're your livestock."

Kevin's cousin Dave leaned down the row of chairs. "You must not have heard. Melinda loves it here, and she's doing a great job. She's planning to buy the acreage in the spring."

There were more stares now, but these were more curious than judgmental. Feeling ridiculous, Melinda ducked her chin and gave a halfhearted wave. Jen motioned for her to come sit on the couch. She hesitated, then hurried through the crowd to take a seat.

The roll call continued. China cups were spoken for, and a vintage toaster Horace confirmed was still tucked away in the kitchen. Elaine was next, her face tired with tears and puffy from grief. In a second, Melinda realized, that wasn't all.

Elaine wasn't just sad, she was enraged. She crouched in her chair by the stairwell as if ready to pounce, the outrageous diamond on her finger flashing a distress signal in the waning afternoon light. Her knuckles were white with fury, her hands clenched around the luxurious handbag in her lap.

She first glared at Melinda, then turned her wrath on the rest of the group.

"Well, I guess it's time for me to tell you what I want." Her voice was angry and clipped. The group's chatter, which had at last turned congenial, died away to anxious silence.

"I want this house."

The air rushed out of Melinda's lungs and the room started to tilt. Ada squeezed her hand so hard that it hurt. Jen swore. Horace's lined face turned white. There was a second of shocked silence, then the house erupted with gasps and jeers. Hobo yelped and ran for the safety of the bedroom, Grace and Hazel two panicked blurs at his heels.

Elaine dumped her purse out of her lap with an angry *thud* and shot to her feet. "Now, listen!" She stomped her designer heel on the oak floorboards. "Before you all get down on me, I have something to say."

She looked at Horace, who was frozen in Melinda's chair. When he only blinked, his face a mask of silence, she glanced around the room, daring anyone to challenge her.

"Last time I was here, I talked to Uncle Wilbur about this very thing." She turned back to Horace, her voice defensive.

"I told him when the day came for you two to sell, that I wanted to buy it. And he said it would be nice to keep this place in the family."

"And when was that?" a woman called out sarcastically.

"Uncle Wilbur hasn't been himself for some time." One man addressed Elaine as he would a spoiled child. "I bet you don't have it in writing."

"This was seven years ago, but it doesn't matter." Elaine raised her chin at the boos and laughter that bounced around the room.

"I'm family, I want to buy it, and Wilbur said I could."

Horace still hadn't spoken, his eyes now focused on the floor. Melinda could see his weathered hand gripping the arm of her chair with surprising strength.

"Edward and I have the financial means to give you a very fair price," Elaine told him, her voice now calm and soothing. "We'll pay full market value, Uncle Horace, more if you want it. You and Wilbur won't have to worry about money again. Whatever the cost, you just say what you want for it."

Everyone stared at Horace. Melinda couldn't breathe, couldn't think. She looked down at her lovely floral rug, the one that was the perfect size for the farmhouse's living room floor, and the tears gathered behind her eyes. Horace gave her a price months ago, but she knew it was only half the acreage's current value. And she couldn't afford much more than that.

She couldn't compete with Elaine's deep pockets. Or her sentimental ties to this land.

Elaine waited, her bottom lip trembling. Finally, Horace looked up. "I've already got a buyer." Someone in the dining room began to clap their approval.

"Uncle Horace!" Elaine shouted, her cheeks turning pink. "This isn't fair! I talked to Uncle Wilbur about this years ago! He promised me!"

"Enough!" Edward tried to grab his wife's hand. "Elaine, please don't ..."

"I sure will!" She was crying now, her voice rising in pitch. "This house means everything to me! Some of my best memories are here. I can't let them slip away. My parents are gone, and now George." Her sobs echoed through the house. "I'm family, Uncle Horace!"

"You're damn right about that!"

Melinda felt the pressure on her hand vanish, and looked up to find Ada on her feet, her jaw tight with anger.

"When did we see you last, Elaine? Do you even call Horace and Wilbur? No, you sure don't. And how do I know that? Because I talk to them almost every day."

Kevin started toward his mom, but Jen was closer. She wrapped an arm around Ada, trying to comfort her. And maybe to prevent her from charging around the coffee table toward Elaine.

"My Kevin came down here several times a month, for *years*," Ada's voice trembled, "to help Horace and Wilbur stay in this house as long as possible. Melinda may not be our blood, but she's done a hell of lot more for this family than you ever have."

"What are *you* going to do with it, anyway?" one man called out to Elaine.

"Edward and I are going to retire," she snapped. "We want somewhere to spend our summers, a special place where our children and grandchildren can gather for the holidays." She gestured around her. "And this is where I want to be."

"This is not a hotel," Edith hissed at her niece. "This house deserves to have someone living in it all year long. And from what I've seen, Melinda cares for it far more than you ever will."

"She won't stay." Elaine directed this at Horace, as if Melinda wasn't in the room. "Why would she? At the first sign of trouble, she'll be gone. And she's got a whole life in the Cities to go back to."

"Melinda loves this farm," Horace said simply. "It's hers if she wants it."

And then everyone was talking and shouting at once. Ada was crying now, and Jen tried to steer her toward the kitchen. Elaine, her arms crossed, began to argue with Edward, who looked like he wanted to vanish down the iron floor register by his feet.

Melinda couldn't pass one more terrible minute on that couch. She ran for the stairwell and pulled the door closed behind her before she began to climb, barely able to see the steps because of the tears pouring down her face.

"That's enough!" she heard Mabel shout above the din. "Stop it, all of you! I'm not family, so I'm going to say what needs to be said: It's time for everyone to go."

Melinda hurried toward the safety of her bedroom, heard the reassuring click of the door latching behind her, and fell across the bed.

"I can't lose this place," she sobbed as she pulled the edges of the comforter around herself, Elaine's cruel words echoing through her mind.

"This is my home. And I can't go back to Minneapolis. There isn't anything to go back for."

Her bedroom was refreshingly cool and quiet. Shadows crept in as the last of the gloomy day's light vanished. She curled up, and waited. For what, she wasn't sure. Large snowflakes began to fall, landing softly on the window panes.

"Horace said he's got his buyer," she reminded herself, wiping at her face with her hands.

"But what if he changes his mind?"

She could hear muffled conversations still going on downstairs. Then the thunk of the back porch door, several times, the muffled hum of car engines warming up for cold drives home.

Home. Everyone else had a home to go to. Even Horace. He would never live here again. But she did. And oh, how she wanted to, now more than ever.

Her energy drained and her spirits low, she closed her eyes and fell into a deep, troubled sleep.

"Melinda?"

A familiar voice. A warm hand on her shoulder, shaking her awake. "Hey, we're leaving soon." It was Kevin.

She raised her head and tried to open her eyes, which were swollen from crying. She sat up slowly, her neck stiff and one knee asleep.

"My God, Melinda, I am so sorry." Kevin settled next to her on the bed. "I brought you some coffee, put it there on the dresser. Jen's helping Mom clean up the kitchen, a few of the other cousins stayed behind, too."

Melinda couldn't speak. Her shoulders slumped as her head dropped into her hands.

"Don't you worry," Kevin tried again. "Elaine's gone. Edward marched her out to the car. Between her crazy outburst and his embarrassment, I don't think we'll see them again for, oh, another seven years."

"What am I going to do if Horace changes his mind?" The tears were back. "What if Wilbur really made a promise to Elaine? I know Horace wants me to have the farm. But he's an honorable man, a promise means something to him."

"But Elaine doesn't," Kevin put in quickly. "And you do. You should have heard him in the car today, as we drove down. 'Melinda's done this and Melinda's done that.' He's so proud of you. We all are." He gave her shoulder a squeeze.

"The chickens!" She sat up, suddenly remembering. "And Stormy and Sunny! I never finished chores. Horace and I started for the house and then ..."

"Mabel fed everyone. And I set out more food for Hobo and the kittens. They're all hiding under the bed downstairs, I just checked on them. I guess it's high enough for Hobo to squeak under there, too. I bet they stay right there until everyone's gone."

He reached for the box of tissues on the dresser and handed her one. "Horace wanted to come up, but it's been a few years since he could do those narrow stairs easily. He said for you to ignore Elaine, forget all about it. Oh, and he wanted me to give you something."

Kevin plopped a stack of seed catalogs on the corner of the bed. "A few of these turned up at the nursing home. Horace said it's time to start planning the garden. Spring will be here before you know it."

* 15 *

The cover of the roll-top desk was dusty from lack of use, the metal slot for its skeleton key scarred with rust and dirt. Horace said it was unlocked, and he was confident the sheep book was still inside. Melinda wanted those records, but part of her hoped the lid was jammed and she'd be able to walk away, continue to ignore the desk and its mysterious contents just as she had for the past eight months.

Because even though Horace gave her permission to open the desk, she still felt like she was snooping into the Schermann family's business. And, after the ugly scene she'd witnessed two days before, all but stealing the farm away from them.

She cringed as her fingers gripped the handle. One tug, and another, and then the cover began to inch upward. Whorls of dust rose from the lid's tracks, and a mournful squeal started up somewhere in the back. Melinda closed her eyes, both against the dirt and whatever private, secret-filled items might be waiting inside.

"It's a Pandora's box. And not just this desk, it's the whole house, and everything in it. It's as if every family feud and long-forgotten promise has come to the surface."

It was silly, she knew, but she half expected to find some horrible thing crouching inside the desk. She took a deep breath and studied a collection of items that were old and worn, but far from noteworthy: stacks of yellowed paper, probably receipts; a pile of old farming magazines; and on the far left, a collection of leather-bound books that looked to be her best bet. Maybe she wouldn't have to sift through everything to find what she wanted.

Even so, she put a hand over her face as she recalled the stunning range of emotions that swept through the house Monday afternoon: Grief, and a bittersweet yearning for how things used to be. Then, the arrival of the ugly spirits of greed, bitterness, jealousy and resentment. And from what Kevin said last night on the phone, the battle over the family's antiques, and the uproar over Elaine's demand that Horace sell her the acreage, had not ended when Mabel kicked everyone out of the house.

Kevin's phone was blowing up with calls, emails and texts from his relatives. People who'd missed the funeral were making demands on this or that heirloom, the procedure to request items getting lost as word spread about the showdown at the farm. Many relatives, however, simply wanted to express outrage over who might take ownership of the property.

"You'll be glad to know you're leading Elaine by at least a five-to-one margin," he reported.

"The few on the other side have made it clear they simply don't like the land passing out of the family. Believe me, it's not Elaine they care about. I won't repeat some of the things I've heard, but you get the idea."

"Well, I guess it's good to have the majority vote. I'm sorry you've been caught in the middle of all this. I know how busy you are this week."

Kevin had dozens of research papers to grade for the classes he taught at the community college in Mason City, but refereeing this family fight had put him behind.

"And by the way, I talked to Ron again. You know, my cousin who's a Realtor here in town? He checked with an attorney to be sure, but Elaine has no legal claim to the acreage. Nothing's in writing. And Wilbur's dementia makes it impossible to verify if their conversation seven years ago went down as Elaine claims, or if it even happened at all."

Melinda had blinked in surprise. "Do you think she made it all up? I don't know her very well," she winced at the memory of Elaine's cruel remarks, "but I don't know if she'd stoop that low to get what she wants. On the other hand ..."

"Here's what I think. She pressured Uncle Wilbur, for sure. Wilbur made no promises, but he didn't tell her no. And in Elaine's world, where she always gets what she wants, she assumed the answer was yes."

Kevin's tone had then brightened a bit. "The only thing that matters now is, what Uncle Horace wants, and what you want. He's so mad at Elaine, and so insistent that you're his buyer, that he won't even discuss it. You don't have anything to worry about. Don't let this stop you, OK?"

As she studied the contents of the desk, Melinda wished she shared Kevin's confidence. There was no doubt she wanted to stay. This was her home. She decided that months ago, at Horace's encouragement and with Ada and Kevin's blessing, and then looked ahead to all the wonderful times she'd have here, and the exciting ways she could restore this charming old house.

She would plant a large garden and care for the animals, just as Horace had, but there was so much more she wanted to do. What if she pulled down that crazy bluebird wallpaper in the dining room? Should she have the outside of the house repainted? Did the oak floors need to be refinished?

Melinda had been so busy making plans for her new life, she hadn't given much thought to how the farm changing hands would mark the end of an era for so many.

And now, the gleaming woodwork and the beautiful dishes in the china cabinet were not just tangible echoes of the farm's past. They were a reminder she lived in someone else's house, a special place that was still the emotional home for dozens of people.

As she began to sort the stack of ledgers, tears blurred her eyes. Kevin confirmed Elaine's claim that the Schermanns have owned this land for over a hundred-and-twenty-five years. No matter how much Melinda loved this farm, or how supportive Horace was of her plans, she would be the one to break that link to the past.

And then, even more troubling, was the money. Or the lack of it.

Elaine's offer came with more than just a promise of the farm staying in the Schermanns' hands. It carried a financial windfall that would ensure Horace and Wilbur's final years would be beyond comfortable. Extended care was horribly expensive, and Wilbur's dementia only added to that staggering bill.

"Wouldn't it be wonderful if Horace and Wilbur were sitting on a hidden stash of cash?" she asked Grace, who had just wandered in from across the hall where the kittens were dozing on Melinda's bed. Drawn in by the protesting screech of the desk's cover and the musty scents coming from its dark interior, Grace's petite nose was working overtime.

"Do you think it's possible? You know, like those elderly people who never bought new clothes and always drove a beat-up truck, then when they pass on, they had millions tucked away at the bank? If only that were true in this case."

The farm's genteel shabbiness was a bit misleading, Melinda knew. The house was shaded by dozens of mature trees, enjoyed sweeping views, and sat on some of the most fertile farmland in the state. If this acreage ever made it onto the public real-estate market, it would be snatched up quick. Even so, nothing in this house hinted at hidden wealth. She glanced around the simple office, a compact room walled off years ago when the upstairs bathroom was created above the kitchen. Not an inch of space had been wasted.

And given the humble selection of second-hand housewares and furnishings that greeted Melinda on her arrival, she suspected a dollar never had, either. Farming was a hard life, and the family surely had weathered more lean years than prosperous times. No, somehow the idea of Horace as a secret millionaire didn't fit.

Sure, Melinda renting the farm had allowed Horace to move to the care center and not feel like he was abandoning his animals or his family's home. But in return, he'd already done so much for her.

Her rent remained at a laughable hundred dollars a month, plus only a portion of the utilities. Horace had gently dismissed her offers to pay more with a wave of his hand, mumbling something about how hard it was to find good help these days and that he needed a reliable tenant. He'd also paid Nathan in advance to mow the lawn all of last year, then provide snow removal this winter.

And it had only been in the last three months, and at Melinda's firm insistence, that John Olson handed her the bills for the hay and straw he delivered rather than mail them to Horace.

No matter how she looked at it, she owed Horace. But even with her side income from marketing projects for Susan's firm in Minneapolis, Melinda could never give full-market value for this place, much less compete with Elaine's offer. Prosper Hardware just didn't pay enough.

Grace bounded into Melinda's lap and batted at the fragile papers hiding under the desk's hood. "I don't know what we are going to do, Grace. But first, we need to find this sheep ledger. Maybe it would be better for me to look on my own, though."

She gently placed the kitten on the floor, and kept searching. Nothing shocking passed through her hands, and she soon realized why. If there had been anything too personal in this desk, Ada would have been savvy enough to remove it before Melinda's arrival.

"Here it is! Or at least, this is the newest one." The dates in the leather-bound ledger appeared to run from the late 1970s up until just a few years ago. "Let's see what it says."

The size of the flock was noted every January first, the tally updated with any lambs from the previous year not sent to auction. Throughout the year, sale and purchase prices were carefully noted for every sheep that changed hands.

She recognized Horace's handwriting in the notes about the pedigree of the rams the family owned over the years. Some details were in a determined scrawl that must have been Wilbur's.

Melinda smiled at the carefully calculated date when the ram was first allowed to mingle with the ewes every fall. That interaction was normally controlled by the farmer, rather than the surprise Melinda received one warm September afternoon. The buck in the rented pasture across the road had broken out of his fence, and some of her ewes had pushed through a patched-up gap on their side of the gravel.

The meticulous notes about each lambing season received her full attention. The reports included each ewe's delivery date, the number of lambs born and, to Melinda's horror, the various complications that occasionally occurred.

#6: Twins, stillborn. Second year in a row for this ewe. No more breeding.
#58: Breech lamb, male, very large. Got the vet. Lamb lived. Ewe died.
#15: Quads. Two of each. Lost one female first day. Rest OK.

"Four?" Melinda gasped. "That ewe had four? Whatever would I do with four all at once?" She glanced out the office's lone window, which looked west over the garage and toward the horizon. "I just hope the weather stays decent, so I can get help out here if I need it."

She tried to focus on the fact that most of the entries recorded no signs of trouble. There were more sets of triplets than she expected, but otherwise, the book told the story of a healthy, expanding flock cared for by two very capable farmers. And, she reminded herself, Horace was confident the current batch of ewes would be good mothers. Instinct would take over, just as he said it would.

The last entries were made three years ago. There were Numbers 21 and 33, with notes about their healthy, thriving babies. Melinda could only hope for similar outcomes this time around. One other entry caught her eye.

> *#26: Triplets. Two males and a female. Small one needs a bottle. Named her Annie.*

✳ ✳ ✳

Melinda could hardly believe it. Was that *drip, drip, drip* the sound of snow melting from Prosper Hardware's eaves? And already at seven in the morning?

Maybe it would turn into a true thaw, instead of just one brief day of warmer weather. The skies had already been clear for several days, the snowy fields along her daily route sparkling as if studded with billions of diamonds. But this morning, the sun promised surprising strength for mid-February. She found herself humming as she unlocked the store's back door and came through Bill's workshop, a pan of frosted cherry squares balanced in her arms. Valentine's Day had fallen on Sunday, when the store was closed, but there was no reason they couldn't celebrate two days late.

"A warm-up this time of year gets people out and about," Jerry was telling Auggie as they filled their coffee cups at the sideboard. "That bright sun gets people moving again. It's a reminder that warmer days are coming for real, if we just sit tight. At the very least, it's a chance to run errands before the next storm blows through."

Auggie was in an especially cheerful mood. "I don't think we'll get anywhere near the record, but it's sure warming up out there today." His head snapped around when he saw the pan in Melinda's hands. "So, what do we have here?"

"Cherry squares." She set the treats the sideboard's counter. "A little late Valentine's celebration, if you will."

"Do I see something good?" George called out as he came up the aisle. "I've already put away three eggs and two slices of toast, but I guess there's always room for a little more."

Auggie cut himself a generously sized cherry square and settled in his chair. The way he gulped it down, Melinda thought, you'd never guess his wife, Jane, loved to bake. She smothered a snicker behind the rim of her coffee mug, and admired the delicate etching of frost that still bordered the store's front windows. Today, it might melt away before ten.

"You know," Auggie wiped his hands on his jeans, "it's not just the thaw that's bringing people to town by the dozens. We're smack in the middle of a full moon. Better look out, people get all-kinds-of-crazy this time of the month."

"Oh, come on." Jerry shook his head. "That's an old wives' tale. It's the warmer weather for sure that's bringing people out, and the fact there's an assembly at the elementary school later this morning. A traveling theater group's putting on a production of fairy tales, and all the parents were invited."

"Nope." Auggie was adamant. "The full moon is when the weirdoes show up."

When Melinda laughed, he turned in her direction.

"I'm serious. And I don't just mean the eccentric people. There's a lot of those around here. I mean the real nuts, those folks living out in the middle of nowhere that don't work away from home. This time of year, I think some of them go days, or weeks, without seeing other people. I swear, some of them look around at Prosper like they've never seen it before. Nothing changes, it's not like there's anything new to see."

Auggie got up and topped off his mug. "And I can spot them right off when they come in the co-op, too. They're wandering the aisles, overwhelmed, when everything's stocked in the very same place it was twenty years ago. I guess as long as they purchase something, I can't complain. Dan and I keep an eye on them, though."

There was no mention of Evan. He was still working part-time at the co-op and occasionally had dinner with his parents, but it was little Chloe who Auggie tried to insert into every conversation. He loved his granddaughter, that was plain to see. Melinda only wished he would extend the same open arms to his son.

She and Evan had been texting back and forth, and finally made plans to meet for lunch at the Watering Hole that very day. She brushed aside her nervousness and tried to enjoy how her friends devoured the treats she'd brought in, but her mind kept jumping ahead of the clock.

Only Karen knew about her lunch with Evan. Melinda wanted to keep this under the radar, which would be nearly impossible if she told anyone else. But really, why did it matter? They were meeting in a public place, two friends hanging out for an hour, at most. Maybe it was because she found herself so eager to see him. She told herself it was just because winter had dragged on so, and there wasn't much else to do. Karen had been forced to bail on their last two lunch attempts, she and Doc struggling to keep up with farm calls that took much longer when the weather was rough.

How nice it would be to sit down, with someone whose company she enjoyed, and eat a meal she didn't have to make herself. Her day, Melinda decided as she gazed out at the cobalt blue sky, was certainly looking bright.

Doc wandered in and removed his knit cap and coat. Despite the lines of fatigue around his eyes, even he was grinning. "Nice day out there, hope this lasts the rest of the week. Personally, I'm sick of the snow and the ice. What we've got underfoot is enough. Auggie, when will spring get here?"

"He's not focused on that right now," George cut in with a chuckle. "He was just telling us how we're in danger of some sort of zombie apocalypse, since all the crazies come out during a full moon."

Doc shrugged as he helped himself to two cherry squares. "Melinda, these look great. Just what I needed this morning. Well, I have to say, animals sometimes get antsy when the moon is full. I've always known it to be true." He settled into his folding chair with a resigned sigh.

"And those odd people Auggie's talking about? They're for real. I know, because they call me at the oddest hours with the strangest requests. So hold on, everybody, we might have a few rocky days ahead. No telling what might happen."

* * *

The Watering Hole was packed, thanks to it being Prosper's only restaurant and because the warmer weather had drawn area residents off their farms and into town.

Evan was already there when Melinda walked in, waiting in a booth along the far wall. She liked the spot he'd chosen, not only because the padded brown-vinyl benches were comfy, but because the high seat backs would give them a little privacy. She felt silly for being skittish, but was reminded of why she was so concerned when several people turned to see exactly who was coming through the door.

She had lied to Bill, telling him she was meeting Karen for lunch, a fib that Karen would back if questioned. But the Watering Hole's regulars, perched on their stools at the bar, would have no doubt who she was meeting. And, as Evan had wryly explained, he'd become somewhat of a notable figure in town. Between his visible role at the co-op, being the son of one of Prosper's best-known residents, and the commotion caused by his sudden appearance out at the Benniger farm, Evan often felt as if both old friends and total strangers were scrutinizing his every move.

"God knows what rumors are going around town," he'd said the other night on the phone. "People have been friendly, of course, but I can tell they are dying to pry for all the info they can get. Chloe's found it easy to make friends at story hour, thankfully, but I can't say the same. Except for you, of course."

Melinda had smiled at that. "It can be tough to get on equal footing here, at first. Who knows? Maybe the gossip is really exciting, like you embezzled money from your old job and squirreled away your millions in the basement of that old house. Or you witnessed a terrible crime and you're hiding out from the bad guys."

She was pleased that he'd laughed at that idea. While Evan was in much better spirits than when he and Chloe arrived in Prosper, things were not easy for him. He was a single parent, searching for full-time work while maintaining a tentative truce with his mercurial father. And then Carrie ...

Evan had mentioned she was still at the rehabilitation center near Madison, but Melinda hadn't pressed for details.

"You know," he'd said then, "why don't we meet up for lunch, and I'll tell you where the money's buried?"

Today, Evan was clean-shaven and wearing a tan sweater that set off his kind brown eyes. He looked up from studying the menu and smiled at her. All the sudden, Melinda was really glad she'd agreed to come.

"Do you think we're being watched?" he whispered in a too-loud voice, smirking. "I got us both a Coke, by the way. Your favorite, right?

"Yes, thanks. And as for the stares? Absolutely." She stuffed her coat down her side of the booth and slid in. "That one guy at the bar, in the blaze-orange cap and navy coveralls? He's undercover FBI, I'm sure of it."

"Well, I guess we'll give them something to talk about." Evan rolled his eyes, then stopped. "Really, I shouldn't be so snarky. People have been very kind to Chloe and me. But in Madison, I'm another face in the crowd, you know? Here, I'm Auggie Kleinsbach's wayward son." He tapped his napkin-and-cutlery roll on the Formica table for emphasis. "I've only been here once since I came back. So, what do you usually get? Something fried, I suspect."

"True, but that doesn't narrow it down much." She picked up a laminated menu and flipped it over, suddenly starving thanks to the tantalizing aroma of French fries wafting from the kitchen. "The burgers are always good, of course. Sometimes Doug, the guy who owns this place with his wife, Jessie, gets a wild hair and offers a special. His hot beef sandwiches are amazing."

Jessie Kirkpatrick was on her way to their booth now, her dark curly hair pulled up in a ponytail. She and Doug were in their late twenties, and possessed both the energy and business savvy to maintain the Watering Hole's dive-bar traditions while expanding its menu to draw a wider net of customers. While many small-town eateries were languishing, the Watering Hole was on a roll.

"Hey, Melinda. Hey, Evan." Jessie pulled her order pad from her jeans' pocket. "What'll it be?"

Melinda was sure Jessie gave her a sly look as she waited, pen in hand. But Doug and Jessie had a pact to not spread even one bit of what they saw and heard in the Watering Hole. "It's bad business," Jessie had told Melinda one day. She would be discreet.

"I was just telling Evan about the hot beef," was all Melinda said as she returned Jessie's smile.

"Oh, sorry, we ran out maybe ten minutes ago." She tipped her head toward a group of retired-farmer types around three pushed-together tables in the back. "Those guys wiped us out."

"I'll have the grilled chicken sandwich, then," Melinda decided. Evan ordered a burger.

"Both come with bottomless fries," Jessie said before she started for the next booth. "A new feature we're trying out. Good thing potatoes are cheap these days, though. Word's getting out about it."

"It's great to see the place is so busy," Evan told Melinda as he tucked the menus behind the napkin dispenser. "People of all ages, too. I remember this being a bar first, a restaurant second."

"Doug and Jessie are making changes around here. She put those new gray-blue curtains up in the windows just last week. Next, they want to paint this dark paneling a soft cream, class this place up." Melinda gestured at the walls, which still sported a hodge-podge of vintage beer advertisements. "They moved here from Mason City last year, after the guy who owned this place for thirty years died, and it came up for sale. You'd never know they weren't from Prosper, the way they've fit in so easily."

"Yeah, I can't say the same," Evan admitted. "But still, I'm glad I came back when I did." He looked her in the eye, but didn't say more.

She found herself starting to blush just a bit, then even more, this time mostly out of embarrassment. Had she become so painfully single that a handsome man smiling at her turned her into an awkward teenager?

"I wonder sometimes what I would've done if I'd stayed in Minneapolis," she said, trying to steer the conversation to safer territory. "What if I'd taken that job at my friend's firm? Would I have stayed in my apartment, which I loved, a little longer, or made the leap and bought a house? But then I think, it doesn't matter, I'm right where I'm supposed to be."

Evan was quiet for a moment, then looked down at the table. "Do you ever think about moving away, even to another city? You told me about that one woman, Horace's niece, I think? What a mess. Is she still pushing to get the farm?"

"Yes, unfortunately. Elaine called Horace again the other day, crying, saying she really wants the acreage. I think she's decided if she can't hold the family to whatever Wilbur allegedly told her, she'll try to guilt Horace into selling it anyway."

"So what happened?"

Melinda shook her head. "Horace hung up on her. I know, because he turned right around and called me. I've never heard him that angry. He's usually quiet, you know? He told me, 'The farm's yours, and for the price we agreed on. She better not call you. But if she does, you tell her to go to hell.'"

Evan laughed heartily. "Excellent! Sounds like she needed to be put in her place. Well, it's settled, then. Wait, what's wrong?"

Melinda rubbed a hand across her forehead, a headache coming on.

"I feel so guilty. I want the farm, I want to stay, of course, but I hadn't thought about how much that land meant to all these people. And Elaine can pay so much more than I can."

"That's true, but ..." Evan suddenly reached across the table and covered her other hand with his own. "I think it's meant to be yours. Horace obviously thinks so. You'll keep things going, it won't sit empty most of the year, like what that relative wants to do with it. Think of the animals, too. If you stay, they get to stay."

Melinda nodded. He was right.

"Besides," he went on, not letting go. "You're one of the toughest people I know. You're smart, and funny, and, well, really special. To me, at least."

She looked down at the table, at how he was holding her hand, then up at his face. What she saw in his eyes thrilled her, and scared her, all at the same time.

And here was Jessie, with their lunch platters balanced on her arm. She widened her eyes at Melinda, but there was a look of genuine excitement on her face. The older women at the table across the aisle, however, were less supportive of what they saw. The one on the left pursed her lips, then muttered something to the other woman, and they both deliberately turned their heads away.

Melinda slowly pulled her hand back, then busied herself unrolling her napkin. Evan said nothing, and did the same.

"Here we are." Jessie's tone was one note too cheerful. "Burger for you, chicken for you, fries all around. I'll check on you later." She hurried away.

Melinda took one bite of her sandwich and chewed slowly. Evan had all his attention focused on shaking the ketchup out of the bottle. She had to say something. Anything to break the tension. She might as well be honest.

"Evan," she started to say, then lowered her voice to just above a whisper.

"I ... we ... I can only be your friend. I'm sorry."

The women across the way were pretending not to listen. Melinda gave them a hard look, and they went back to their sandwiches. Would these nosy people ever mind their own business?

She waited for Evan to protest, to laugh it all off and make some joke, but he didn't. The disappointment was all over his face. Melinda's instincts had been right.

That made her both sad, and just a bit happy, to know Evan thought so much of her. But she and Karen had discussed this very thing. She had to put an end to it, right now, before things got messy.

"I know," he finally said. For a moment, he seemed to be thinking something over. "But ..." Then he nodded, as if checking himself.

"I know. You're right. I'm not good enough for you. I don't have it all together. You've got your new life all planned out, and it's a great one, and there's no room for me in it. I'm just sort of at loose ends, no matter how much I wish I wasn't."

"That won't last forever." She shook a fry at him for emphasis. "You'll sort things out, it'll all fall into place. It just might take a while. Or, who knows? Good things could arrive very soon. Mine came out of nowhere, it seemed. When something feels right, you'll know. You'll know what to do."

He managed a small, rueful smile. "Well, I'll take your friendship, no matter what. Sorry, I shouldn't have done that, I shouldn't ..."

"Don't worry about it," she told him, then smiled. "I was kind of glad that you did. It's been a while."

Then she had to laugh. "You know, your dad was saying just this morning how there's a full moon, and people are acting a little, well, impulsive."

Evan snorted, shook his head and picked up his burger. "Well, I'll use that as an excuse, then. You know, I don't have to be back at the co-op for another half an hour. I think we'll have time for some of Jessie's homemade pie."

* 16 *

Melinda stared at the calendar tacked up by the wheezing refrigerator. It was Sunday, two more days until February 23, Karen's calculated target for the earliest the lambs might arrive. The months of wondering and weeks of preparation were all leading up to that date circled in red. She'd studied the birthing process, consulted several veteran farmers, and cleared a shelf in the back porch closet to keep her supplies at the ready. All she had to do now was wait.

And be patient, she reminded herself. Karen had cautioned that any lambs arriving early might be too small and weak. A few days' delay would be best for everyone.

"If only they'd all go into labor sort-of soon." Melinda made a praying gesture with her hands and glanced up at the kitchen's plaster ceiling.

"But not *too* soon. And just one at a time, please. And not in the middle of the night. Thanks and amen."

Her parents came over that afternoon to help with last-minute preparations. The lamb bottles were scrubbed and sanitized, and set out to dry on the metal-topped canning table in the basement. That room had a door that latched securely against the curious paws of Hobo and the kittens.

Out in the barn, there wasn't much left to do. The new heat lamps' bright metal shades glowed like jewelry against the barn's weathered walls and pens, their lights strung together with the cheerful electric-blue insulated extension cords. Melinda, Roger and Diane gave the cleaned-out pens one last vigorous sweep, then focused on stocking the extra compartment with straw and hay.

"I wouldn't worry too much," Roger comforted his daughter as they lugged straw bales across the haymow floor and dropped them through the trap door. Diane waited below to stack them on the wheeled cart. "Sheep are usually healthy animals and excellent mothers."

"That's what everyone says." Melinda reached for the next bale, shooing Sunny out of the way before lifting the bulky rectangle by its twine strings. When she arrived at the farm, it took her a great deal of effort to lift a bale. Now, she managed them with ease. "And I want to believe that, I really do. But you should see this sheep ledger, Dad. Most of the births went off without a hitch, and I keep reminding myself about that. But the rest of them? They're like a hit list of every nightmare scenario you could imagine."

"Well ..." Roger hesitated. "It's true, there can be problems once in a while. We raised sheep off and on when I was growing up, you know. Your Grandpa Foster always said sheep were either healthy or dead."

"I heard that!" Diane shouted from below. "Not helping, honey!"

He sighed and patted Melinda on the shoulder. "I'm not trying to scare you. All Grandpa meant was, sheep are usually low-maintenance creatures. But if they do get sick, they can go downhill fast."

"I thought you were here to help me get ready." She gave her dad a warning look and shoved the next straw bale into his hands. "I'm about to stuff that sheep ledger back where I found it."

"Not a bad idea, if you ask me." Roger moved on to the stack of hay bales in the other corner of the loft, and began to count them out. "You don't need it. You know what you're up against, you're well-stocked, and help's only a call away. Horace must be awfully proud of this barn; it's still snug and sturdy, even for one this old. And those cleared-out pens? I don't know if I've ever seen any that spotless. Those ewes will think they've checked into some sort of sheep spa."

Melinda only smiled and tipped her chin. She didn't want to admit she'd maybe gone a bit overboard. Her cleaning hadn't stopped with removing the old straw and sweeping down the pens' walls and floors. The half-walls and feed bunks had also received a vigorous scrub-down of hot water spiked with bleach.

"I want the mamas to really be comfortable," was all she said. "We can bed down the first two stalls today, and I'll get the others filled once we get closer. That'll keep the straw cleaner, if I don't spread it all right away."

Now it was Roger's turn to hide his laughter. "Yes, ma'am. You're the shepherd. Let's get the rest of this hay and straw moved, and get inside for a hot cup of coffee and some of that spice cake I saw cooling on the counter."

Tuesday morning finally arrived. Melinda hurried into her chore gear and rushed out to the barn, her heart pounding with expectation. Nothing. The evening brought no sign of impending change, nor did her pre-bedtime inspection.

Ed had offered to do midday barn checks on the days she worked at the store. He and Mabel still had a few beef cows, as a hobby for Ed and to keep the pasture grass chewed down, but had sold the rest of their livestock when they retired five years ago. Ed was nearly as excited as Melinda was about the lambs' arrival. Which was saying something.

"Just you wait," Doc told her Wednesday morning, gesturing with his coffee mug for emphasis. "You'll be busy soon enough. Enjoy a few more nights' of uninterrupted sleep while you can."

"Look at you," Auggie snorted. "You're so wound up. Calm down, Melinda. Those sheep will come through just fine. Tell you what, when one of them gets as antsy as you are right now, pacing around with that crazed look in their eyes, then you'll know there's lambs on the way."

"OK, OK. I just feel so responsible for them. They trust me and I don't want to let them down."

"That's just the sign of a good shepherd," George put in gently. "It'll be all right. Distract yourself with one of these apple-cinnamon muffins Mary sent along. She baked a double batch for some reason, and told me not to bring any of these home." He reached for a paper plate. "Here, take two. You need to keep up your strength."

Thursday morning, Number 18 didn't rush to join the line at the trough. While the other sheep jostled at the fence to get their noses petted, she hung back from the crowd. The ewe was ... antsy, Melinda decided. And her sides, while still swollen, looked a bit different.

She fed the rest of the flock, stocked the first pen with feed and water and fluffed its fresh straw, then reached for one of the heavy rope halters waiting on a nearby hook.

"All right, Mama," she cooed. "I think it's time you get a private room." The ewe was so distracted she barely noticed the halter sliding around her neck, but the scoop of shelled corn waved under her nose got her attention. With the other sheep busy with their breakfast, Melinda easily guided her through the gate and around the corner to the birthing stall.

"Not so hard, was it? You're new at this, but Horace says you'll do just fine. Ed will come over midday to check on you, and I'll be home as soon as I can."

She was leaning over the store's counter visiting with Gertrude, who cared for a colony of feral cats along the railroad tracks on the edge of town, when her phone buzzed.

"You better take that, honey." Gertrude reached for her purse and started for the door. She always purchased the economy-size bag of cat food, and Bill was about to load it into her car. "From what you've said about your sheep, that's probably Ed. Good luck!"

Ed was exuberant, practically shouting over the din. Melinda wiped away a few happy, relieved tears as she heard the ewe calling her lambs, then two high-pitched responses. "Twins, one of each!" he hooted. "The babies and their mother are all fine. They're just about perfect, I can't wait for you to see them!"

Neither could Melinda. It seemed as if four o'clock would never arrive. At three-thirty, Bill came up from the woodshop. "It's a little slow this afternoon. I'm closing, anyway. Why don't you just head out?"

Melinda parked in front of the garage, not bothering to put the car inside or change her clothes, and ran for the barn. Hobo charged through his doggie door, barking with excitement, and caught up with her halfway across the yard.

"Have you seen them yet? No, I bet Ed didn't want you underfoot. Oh, I can't wait any longer!"

The flock raised their usual greeting when she opened the barn door, but the sight of her nicer coat and different knit cap gave them pause. Ed showing up in the middle of the day, plus all the commotion in the back part of the barn, already had them stirred up. "It's just me!" she told the sheep, reaching over the fence to hand out some reassuring nose pats. Then came the call of the new mother, and the sweet sound of baby lambs.

Ed had turned on the heat lamp and gave the ewe more feed before he went home. The lambs seemed to be all black legs, their tiny hoofs exact replicas of their mother's. Their heads were also dark, but their peach-fuzz wool was more gray than cream. With curious eyes, they starred first at Melinda and then Hobo. One of the lambs shook its tail, stuck out its tongue and let out a cute, high-pitched "baaa."

"Look at you!" Melinda gasped. "Oh, you are both so beautiful. Good job, Mama!"

Hobo had turned up at the farm as a stray puppy only a few years ago, just missing the last lambing season. Although Melinda allowed him to approach the pen, she watched him closely. He raised his ears but didn't bark. Then he settled on the floor next to the gate, sticking his nose through the panel to give both babies a curious sniff.

While Hobo showed no signs of aggression toward the lambs, she was glad the barn's pet entrance was already walled in so only Sunny and Stormy could pass through. He could visit the lambs, but only if she was there to supervise.

There was a loud knock on the barn door. Ed and Mabel let themselves in.

"We were watching at the front window for your car to go by." Mabel gave Melinda a joyful hug. "I was dying to come down and see the babies. And I brought you a casserole, dear. It's in the car. You stuff that in the freezer and some night when you need it, it's all ready to go."

"Oh, that's wonderful! And Ed, thank you for coming down." Melinda was so happy she thought her heart might burst. "I wish I'd been here, but it meant so much to know you were checking on her for me."

"They'd already shown up." Ed shrugged, but he was grinning from ear to ear. "Mama had it all under control."

"I think Hobo would keep watch all night if you let him." Mabel reached down and rubbed Hobo's ears. While he loved Mabel, Hobo was so focused on the new lambs he barely looked up. "He doesn't know what to make of all this."

"Those are some fine twins." Ed whistled. "Good-sized for newborns, and strong. If you had to end up with unexpected lambs, that buck across the road was the perfect ram. And if the other deliveries go as smoothly as this one did, you'll be done in no time."

After Ed and Mabel left, Melinda settled down and finally went inside to change into her chore clothes and make her rounds. The other pregnant ewes showed no signs of impending labor. With a sigh of thankfulness and relief, she sat down to a leisurely supper of leftover lasagna and salad.

The sheep book waited on the other side of the kitchen table. Once her meal was finished, she picked up the ledger and flipped to the first blank page.

"It's time for us to make an entry," she told Hazel, who bounded into her lap and tried to bat at the pen. "One down, three to go."

* 17 *

Melinda rolled out of bed at the silent hour of two in the morning, eager to pull on her boots and take a sleepy walk to the barn to check on the newborns. And anyone else who might be on the way.

A few more nights of this and it wouldn't be so much fun, but this trek was surprisingly pleasant. The sky was clear, the stars close. And it wasn't as cold as it could be. Hobo hadn't stirred from the crazy quilt on Horace's old bed, tired out from all the day's excitement, so her only companions were the cool beam of the yard light and the warm glow from the headlamp strapped around her knit cap.

At least, she didn't see anything else. The gangly baby lambs had her on guard, as protective as their mother. She remembered the night she and Hobo watched the deer feeding, and scanned the yard again. She'd found a swath of strange tracks that next morning, but they were soon muddied by a warm spell. Another round of fresh snow, and the paths of all the other wildlife calling this farm home, had erased them completely.

The three pregnant ewes didn't seem any closer to labor, so she focused her attention on the mama and babies in the back. The twins were barely twelve hours old, but had already discovered it was fun to run to the stall gate and greet Melinda when she came for a visit.

Satisfied all was well, she turned off the lights, checked the barn door was securely latched, and hurried back to the house and the warmth of her down comforter.

Saturday morning, it looked like Number 7 was the next mother-to-be. She was younger, Annie's age, and also new to lambing. Melinda took no chances, and penned her up before she went to work. Sunday and Monday were her weekend, and the odds were good she would be home when this ewe went into labor.

"See, it's all going to work out," Auggie told her that morning. "Maybe the other lambs will follow soon, and you'll be done. You've had good weather so far, it's pretty warm. It'll rain later today, and then maybe a bit of snow tonight, but there's no blizzard on the way."

Ed checked the young ewe at noon, and reported there was little change. Melinda wanted to rush to the barn the minute she got home, but made herself go inside and change her clothes. By the time she'd warmed up some leftover chicken gravy for part of Sunny and Stormy's supper, a steady rain had started to fall.

Her rubber boots sloshed through the water ponding in the farmyard, the rain filling in the rough craters left by the partially melted snow. It was a slow, careful trip, and she was soaked through by the time she got to the barn. The pregnant sheep was now pacing in her stall, calling out to Melinda and the mother in the next pen. The other ewe answered with a low, reassuring bleat, then turned back to her lambs.

The smaller ewe was of a gentle sort, not a diva like Annie. Melinda climbed into the stall and approached her easily. Even better, she graciously allowed Melinda to gently pat her sides and stare at her bottom. From what Melinda could see, things were progressing nicely.

"You'll do fine." She looked the ewe in the eye and rubbed her head. "It shouldn't be long now. Sometime tonight, you'll be a mama. Here, I set out your supper, and you've got plenty of water. I'll even turn your heat lamp on early. See? Nice and cozy. I'll come out later and check on you again."

Once the other sheep were fed and the cats settled in the grain room, Melinda gathered her buckets and raised the hood of her coveralls, bracing for the chilly rain tapping on the north side of the barn. She turned the door latch, stepped out, and nearly slid off her feet.

The yard was now a pockmarked field of ice, the light by the garage feeble in the rain-blurred twilight. How long had she been inside? She couldn't be sure. Steadying herself by hanging onto the door's iron latch, she aimed her headlamp's beam skyward and saw shiny patches spreading on the rough boards of the barn.

A blast of damp wind slapped her face, and she pulled her scarf closer to her nose and set out for the chicken house, trying to keep her steps deliberate and her pace steady. It would be fully dark soon. She had to get to the coop, and back to the house, as quick as she could.

When had the forecast changed? It had been a busy day at Prosper Hardware, since it was a Saturday and not terribly cold. And Auggie had been so confident this morning ...

The snow between the garage and chicken house hadn't melted as much before the rains came, and provided more traction. The hens were agitated and skittish, squawking more than usual, but they were all safely inside. She set out generous rations and stumbled across the yard to the house, her thick scarf crackling with ice by the time she reached the back steps.

Melinda groaned when she pulled her phone from the inside pocket of her coveralls. She'd forgotten to switch it out of silent mode when she left the store, and missed the alert sent out just twenty minutes ago: An ice storm warning had been issued, effective until tomorrow morning.

She sank down on the porch bench, tears forming in her weary eyes. "Why hadn't I paid more attention? The weather can turn on a dime this time of year, I know better than that. I'm just so tired."

Hobo slipped through the doggie door from the kitchen, then sniffed cautiously at her soaked boots and discarded hat and gloves. She sat up straighter and wiped at her cheeks. "If you need to potty, let's try to go soon, OK? It's getting icy out there. And I won't let you go out alone until this blows over."

Hazel met them in the kitchen, and Melinda picked her up. Grace was snuggled in her favorite corner of the couch, her orange front paw crossed over the black one, sound asleep. Melinda settled Hazel next to her sister, popped a pizza in the oven, then looked around, thinking.

With Hobo and the kittens in the house, candles would be a last resort. She needed the flashlights, and the battery lantern.

Auggie had laughed last fall when she insisted he sell her a gallon of kerosene, but she was glad it waited for her out in the garage if she needed it. The two antique lanterns she'd found in the house were clean and ready, thanks to an assist from George one morning at the store.

There were gallons of drinking water in the downstairs bedroom's closet, and some clean pails in the basement she could fill at the utility sink. She'd taken advantage of one of the nice days earlier that week to bring up more wood from the generous pile behind the machine shed, and stack it inside the back porch.

Mabel called, then Angie, then her parents. Melinda told everyone she was as prepared as she could be, and that the second ewe was on track to deliver yet that night.

"Sometimes a storm gets them stirred up," her dad said, "but that doesn't mean they can't have a normal delivery. Just be careful in that icy yard."

Hobo shadowed her as she crisscrossed the house, then sat by her feet while she ate. "You're in charge of Hazel and Grace, OK?" She gave him a hug. "I'm going to be in and out. I need to get to the barn every two hours, no matter what."

A gust of wind slashed the side of the house, and the pitter-pat of the rain turned into an icy rattle. For just a second, the lights flickered.

Suddenly, Melinda was no longer hungry. She tried to watch television and flip through a magazine, but kept one eye on the mantel clock. Promptly at eight, she braced for the chill of her damp overalls and slid on her still-soaked boots.

"Please God," she whispered before opening the back door. "There's lambs in the barn, and more on the way. Please keep the lights on, the heat on. I'm sorry I ever laughed about Horace still having that old wall phone. He was smart to keep it. He knew what could happen."

The ewe was still pacing, but there was no sign her lambs would come soon. Melinda hesitated, sick at heart. She hated to leave the sheep's side, but it could be hours until the babies arrived.

Another dark, icy stumble across the yard, another gasp of relief when she reached the back porch steps, which were now so treacherous she had to cling to the handrail. It was too late to spread ice melt, too late to do anything but wait.

She wiped the icy rain from her face, which flamed in the sudden heat of the kitchen, and plugged her smartphone into its charger. Hobo ran in from the living room and bumped his nose against the leg of her jeans.

"I'm back," she told him. "But I don't know for how long."

The lights blinked again. Melinda set her best flashlight on the coffee table, started a fire and huddled on the couch, Hobo at her feet and Hazel and Grace in her lap.

The warnings scrolled across the television: numerous power outages had been reported, roads were impassible, and everyone was urged to shelter in place. The wind was howling now, and the ice pellets bounced off the house and flung themselves at the windows.

And then, like someone blowing out a candle, the house went black except for the small blaze burning in the hearth. Hobo whimpered. Melinda's hand shook as she gently placed her palm on his head. "It's going to be OK, it'll be back on soon," she whispered, knowing it wasn't true. All it took was for one power line to snap somewhere, even a mile or two down the road, and everyone was left in the dark.

She turned on the lantern and sat there for a moment, helpless. But then, there was something she could do.

"I might as well go to the barn now," she told Hobo and the kittens. "And I might have to stay away longer than before. But I will come back, I promise."

The landline phone still hummed its soothing dial tone, but her once-cozy home was shadowy and surreal. There was an uneasy silence under the rage of the ice storm, with Horace's wheezing old refrigerator suddenly mute and the furnace no longer purring in the basement. Even with the thick fleece curtains pulled tight closed against the cold, the temperature in the house would soon start to drop.

This time, she packed a tote. A stack of worn-but-clean towels, antiseptic, rubber gloves. She mixed a small batch of milk replacer, using some of her precious jugged water, and added a second, empty bottle to her stash.

With the power out, the yard light was also gone, her path so black she couldn't even make out the barn's outline from the back steps. Her lantern and headlamp offered only weak circles of light in the howling storm.

At last, the barn door. She turned her back to the wind and busted the ice off the latch with her gloved hand, the oil she sprayed on it a few hours ago already worthless against the driving sleet.

The flock was restless and shifting, only a few of the ewes greeting Melinda as she wrestled the door out of the gale's grasp and latched it tight. She turned off her headlamp to conserve its batteries. The inside of the barn was as dark as the yard, heavy shadows snaking through the corners as she shuffled down the aisle with her lantern. The sudden beam of light startled the first ewe and the twins and they called out to Melinda, but there was no sound from the second pen. She hustled around the corner, trying to pull away her hat and gloves as she went.

The other ewe was down on her side, breathing heavily. Her eyes were wild in the thin glow of the lantern.

"Hold on," Melinda gasped. "I'm here. And just in time."

She put down the tote and climbed into the pen, swinging the little lantern to get a better look.

The sheep was in full labor at last. Melinda knelt in the straw and stroked the ewe's nose.

"You're doing great," she whispered. "Just hang in there. Your baby, or babies, are on the way now. It'll be over soon. I'm not leaving you." Her voice caught in her throat. "Not again."

The ewe panted and shifted, her grunts drowned out by the rattling sleet pounding on the barn's roof.

Melinda curled up along the side wall of the pen, grateful for something solid to lean against, as the heat lamps dangled, useless, above her head.

Sunny and Stormy padded out from their darkened house, eager for the relative warmth of Melinda's lap. Gathering her courage, she snapped off the lantern. She would need its light later.

Minutes passed. With her phone turned off to conserve power, she wasn't sure how many. Every so often, she flipped on the lantern to take a look. Should the lambs have been born by now? Was the ewe in danger? She wasn't sure, and it frightened her. Because if there was trouble, no one would be able to come.

Then the grunting and pushing escalated, and Melinda sensed movement. She powered up the lantern and soon saw a lamb, covered in fluids, slide out into the straw. It was smaller than either of the twins were at birth, and she feared the worst.

The ewe staggered to her feet and licked the newborn clean. It gave a weak answer to her greeting, but at last stood on its wobbly legs.

"There you go!" Melinda whispered. "Good baby!" The lamb nudged its mother's side and took its first draw of milk, getting the colostrum it needed to thrive. Mama let the baby nurse for a few minutes, then grunted and eased herself back into the straw.

"There's more," Melinda told Sunny and Stormy, who now watched from outside the pen. "Come on, girl, you can do it. You're almost there."

More pushing, then a second lamb appeared, even smaller than the first. The ewe cleaned the tiny newborn and urged it to stand.

The roar of the storm filled Melinda's ears, and she wasn't sure if the lamb had answered. At last, there came the smallest lift of its wooly flank, then another. But were the breaths too far apart?

The ewe called again, more insistent, and nudged her little baby. It lifted its head, then slumped back into the straw.

Melinda reached for the lamb, afraid of how fragile it felt in her hands. It was very weak, so feeble compared to the other newborn that was already exploring the corners of the pen. "You have to get up. Baby, you have to!"

This tiny one needed to drink from its mother, and soon. Melinda lifted her tote bag over the gate, then fished out the empty bottle. She had to hurry.

"I'm sorry, mama, but I've got to do this." She moved her lantern in close and watched how the first lamb pulled on the opposite teat, its tail wriggling with satisfaction.

Horace said it was easy, told her she could do it. She had no choice but to get it right.

The roar of the ice storm fell away as she focused on her task. The milk streaming into the bottle was thick and rich, the ewe silent and still as if she understood. Melinda slid back on her heels and stretched the rubber nipple over the bottle, then crawled to where the weak lamb lay in the straw. She let out a deep breath as she saw a faint rise and fall in its wool. It wasn't too late.

"You have to drink, baby. Please, take a little, OK?"

The newborn took a tentative pull on the bottle, then turned its head away. Melinda felt panic rise in her chest. If she couldn't get milk in the lamb and get it warm, it was going to die. She set the bottle down and tried her phone. The signal was scratchy, but there. Karen picked up on the second ring.

"Melinda! Are you OK? Are you at home?"

"I'm out in the barn. Oh, Karen, I don't know what to do."

Karen confirmed what Melinda suspected: Her only chance was to get the lamb to the house and by the fire.

"What if it gets too cold and wet on the way? It takes ages to get across that yard tonight."

"It's the best of two bad options. It's the only chance you have. No one can get to you, I wish I could. Power lines are down all over, the roads are covered with ice. Everyone's trapped right where they are."

"I know, I know." Melinda signed, blinking tears away.

"I've got two other farmers with babies coming in this storm." Karen's voice wavered. "One cow, another ewe. Both are struggling. And I can't get out of my driveway to help anyone. You're doing everything right. Don't give up."

Melinda rolled her towels around the tiny lamb, wishing they were warm, then placed the bundle gently inside the canvas tote. The ewe called anxiously to her baby, but there was no answer. Melinda tucked the bottle of colostrum under her arm and left the milk replacer in the aisle. There simply wasn't room.

"I'll do all I can to save your baby," she promised the ewe, then started for the door. She worried the lamb would toss and thrash inside the bag, scared and unsure about being taken from its mother, but the baby was silent and still.

Her shuffle to the house was worse than before. The howling wind tried to push her back and the driving sleet pummeled her arms and face. She held the tote close to her chest, hoping to keep the lamb dry and not lose her balance on the ice.

Finally, the back steps. Not bothering to remove her bulky layers, she waddled through the dark house to the fireplace. Hobo leaped off the couch to sniff the toweled bundle in her arms. She set the baby as close to the grate as she dared, willing the fire to get it warm.

The lamb's eyes were partially open. She had to wait, but then saw the rise and fall of its side.

Melinda hurried to the kitchen and kicked off her boots and coveralls. She reached for the colostrum bottle, grabbed all of her spare towels, and rushed back to the lamb. The antique mantel clock ticked on, oblivious to the loss of electricity. It was just after ten.

"Come here, baby." She lifted the feeble lamb and its cocoon of towels from the rug and snuggled it in her lap. She gave the milk a shake, and squirted some on her finger.

The lamb wriggled and lapped up the milk. She tried again, this time with the bottle. It hesitated, then took a half-hearted pull.

"There you go. Will you take a little more? Please drink a bit more, OK? You're safe here, and we'll get you warm."

The baby took another drink, then leaned its weary head against her shoulder, its gangly legs awkward in her lap. She rubbed the soft towels on the lamb's flank, trying to warm its frail frame.

She swapped out the first towels for the new, warmer ones, then fetched a plastic tote and a throw blanket to make a better nest. The house was colder than before, the residual heat in the furnace ducts already gone.

She closed the bedroom door, then dragged the coffee table sideways and draped it with a blanket to try to keep the fire's heat contained.

With another blanket around her shoulders, she cuddled the baby while the tote warmed. Once it was ready and the lamb placed inside, Hazel climbed in and snuggled against the newborn, Grace right behind.

"That's right," Melinda whispered to the kittens. "You going to help me keep the baby warm?"

A shot rang out north of the house. Melinda flinched and Hobo lifted his head, his ears and tail alert. Then came a rattle and a *whoosh*, then another *crack*, as tree limbs heavy with ice snapped from their trunks.

There was a shift inside the towels, and the lamb bleated weakly. Melinda reached for the bottle, warming by the fire, and the baby drank a little more this time. The lamb studied Hobo, then took in the curious faces of Hazel and Grace as they sniffed its short, curly wool.

"These kittens slept in a tote just like this when they first came to live with me," Melinda told the lamb, who wriggled a bit more before settling into the towels, apparently unfazed by the kittens' purring. "Now that you drank more milk, it's going to be all right."

She added more wood to the fire. Then she curled up again under her blanket, one arm around Hobo and the other around the tote. It was almost eleven now. The storm windows trembled in the relentless wind, the sleet still rattling on the roof. Another round of *cracks* and *pops* echoed from the windbreak. Her mind was thick from cold and exhaustion, too many nights of short sleep. The fire sizzled and hissed, and the flames danced before her eyes.

Her cheek was icy against the hardwood floor, her jaw stiff. Melinda sat up suddenly. The fire still glowed behind the grate. But something had changed, and she listened. The wind continued to howl around the farmhouse's eaves, but the icy rattle was gone. The clock's hands had just passed two.

Hobo dozed next to the tote, Grace and Hazel and the lamb still snuggled inside. Grace raised her head and let out a gentle mew.

"Look at my little nurse." Melinda reached out to touch Grace's soft calico fur. "You and your sister are ..."

The lamb was so very still, its eyes closed. Melinda stared at the towels bundled over its wooly back, waited for the reassuring rise and fall.

"The baby's just asleep," she told herself when the towels didn't move. She waited again, longer than before. Counted to twenty, then thirty ...

In a flash, she remembered that heartbreaking day at the vet clinic, Doc working frantically to save Grace and Hazel, the silent bundle on the side of the exam table.

"Nooo!" Her hands shaking, Melinda gingerly pulled back the towel, willed the lamb's thin chest to lift. Nothing. "No, it can't be! Oh, God ..."

She carefully set the kittens next to Hobo and lifted the lamb out of the tote. It was strangely heavy, its limbs already turning stiff. Melinda cried as she rocked it in her lap, rubbed its flank and face with the warmest towel she had. Three minutes passed with no sign of life.

Now fully awake, Hobo and the kittens sniffed the chilled air cautiously, their tails low. *They know*, she thought. *They know the lamb is gone.*

The memory of the ewe's urgent calls to her baby struck Melinda right in the heart. "I'm so sorry," she wailed, reverently folding the towels back around the small body. "I'm sorry I took your baby away. I shouldn't have done that."

The poor lamb's life was so brief, only a few hours. Melinda had been so focused on trying to save it that she hadn't looked to see if it was a boy or a girl. Now, she couldn't bear to check.

What had Karen told her? *You're doing everything right. Don't give up.* But she had. She hadn't meant to fall asleep, but it didn't matter in the end.

Exhausted and heartbroken, her mind rewound the past several hours. Should she had left the lamb with its mother? Did it get too cold during the long, treacherous walk from the barn? The lamb had started to rally, to drink from the bottle. Why didn't she find a way to stay awake? If only the power was still on, if she could have heated the towels in the dryer or warmed the milk faster. Maybe she should have tried harder to get the baby to drink while in the barn, shouldn't have been in such a hurry to get back to the house. Maybe ...

Melinda stumbled to her feet and started for the kitchen with the bundle still in her arms, not bothering with the lantern. Finding one of the kitchen chairs by touch, she sank down into it. The tears came in a rush now, her head bent over her lap.

"Maybe I can't do this. Maybe I can't do any of this. I'm lucky more of my animals aren't dead." Her sobs echoed through the lonely house, rising above the howl of the wind.

"I thought I could just move out here, and pick tomatoes and watch the sunset and, oh, whatever else I planned to do. But I don't know how to do this. And I can't keep asking people to bail me out, to fix things for me. And I'm so sorry," she cried to the lifeless lamb, "I let you down."

Suddenly she sat up straight. *Whatever would she do with the body?*

Melinda felt her way back to the fire and picked up the tote and all the towels. Back in the kitchen, she settled the bundle inside and covered it well, then took it out to the back porch and gently placed it under the bench. She stood there for a moment, in the dark, the tears running down her face, numb with grief and despair.

"Maybe I'm just done," she whispered.

And then, an idea floated into her mind. She pushed it away at first, but then it settled in, forcing her to consider it.

I could walk away. It's not too late to walk away.

It would be so easy, really. Elaine wanted to buy the farm. Why not let her have it?

In mere seconds, everything became so clear: The acreage would stay in the family. Horace and Wilbur would get a windfall that could carry them through the rest of their years. She'd find a house in town, and take Hobo and all the cats with her. Someone would want the chickens. The sheep would have to be sold, of course, but hadn't Horace considered that long before she arrived?

The thought of leaving broke her heart. But maybe, just maybe, it was the right thing to do. It was so dark, there on the back porch, that she couldn't see the sad bundle under the bench. But she knew where it was, and how it came to be there. She'd tried to care for her flock, but failed. Maybe it was time to let that dream go.

She couldn't call Horace at that lonely hour of the night. It would have to wait. The thought of what she would say brought more tears.

Melinda stumbled into the kitchen, locked the door behind her, and wandered back through the house. This dear house, that she had so wanted to be hers. Curled up with Hobo and the kittens on the couch, all of her blankets wrapped around all of them, she cried herself to sleep.

* 18 *

The *bang, bang, bang* on the back door startled her awake. Hobo let out a protective growl and dashed off the couch, then ran into the kitchen.

Melinda raised her head, her eyes swollen with spent tears. Her hands were icy where they had slipped from under the blankets, and the fire was low behind the grate. The light had changed, the cold gloom in the farmhouse now a different, lighter hue. She squinted at the mantel clock. It was almost seven.

"Melinda!"

A muffled yell from the back steps, then more pounding. "Melinda, are you OK?"

She set the sleepy kittens aside and stumbled through the house, the oak floors like ice under her sock-covered feet. Daylight had just arrived, although the sky was still heavy and the house remained unbearably silent.

John Olson was trying to peer through the back door's window, his face grave.

"Oh, thank God!" He put a quick hand to Melinda's arm when she let him inside the porch. "You didn't come to the door, I started to worry ... what happened to you?"

The damp, frozen air that rushed in with John assaulted her senses, and it took her a moment to remember. Then she glanced over to the towel-filled tote under the bench, and the tears started again. John motioned to someone in the driveway and shut the door behind him.

"You look terrible. Here, sit down." He steered her into the kitchen and pulled out a chair. She sank into it, and put her face in her hands.

"The baby lamb died," she sobbed. "It was so tiny and weak. I brought it in last night, kept it by the fire. But it didn't make it. I don't know, I must have done something wrong."

John's face fell. With an understanding sigh, he sat down at the table.

"Oh, I am so sorry. That happens, every so often. It's heartbreaking, I know. Sometimes, you just can't save them."

"It was so small." Melinda wiped her face with her hand. It was so cold there in the kitchen. Would she ever get warm? "At first it was breathing, I tried to get it to drink, I got the milk from the ewe and ..."

"You did?" John gave a low whistle. "That was the right thing to do. How did you know about that?"

"Horace told me."

Melinda's heartbreaking decision flooded back into her frazzled mind. She shook her head, and covered her face with her hands. "Oh, I'll have to call him and tell him ..."

"Not just yet," John said kindly. "That all can wait, there's no hurry. You're exhausted and upset, I can see that. You've been up most of the night, and probably haven't had a solid sleep in, what, two or three days?" Melinda nodded.

"First, you need some breakfast, and more rest." He paused, thinking. "So, was there just the one lamb?"

"No, she had twins." Melinda jumped up from her chair and bolted for the porch door. "I have to get back out there, right now. I should have gone out again, I should have checked on the mother and the other lamb. But I was so focused on the tiny one, and the first one was nursing and ..."

"Then I'm sure it's doing OK." John found her tossed-aside knit cap and gloves and gestured for her to pull on a thick chore coat, rather than her still-damp coveralls. "Those won't keep you warm, all wet like that. And don't worry, Tyler and Dylan are out there now, checking on everything. Watch those steps, they're an awful mess."

Melinda wanted to hurry, but John was right. Even under a cloudy sky, the barn's faded-red boards still glowed with ice. Twigs and tree branches, frosted with sleet, dotted the shimmering yard. She was glad the house and garage blocked most of her view of the windbreak. There would be a terrible mess to clean up once a thaw came. But she couldn't think about that right now.

The glazed-over gravel drive forced their pace to be agonizingly slow, one tiny step at a time.

"Too many trips across here last night," John said as they tacked around his truck, gripping its sides for balance, "and you could have broken a leg, or worse. We're lucky, you know. I called the power company's hotline, sounds like we could be back on the grid sometime tomorrow. Over east of Prosper, some may not get their juice back for a week."

After so many hours alone in the cold and the dark, and the heartbreak that came with them, this sudden burst of conversation and activity had Melinda reeling. She tried to clear her muddled mind, focus on the here and now. The other sheep needed her, and the chickens and Sunny and Stormy. With the power out, their heated waterers might be frozen over. If they were, she'd have to haul buckets from the hydrants and ...

"I'm so glad you came over," she finally said as they slid the last few feet to the barn. "But why are you here? I mean, you could have called, saved yourself the trip."

"Well, we wondered how you were getting on." He paused before the door and turned her way. "And I wanted to see where the power lines were down, how to get to town, if I needed to. There's snapped poles south of our place, a few more down between there and here, and several broken lines. But the roads weren't blocked. As long as I crawled along at, oh, maybe fifteen miles an hour, it wasn't so bad."

Melinda could hear muffled voices inside the barn, John's teenaged sons talking back and forth. She glanced down the driveway, and could see the sagging power lines across the road. *That must be what's making that strange humming sound*, she thought.

When she looked back toward John, he was suddenly grinning from ear to ear. Before she could question him, he turned the door's latch. "Let's see how things are going, huh?"

Was she imagining things? The main aisle was filled with light, far more than what would come through the barn's windows on such a dreary day. Then she saw two unfamiliar heat lamps, blazing bright, tacked on the posts by the sheep's feed bunks. A cheery glow radiated from the back of the barn, where her own fixtures appeared to be on. As she blinked, trying to figure it out, she heard the muffled strains of easy-listening music coming from somewhere.

"We brought you a generator!" John clapped her on the back. "I've got three, thought we might as well share. We're running one in the house and one in the barn. We figured you could use the other one."

Melinda was stunned into silence for a moment, then clapped her hands with delight. "You've brought heat for my lambs! Oh, I can't thank you enough."

John shrugged, still grinning as he paused to offer a few pets to Sunny and Stormy, who watched the goings-on from the haymow steps.

"Oh, it's no trouble. I knew Horace didn't have a generator anymore. His last one wore out two years ago, and he never bothered to replace it. I guess when you grow up without electricity, it doesn't seem like such a priority." John jerked a thumb toward a rarely used pasture entrance. "We set it up out there, slipped the line through a little gap on the bottom of the door."

"We found that old radio in the grain room." Tyler, the oldest boy, gave Melinda a quick nod as he pulled a new bale of straw out of the far stall. "Brought it out here, thought the ewes and lambs might enjoy some tunes. That newest lamb's small, but he's doing fine, as is the ewe. And those twins you've got there?" Tyler whistled. "Show lambs for sure."

"You hit the ram-and-lamb lottery," Dylan hooted, giving the older ewe an affectionate pet as he latched her gate. Both sheep already had fresh water and their grain and hay. "It's a good thing you're too old for 4-H, or we'd have some stiff competition at the fair come July. And there's more lambs on the way."

"I know." Melinda sighed.

"I mean, like, *today.*" Tyler broke open the bale and began to scatter straw in one of the empty stalls. "Number 33? The really big one? She's pacing like it's almost time. Where are your halters? We'll bring her over."

John was still standing there by the stairs, grinning like it was Christmas morning. "Linda sent breakfast. There's coffee, eggs and toast in the truck, and they're hot. Or at least, they were when we left home. I can't promise how they fared in that thermal pack, but it's better than cold cereal. You go inside and eat. We'll finish up the chores."

Dylan and Tyler insisted on staying on through the morning, as it became clear the third ewe's lambs were eager to be born. It was triplets this time. All arrived with little assistance from the boys. Melinda stood back and watched and learned, impressed by how calmly and efficiently Tyler and Dylan worked. *I wish I had their confidence,* she thought.

The smallest new lamb would need occasional bottles at first, but she was as healthy and strong as her sister and brother. The proud mother fussed over her babies and welcomed Melinda's attention, but stomped a hoof when the boys tried to lean over the gate and touch her children.

"She doesn't need our help anymore, and she knows it," Tyler said. "You shouldn't, either. And I think you might get a few days to catch your breath. That last ewe doesn't look anywhere near ready to deliver. I'll call Dad to pick us up."

"Come with us," Dylan suggested. "Mom's making chili in her slow cooker. We've got that extended cab on the truck, you know, there's room for you to squeeze in."

Despite her exhaustion, Melinda found herself saying yes. She wouldn't have to eat a cold sandwich alone. Maybe she could bring Horace's old crockpot out to the barn that afternoon, plug it in, dust off a shelf and cook up something decent for supper.

"Hey, what's so funny?" Dylan wondered at her sudden laughter.

"I like your mom's idea, that's all. And it didn't even occur to me to take the generator up to the house, make more use of it myself. It needs to be out here, helping the sheep."

"That's the farmer way." Tyler gave her a thumbs-up as he reached for his phone.

Melinda only smiled, and tiptoed back to the house to change her clothes and wash her face with a bowl of cold water. She couldn't bear to tell anyone about the storm of emotions she felt this morning: regret, guilt, disappointment and grief. And she was angry, too. Angry at herself, for coming this far, working so hard, yet doubting she could make her new life last.

The chatter around the Olsons' kitchen table, where one plugged-in lamp brightened the chilly gloom, looked forward to spring. An hour with her neighbors, and some hot chili and coffee, provided a quick boost to Melinda's sagging spirits. But when John dropped her back at the farm, she still had to face the fallout from the night before. That included the tote still waiting under the back porch's bench, momentarily forgotten in the morning's rush.

She needed to get the lamb's body out of the house, and away from the other animals. Gritting her teeth, she took the bin down the back steps and transferred the lifeless form to an empty burlap sack.

She double-knotted the twine that tied the bag closed, then carried it carefully across the icy yard, gently depositing her burden next to the woodpile behind the machine shed. Doc answered her text, and said he'd take the remains away the next afternoon when he came to evaluate the ewes and their lambs.

Karen called, but her words of comfort did little to ease Melinda's heartache. She also talked to Angie and Mabel, and her parents. Before she could gather the courage to ring Horace's room at the care center, he reached out to her.

The ice storm had been less intense in Elm Springs, and the community had lost power for only a few hours. He listened to her rundown of the previous night, and she could sense him thinking through every decision she had made.

"That's too bad about the littlest lamb. But I would have done things just as you did. Those things happen, don't let that get you down."

"I know. It's just so sad. The baby was so small and ..."

The tears threatened to return. This time, she pushed them back, along with the doubts still swarming in her mind. Horace was already worried about her, she couldn't drop such alarming news on him right now. Or fully process it herself. It was mid-afternoon, and she could hardly take another step. All she could focus on was her need for a nap, then finishing evening chores before nightfall.

"Sometimes, it's just not meant to be," Horace said. "It never gets easy. Give all the sheep and their babies a 'hello' from me." His tone turned wistful. "Wish I could get out there to meet them. I'm going to call John and thank him for bringing that generator over. He's a good neighbor. You're surrounded by the best."

That was true. But would she ever be as resourceful, as resilient as her new friends and neighbors? She had learned so much in the past several months. But maybe, this life wasn't the right one after all.

Whatever happened, she had some smaller decisions that must be made first. If she was going to slip and slide through another round of chores, there had to be something more than a peanut-butter sandwich waiting when she returned. She'd given up on the idea of taking the slow cooker to the barn to heat up some soup, realizing she might drop it on the ice. Instead, she would use the last outlet on the generator to boost her smartphone.

Picking up a flashlight, she went to the basement stairs and stepped down into the thick darkness. Even some chips with homemade salsa would liven things up a bit. There was some in the canning room.

Mabel had suggested Melinda put her milk, cheese, fruit and some other refrigerated items in a box on the front porch, where the air was cold enough to give them a day's reprieve. Thank goodness she had a package of lunch meat in the freezer. If it would thaw fast enough on the icy kitchen counter, it could edible in a few hours.

Most of her fresh food was spoiling, or about to. One more day without power, and everything in her freezer would also turn into garbage.

She felt her way through the murky basement's rooms, her flashlight's beam catching the dead furnace and the out-of-commission washer and dryer. What she wouldn't give for a hot shower and a warm towel.

She stopped short. The canning stove! It had to be at least fifty years old, a beast Melinda had been happy to let Mabel light when they put up produce over the summer. But it was a *gas* range. There could be a hot supper, maybe soup with a grilled-cheese sandwich. She had instant coffee upstairs, would only have to boil some water. And no more ice-bath facials! If the hens had a fresh egg or two tomorrow, that would be the start of a better breakfast.

But first, she would have to light the darn thing. Mabel could walk her through it. And there was that gallon of kerosene out in the garage, and the two antique lanterns on a closet shelf. They would save battery power. She had these things at her disposal, she needed to use them.

"When Horace was a boy, that was all they had," she reminded herself as she found her way back to the stairs, just a bit of spring in her step. Hobo and the kittens were waiting for her in the kitchen, curious about what she was up to but unwilling to pad down into the darkness to find out.

"We are going to party like it's, oh, nineteen-thirty," she told Hobo as she petted his head. "Maybe tonight won't be so terrible. And maybe tomorrow, if we're lucky, we'll be back in the modern world."

The kerosene lamps were a bit smelly, but she didn't mind. They spread more light than her flashlights, and allowed her to save the battery lantern for use outside. If Horace and Wilbur had been able to do their homework by these lamps, she could surely distract herself with a good book. She splurged on a few minutes of music from the dusty radio in Horace's bedroom, its batteries old but with just a bit of power left to burn.

It was the very last day of February, a fact Melinda only realized when she sat down for supper and noticed the calendar, waiting there in the gloom by the refrigerator.

She nearly cried with relief as she devoured her hot meal and sipped a steaming mug of coffee. If things would just get back to normal, if she could just get through all this, maybe she could find a way to hang on.

The mantel clock's hands showed only nine o'clock when she banked the fire, carefully extinguished the kerosene lamps and let the darkness drape around her like a blanket. The night was so quiet, only the comforting tick, tick, tick of the clock and an occasional sigh from Hobo. Tonight, maybe she could sleep.

Tomorrow has to be better, she thought as her mind finally began to relax.

If it isn't, I don't know what I'm going to do.

✳ 19 ✳

The house was still frigid in the morning, the power out for thirty-six hours and counting. On the front porch, where only a wall of flimsy metal-framed storm windows kept out the cold, icy chunks floated in the half-gone gallon of milk. Melinda built up a blaze in the hearth, wondering how she ever would have managed this long without a fireplace. She'd need to bring in more wood that afternoon if something didn't change.

But there was hope. She flipped the kitchen calendar over to a fresh month, welcoming March and its promise that spring would someday arrive. The sun at last showed its face that morning, giving a luminescent glow to the ice still coating every surface.

She was shuffling across the farmyard when there was a roar in the distance, then the wonderful sight of a boom truck creeping down her gravel road. Crews had worked around the clock since early yesterday morning, replacing broken power poles and stringing new electrical lines, and had at last reached her rural neighborhood. Aunt Miriam called to say the lights were back on in town, and Prosper Hardware would open today as usual. She insisted, however, that Melinda not try to make it in.

"It'll be crazy at the store, but you're off until tomorrow, like always. Esther's coming in to help. And it sounds like you've got your hands full out there, honey. The store's generator kept our refrigerator case going, but it'll be cleared out soon, I'm sure. What are you running out of? Milk? I'll hide it in the office fridge for you. Lord knows when we'll get a truck this week."

Melinda gave the smallest triplet lamb a bottle, and was relieved to see the last ewe was not yet in labor. "Don't wait too long, girl," she told the sheep as she patted her wooly head. "But I have to say, I'm thankful to catch a little break. Doc's coming this afternoon, he'll give you a look-over."

There was only one egg in the coop, but Melinda scrambled it and made a breakfast sandwich. The clock was ticking on the basement freezer, so she pulled out a beef roast and dumped in a pint of garden tomatoes and some seasonings. Tucked in the gas range's oven, it would slowly heat through by supper.

She was at the kitchen table, her gloved hands wrapped around her second cup of coffee and wondering what she could scrounge up for lunch, when the sudden rumble of Horace's old refrigerator made her jump. In a second, everything changed as the furnace started to hum and the lights snapped back to life. Hobo began to bark, and she ran into the living room where he and the kittens were swaddled in layers of blankets on the couch.

"We made it!" Melinda squeezed in and settled Grace and Hazel in her lap. "Oh, girls, it's over! Look, do you see that water dripping off the eaves there? It means the ice is starting to melt." Then she paused, thinking. "Where do I start? That's easy, really. I desperately need a shower."

She had never been so excited to do laundry, or to put fresh sheets on her bed. Trying to hold her breath, she lifted the toilet seat off the five-gallon bucket wedged in the downstairs bathroom and flushed its contents, a bit at a time. The blankets on the couch were fluffed and folded into a neat stack, and the kerosene lamps' chimneys cleared of soot. Melinda set them back on the shelf in the downstairs bedroom's closet, then cleaned out the refrigerator.

The farmhouse was nearly set to rights by the time Doc's truck chugged up the lane late that afternoon. She pulled on her boots and left an unhappy Hobo waiting on the wrong side of his suddenly locked doggie doors.

"You can see Doc another time," she soothed him as she zipped up her coveralls. They were filthy; maybe she could work in another load of laundry yet that night. "He needs to look the lambs over, and you might get in the way."

The triplets' mother didn't want Doc to even glance at her babies, much less touch them. He just laughed and reached for a rope halter. "I'll tie her up in the corner, then, until I'm done examining her kids."

Doc went from one birthing pen to the next, checking each lamb. Much to Melinda's relief, he found all six to be thriving. The ewe that had yet to deliver was also healthy, he said, just taking her time. He then spent several minutes examining the mother who'd lost one of her babies.

"You're right that this live lamb's smaller than average. Mama is, too," Doc said as he let himself out of the pen. "But they're doing well. It might be a blessing the lambs were undersized," he added gently.

"If they had been significantly larger, she might have found herself in a dangerous struggle, something you never could have handled alone. You might have lost the other baby, too, or even the ewe."

With tears stinging her eyes, Melinda watched the single lamb nuzzling its mother. All she could do was nod.

"Well," she finally said in a shaky voice, "I've got that ... the sack is around back of the machine shed."

"Let's get it." He gave her an encouraging pat on the shoulder. "It'll do you good to get that out of here, I think."

They moved slowly in the slush and snow, picking their way along the pasture fence then turning toward the machine shed. Beyond the windbreak, the western horizon blazed with red and orange, sunset coming on in less than an hour. "I wasn't sure where to put it," Melinda tried to fill the silence, "so I just ..."

She gasped and jumped back, moving her right boot just in time and nearly losing her balance.

A dollop of dark blood, clotted and brittle, poisoned the ice-crusted snow behind the corner of the shed.

"Good God," Doc whispered.

A few feet away, another quarter-sized blob of red. Then a pink streak, a dragging slide pointing into the stand of broken-limbed trees.

And animal tracks. Large, and round.

The burlap sack still leaned against the shed's foundation, the weighted tarp protecting the firewood next to it undisturbed. They stumbled over to the bag, and found more red flecks sprayed in the snow.

"I can't look," Melinda gasped, feeling dizzy. "I can't. Oh, my God ..."

Doc lifted the bag and swore. The sack hung empty. He turned it to the side, and she saw it: A long, jagged slash through the burlap. The kind made by claws, not a knife.

She spun around, scanning the edge of the frozen yard for any movement. Nothing. Whatever had come here, and snatched the lamb's lifeless body, had already moved on. Or at least, was crouching where it couldn't be seen.

Doc glanced at the setting sun, then into the windbreak and down at the ragged, dirty burlap bag in his hand. "Are the chickens all locked in?" His voice was calm, but cautious.

"Yes," she managed, her pulse throbbing in her neck.

"Where are Sunny and Stormy?"

"In the barn." She tried for a calming breath. "I shut their door Saturday and they haven't been out since."

"Good." She had never seen Doc so rattled. It scared her.

"Melinda?" His voice was barely above a whisper this time. "Do you have any trash to burn? The wind's down for once. It's a good time for a fire."

She stared at him, then caught his meaning. "I do. And I just cleaned out the fridge. The barrel's behind the garage."

By the time she came back from the house, a lumpy paper sack in her arms and her hands shaking, Doc had a blaze going in the incinerator. The burlap bag was already scorching in the flames. She added to the pyre and they stood there, helpless, watching everything burn, a grim column of smoke rising in the calm, cold air.

And then Melinda was crying, deep, trembling sobs. "I don't know if I can do this," she blurted out. "I want to, but I just can't."

"It's the best way." Doc nodded, as if to reassure himself, then stuffed his gloved hands in his coverall pockets.

"We've got to get rid of anything that might carry a scent, that might bring ... whatever it was ... back here, looking for another easy meal. Before I go, I'll scoop up that bloodied snow and toss it out in the windbreak."

"No." She hugged herself, trying, and failing, to make everything OK. "No, I mean, I don't know if I can stay out here. It's too much. I'm not cut out for this."

The incinerator belched and growled, the putrid stench of scorched food creeping into the billowing smoke. What had she done? She should have put the lamb's body in the shed, not left it out there, where it would draw the attention of a predator. She should have known better than that.

"That little lamb was alive when I took it from its mother." She covered her face with her hands. "I shouldn't have tried to bring it to the house. It got cold, I know it did."

The understanding on Doc's lined face didn't ease her grief. "You did the right thing. I would have done the same. It was the only chance that lamb had."

"But it died anyway," she cried, the acrid smoke filling her lungs. "No matter what I tried. I thought it was doing better, it took some of the milk, lifted its little head and put it on my shoulder. And then I fell asleep. I shouldn't have fallen asleep. I woke up, and it ... it wasn't breathing. I waited, and waited. But it was too late."

Doc stared at the frozen ground. "Death is a hard thing. You never get used to it. But it's part of being out here, it's part of life. I wish it wasn't, but there's no way around it."

She didn't answer, her hands still over her face.

He looked up, his brow furrowed. "It's not just that, is it? Something else happened. What's going on?"

"Horace's niece says she wants the farm." Melinda's voice rose in pitch as she sobbed.

"Elaine says Wilbur told her years ago she could buy it someday. She's family, and she's got money, more than I'll ever have."

Doc was clearly shocked. When he didn't respond, Melinda kept talking. And then, she couldn't stop.

"Horace and Wilbur need that money, the nursing home is so expensive. And this farm has been in their family for over a hundred years. How can I take that away from them? And then, the baby lamb ... I have to leave, Doc. I can't stay here, I can't do this."

She looked around the yard, over to the strong-shouldered barn and the cozy farmhouse, and the tears started again. "I thought this was my home, but maybe I was wrong. Maybe I was wrong about lots of things."

"Wait." Doc put up a hand. "Just wait a minute. What are you saying? Horace wants you to get the acreage, you said so yourself."

"But everything's different now."

"Are you sure?" He raised an eyebrow. "I've known Horace for years. When he sets his mind to something, no one can change it. So, what does he say about all this?"

She looked away and didn't answer.

"Good. You haven't told him yet. Don't. At least, give it a few more days. Don't throw it all away now. You've worked too hard."

"That's just it. I'm so tired." Her shoulders slumped in defeat. "Tired of the cold, tired of fumbling around, not knowing what I'm doing. Look, I've got this worked out. I just get a house in town, is all. John Olson might buy the sheep. He's impressed with the lambs and I know he's looking to expand. I can find someone to take the chickens. Hobo and the cats would go with me."

"So you'll just walk away, then."

"What else am I going to do? How can I stay on here? It's been so hard, Doc. Harder than I ever thought it would be."

"You're right." Doc set his jaw. "It's damn hard. And it's not for everyone. But you're cut out for it. I know you are. So does Horace. He believes in you. You just have to believe in yourself a little more."

"I wish I did. I wish I could."

"So that's it?" Doc threw his arms up in frustration. "That's your plan? To give up?"

"It's not like I haven't tried," she said defensively. "I've tried to learn how to do things. I pray for my animals all the time. I set out the hay on Christmas Eve, to catch the special frost that might keep them safe. Angie and I even blessed the animals ... last month ... during the Feast of St. Anthony ..." Was Doc trying to hide a smile?

"It's not funny." She shot him a look. "I've tried everything. But it hasn't been enough."

"Well, before you start packing, let's get inside for a cup of coffee. I think this is the most depressing call I've had all day, and it's been a doozy. Half the places I've been to don't have power yet, and a heifer stepped on my foot this morning."

They sat at the kitchen table, trying to warm their hands and feet, while dirty puddles gathered under their boots on the back porch.

"It's hard to lose a patient," Doc said, then paused to pat Hobo on the head. "But you learn from each case, and you apply that knowledge to the next one. And sometimes ... most of the time, if I'm honest with myself ... it's in the hands of someone far more powerful than I am."

Melinda gripped her coffee cup with stiff fingers, embracing the steam that rose from its rim. "I know. But I was here, all alone, and it was on me to fix things."

He acknowledged her point with a slight nod. "Well, look at this way. All the sheep you fed the special hay to, and that received the blessing, are alive and healthy. You're lucky things didn't go six-ways-from-wrong with that smallest ewe. There's only one left to lamb, but she looks good and you said she's been a mother before. You can't control every situation. You did everything you could. That has to be enough."

Melinda could only shrug.

"And as far as all that other stuff," he leaned over the table, "there's a fine line between habit and superstition. I'm a man of science. But I still watch the animals, study the weather. If you pay attention, if you give nature the respect it deserves, your efforts will be repaid. But Melinda," his tone turned cautious, "you cannot let fear get the upper hand."

"I'm afraid sometimes." She looked out the window, to where twilight was coming on fast. "I'll admit it."

"Let me tell you something." Doc set his mug down. "A long time ago, I was out on a call. It was early spring, much warmer than now. I was just out of vet school, green as could be." He shook his head, remembering.

"I go out to this farm, and the old man had sheep. He was, oh, at least eighty. The first lamb of the season had just arrived, and it was born dead. He was upset, of course, but he was also afraid. 'It's a bad omen,' he told me, 'and I need to make it right.'"

Melinda's head snapped up, her eyes wide.

"So he totters over to the wall and pulls down two shovels, hands me one, motions for me to follow him," Doc continued. "He goes out the barn door, right in front of the threshold, and says, 'start digging.' He was so scared and determined, I couldn't say no."

Doc looked down in his coffee mug, as if seeing something in its depths.

"His grandfather swore the only way to break such a curse and protect the rest of the lambs was to bury the body right there, in front of the barn. So that's what we did."

"You've got to be kidding." Melinda slapped the kitchen table with her palm. "You're giving me the creeps, Doc. What ... what could that mean?"

"Old Pennsylvania Dutch superstition, he told me when I pressed him on it. But here's the thing: he couldn't tell me exactly what it was supposed to accomplish. Would the lamb's spirit guard the door and keep Death away from the rest of the flock? I don't know. He didn't, either, or wouldn't say."

Doc crossed his arms as if he felt a chill, even though the house had already warmed back to its usual temperature.

"But my point is," he shook a warning finger at Melinda, "he was scared enough that he felt compelled to do it. When we finished, he said a prayer and tamped the dirt down with his boot. 'There'll be no more lost now,' he told me. And you know what? All the rest of his lambs came just fine."

Melinda tapped the rim of her mug. She understood the old man's fear, the feeling that forces beyond your control were at work, and maybe not for the better. Could she admit that to Doc? She decided she could.

"There's been a few times, always at night, when I've felt something ... strange out here. And it scared me."

He nodded, encouraging her to continue. She told him about the night of the blizzard, the feeling that she and Hobo were being watched when they went outside, and the unearthly tapping at her window.

"I know it sounds silly. But then, other times when I've been out in the yard at night, I feel so small and afraid. What if something doesn't want me here, doesn't want me to stay?"

"It's not silly at all. I know that feeling," Doc admitted. "But it's just your own fear. Nothing more, and don't you scare yourself into believing anything else. Just remember: Fear thrives in the dark. If you face it, you can beat it."

He took a hearty gulp of his coffee. "As for the rest of it, I believe those who've gone on might be able to reach out to us from the other side. But if anything, you're staying on here would make them proud, I'm sure of it."

Melinda nodded. Maybe Doc was right. She hoped so. If only she could really believe it, know it to be true.

Doc eased out of his chair and took his empty cup to the counter. "And whatever animal took that dead lamb, it was just that: A wild animal, hungry and exhausted from tracking prey in all the snow and ice. It was probably a bobcat or a coyote, but those tracks ..." He let out a whistle.

"You hear about cougars passing through, but who knows? Whatever it was, it means you no harm. Keep your critters in at night. That's all you can do."

Grace and Hazel romped into the kitchen, then stopped short when they spied company. Grace let out a tiny mew, and rubbed against her sister.

Doc's face lit up. He crouched down, gingerly picked up Hazel and held her close. She stared into Doc's kind eyes and put a fuzzy brown paw on his coveralls, as if she remembered him. Melinda felt the icy unease in her heart begin to thaw.

"And if you ever again feel like a failure, you just look at these babies. I couldn't save their brother, but you saved the both of them." He set Hazel on the floor, then gave Grace a gentle pet. "Well, I better get going. I'll shovel that snow away before I do."

"Thanks, Doc, for everything." Melinda rose and offered her hand. "Let me know what my bill is. I'm sure you charge extra for snow shoveling and life coaching."

He shook it heartily, then patted her on the arm. "Nah, it's all covered under my standard farm-visit fee. But, if you really want my advice ..."

She nodded vigorously and waited.

"If I were you, I'd cut myself some slack." Doc grinned, and pulled his knit cap over his head with a quick snap of the wrist. "And then? I'd call Horace and the bank, and set a date to sign those papers before Ms. Fancypants can raise any more hell. Well, I'll see you tomorrow."

* 20 *

The last of the ice melted away over the next two days, erased by a sudden warm-up that had Melinda yearning for spring and searching for answers.

Twice she picked up the phone to call Horace, but couldn't bring herself to dial his number. What exactly would she say? That she had to move on? That she was having second thoughts, and ask him for advice?

But she already knew what his response would be: He'd tell her not to give up, that the farm was hers if she still wanted it. In his mind, their agreement hadn't changed. She shouldn't call him, not yet, unless she was really sure she had to walk away. And she wasn't.

"I can't imagine leaving here," she told Hobo Friday morning as they crossed the muddy, slushy farmyard on their way to start morning chores. "You'll always have a home with me, you and all the kitties, no matter what. Oh, I don't know what to do."

A new day was about to begin, a faint line of light appearing on the eastern horizon. She had a bottle under the arm of her coat, another round of formula for the smallest triplet lamb. The little girl was gaining. All the lambs were. And the pain Melinda felt when she looked at the mother with only one baby? The despair was still there, but its edges cut her less as each day passed.

Maybe Doc was right; maybe the biggest challenge she faced was her own fear. She wanted nothing more than to get back into her regular routine, to pick up where she'd left off before everything spun out of control. Three of the ewes had lambed, there was just one more to go. She was so close. Could she lean hard enough on her faith, and find enough courage, to see this difficult season through?

"We've come so far," she told Sunny, who was waiting for her on the other side of the barn door. "But I just can't get over the feeling that I'm selling Horace short. Or that he's selling himself short. I wish I could pay him a fair price for this place, but I just don't have the money."

She couldn't get a larger loan, but that was only half the problem. Farm life had so many expenses she hadn't expected. The lambs would need their vaccinations. And then there was the cost of oats and hay and straw, not to mention food for the rest of her animals and the updates the farmhouse needed. Susan's firm had come through with another round of contract work, but that extra income would never be steady.

"We're almost out of milk replacer, too." She sighed as she fed the little lamb her bottle, saving the last few pulls to pacify the baby's jealous brother and sister. "Guess I'll need to stop at the co-op after work."

She dreaded that errand. Not just because the powdered formula was expensive, but there was always the chance she might run into Evan. He usually helped his dad on Fridays. They had left the Watering Hole as friends, and had texted once a few days later, about something insignificant. But when had she heard from him last? She couldn't even remember, it seemed so long ago. According to her phone, it had been nine days. If she ran into him, what would she say? She didn't know, but it didn't matter. She needed that milk replacer, and today.

The co-op was packed that afternoon, the aisles filled with customers stocking up on supplies and trading war stories about the ice storm. She marched over to the sheep aisle, trying to keep an eye out for Evan as she scanned the shelves of ointments, medicines and supplies. What was all this stuff for, anyway? One item's label showed a smiling woman with glossy blonde hair, the arms of her stylish plaid coat wrapped around a newborn lamb with a spotless white fleece.

"Marketing." Melinda snorted, pushing down her sheep-mama guilt as she passed over everything else and reached for a bag of powdered milk replacer. There was only one on the shelf, and another customer was coming down the aisle. She snatched up the sack and turned away.

Dan was at the register, but the line was deep even though he tried to keep it moving. He wouldn't have time to run to the back and restock.

The office door was open. Auggie glanced over his glasses and grinned when he saw Melinda.

"I hope you have more." She adjusted the bag on her hip. "I took the last one."

"Yep, sure do. I'll get us a refill. Been swamped all day, but that's good, I guess. Can hardly get the feed loaded fast enough. Good problem to have."

Melinda saw her opportunity and took it. "Now that you mention it, I didn't see Evan loading at the side door when I came in. Chloe isn't sick, is she?"

Auggie's jaw tightened and his fingers froze over his keyboard. Melinda's stomach dropped. He gave her a long stare she couldn't quite read, and motioned for her to close the office door. She took a seat in the worn chair next to his desk, her heart thumping. "Something's happened," she said flatly. "Is everyone OK?"

"Well, I hope so." He sighed and started to crack his knuckles. "Seeing as they're gone."

The milk replacer slipped from her lap to the floor. She couldn't speak. *Gone?*

"I guess I thought you knew." His voice was so quiet she could barely hear him over the muffled chatter coming from the other side of the door. "I know you and Evan, well, talked to each other and ..." He looked away.

"We were just friends. Only friends, ever," she said firmly, her mind still grasping for answers. "Wait. Where are they? What's going on?"

"They went back to Madison." Auggie removed his glasses and rubbed at his eyes.

"Evan's old company called late last week, said someone's retiring. They wanted him back. He had to take it on the spot, or they'd go down the list to the others that got laid off. He was smart to grab his chance, I'll give him that." Auggie's tone, however, wasn't as understanding as his words.

"But, where will they live? They got kicked out of their rental house and ..."

"Evan found an apartment online right away, a complex not far from Chloe's old daycare that had a lucky opening. They allow cats, too. Jane gave him the money to pay off the rest of what he owed the other landlord, so he'd get a decent reference." Auggie frowned and crossed his arms.

"That's wonderful." Melinda tried to keep her voice light. "I know that ... well, I know Evan wasn't sure about staying around here for good."

"He's damn lucky, that's all." Auggie's voice was icy. "I don't know how many more breaks he's going to get. And then there's Carrie."

He snorted. "She's doing so well in rehab that she wants to come home. Evan says Chloe needs her mother. I can't believe he'd even think about taking her back."

Something cold and hard settled in Melinda's stomach. Was it anger? Relief? But her feelings, at least for the moment, didn't matter. The hurt in her friend's eyes was heartbreaking. Auggie had tried so hard to give Evan another chance, to open his heart to his wayward son.

He gave her a thoughtful look, then leaned over the desk.

"It's none of my business," he said quietly. "And he may be my son, but I'll tell you this: He's not good enough for you, Melinda, not by half. He didn't even tell you he was leaving, after you've been so kind to him? It's a disgrace, I say, that's what it is."

Melinda took a deep breath and tried to steer the conversation away from herself. "I know how much it meant to you and Jane to have Evan back, at least for a few months. And Chloe, she's such a sweet little girl."

Auggie set his jaw again but this time, Melinda thought he was trying to blink back tears. "She's that for sure. I don't know when we'll see her again." Then his face clouded. "Don't say anything, but Jane and I have talked this through. Chloe needs a stable home. If Evan takes Carrie back, and they don't straighten themselves out, we might try to get custody. She deserves better."

All Melinda could do was tell her friend how sorry she was, then go back out and get in line. It seemed to take forever to get to the register, the bag of milk replacer suddenly so heavy it made her arms ache. Dan's hearty greeting forced her to smile and nod as if nothing had changed. It was a relief to stumble out to the car, drop her purchase in the passenger seat and let the tears come.

She sat there for several minutes, the afternoon sun beating warm through the windshield, and cried. It hurt, of course, that Evan had left town without saying goodbye. But maybe it was for the best. After all, she was the one who said they couldn't be more than friends.

And as much as she liked Evan, this news confirmed what she always suspected: He wasn't over Carrie. She had dodged out of the way, just in time, before things got complicated.

"I was right about that," she whispered and crossed her arms, nodding to herself. "I did the right thing, putting my foot down. He's not worth my time, anyway."

And then she thought of Auggie, of his disappointment with his son. The bitterness was already creeping back into his heart, like an oozing poison.

Melinda let her arms fall to her sides. She decided right then she could be alone if she had to, but she couldn't afford to be bitter. She couldn't let her heart harden to the point that, if and when someone special came along, she would be too afraid to take that chance.

"Besides, everyone has to make their own way in life," she reminded herself as she wiped at her face with the back of her hand. "Evan has the right to make his own choices. He has to do what he thinks is best, whatever that is. We can't let other people make our decisions for us."

All of the sudden, just like the other night on the cold, dark porch, Melinda could see everything clearly. But this time, the vision was much different.

She could stay.

She should stay. Had to stay. No matter what happened, no matter what anyone else thought or did or said.

"I can't let other people choose for me, either," she said at last, then waited for a contradictory emotion to arrive, whether it be fear or doubt. But it didn't.

"That farm is my home. I can't let Elaine stop me, bully me into walking away. As for Horace ..." She gripped the steering wheel and squared her shoulders.

"He's losing a ton of money by letting me have the farm so cheap. There's no getting around that. And I'm going to feel guilty about that for some time to come. But Horace gets to make his own choices, just like everyone else, and he's already decided what he wants to do. Maybe at his age, money doesn't matter anymore. Maybe for him, it never really did."

* * *

The minute Melinda arrived home, she ran to the barn. Ed reported all was quiet at midday, but he expected the last ewe to go into labor soon.

The mother-to-be was pacing and grunting, but thankfully didn't fight the rope halter slipped over her head. "There you are." Melinda let out a sigh of relief as she secured the fence panel over the end of the lambing pen. "You're the last one, and you're all set."

She glanced out the barn's rows of small windows, comforted by the cheerful light that poured through at this golden hour just before sunset. There would be no storm tonight. Not outside, at least.

She pushed that thought away and petted Sunny, who lounged in the aisle, his golden eyes focused on the restless ewe. "I'll check on you again soon, mama. Sunny, you're in charge until then."

Two hours later, the ewe was fully in labor. She had lambed before with no complications, according to both Horace and the sheep ledger, but Melinda was still worried. She snapped on the spare heat lamp in the adjoining empty pen, slid a straw bale under the warmth, and settled in.

"I'm not leaving," she cooed to the ewe, whose grunts elicited "baaas" from the three mothers nearby. "I'm not heading back to the house until you're done."

Stormy and Sunny joined Melinda in the waiting room, only leaving her lap when she stood to lean over the fence. At last, there was the unmistakable appearance of two tiny hooves, then a lamb's nose. Melinda waited, hardly able to breathe, but it didn't seem like much was happening.

She could call Doc or Karen, but it might take them half an hour to get to the farm if they were even available. What about John Olson and his sons? It was Friday night, and there was a basketball game. They wouldn't be home. Ed might be, but Nathan had the flu ...

The ewe grunted, puffing with exertion as she lowered herself to the straw. The lamb was coming the right way, as far as Melinda could tell. Its face was at last starting to show, but there was much more to come. She ran back to the house, her headlamp bobbing through the darkness, and fetched a clean pair of rubber gloves. By the time she returned, the ewe's grunts had increased in pitch and frequency.

"I'm on my way!" Melinda gasped as she climbed over the fence and into the pen. "Hold on." She said a quick prayer, grimaced, reached in and put her gloved hands on the sides of the baby's head.

"OK," she whispered to the ewe. "You push and I'll pull."

As if she understood, the sheep let out a bellow. Melinda sensed the ewe's muscles contract, and did her part. The head was free now.

Another contraction, then another. She reached for the baby's shoulders, trying to balance this newborn's surprising weight. Then the lamb was coming right at her, and slid into her lap. She gently released it and crawled back and away, knowing the mother had to quickly clean the lamb and claim it as her own. The ewe let out one final sigh, staggered to her feet and began to nuzzle her baby.

"Good job, mama." Happy tears filled Melinda's eyes. "Your baby is just huge, I must say. I can't imagine there's another one in there."

The lamb began to bleat, wavered a bit, then stood up for the first time. It was a boy, strong and healthy, and almost as tall as the lambs in the next pen, the ones that were a week old. He instinctively pushed at his mother's side, then began to nurse.

"We're done!" Melinda raised her still-gloved hands skyward, oblivious to the mess all over the front of her coveralls. "Everyone's done!"

Her whoops of joy set off a chain of responses from the mothers and lambs in the adjoining pens, as well as the rest of the sheep.

She carefully peeled off the rubber gloves, making sure they stayed inside out, then climbed over the fence.

"Seven babies from four mamas. Not bad." She reached across to the ewe that lost one of her lambs, giving both mama and the now-thriving little one comforting pats on their heads. "You take such good care of your baby," she told the sheep. "You're such a good mama, and you did your best. *We* did our best, right? I guess that's all we could have done."

Her focus on that family brought bleats of jealousy from the triplets in the next pen.

"No, no, you don't get another bottle tonight," she gently told the littlest girl, who pushed her black nose through the fence slats and nudged Melinda's hand.

"You had one at chore time. You're getting so big now, and strong. You only get one twice a day, remember? And soon, you won't need one at all."

Melinda rubbed her face after she latched the barn door tightly behind her. It couldn't be that late, maybe nine or so, but she was exhausted. Exhausted, but relieved. And elated. It was clear the last ewe would only deliver the one lamb, and both were doing well, but she would take no chances. She'd come out later, just before bed, and check on them again.

What would it feel like to sleep through the night, her mind clear of worry and fear? Somehow, during the last few weeks, Melinda had forgotten. But she couldn't wait to remember.

The kitchen was warm and bright, the furnace humming its gentle tune in the basement. Hobo greeted her at the door, curious to smell her chore clothes for any hint of what was happening in the barn.

"You'll have to see this one to believe it." She rubbed Hobo's ears while she sat on the porch bench to kick off her boots. "He's the biggest lamb I've ever seen. Granted, I've seen very few. But he's just huge. I'll introduce you in the morning, OK?"

She peeled off her layers, took everything down to the laundry room and tossed them in the washer, then scrubbed her hands at the utility sink. It was time for a treat. The power had come back on just in time the other day, allowing her to salvage most of the items in the basement freezer. That included the ice cream.

In the canning room, the rows of filled jars glowed in the light from the ceiling's bare bulbs. She reached for a pint of strawberries, their ruby shapes suspended in thick, sweet juice, and smiled as she remembered the June afternoon when Mabel and Angie helped her preserve gallons of fruit from Horace's patch.

That had been a special day. It was the first time she felt a real connection to this farm, and discovered the sense of accomplishment that could only come with a counter full of cooling canning jars. She hadn't known it then, but it was also one of the first steps toward her new life. A life she was not willing to give up.

Upstairs in the kitchen, the jar lid gave away with a satisfying *ping* and the sweet aroma instantly took her back to last summer.

How the hot sun felt on her shoulders as she weeded the garden. She heard the crickets' evening song, punctuated by the rhythmic squeak of the porch swing's chains. Remembered the heavy feel of a hazy afternoon as clouds approached from the west, bringing the promise of rain and a refreshing breeze.

"Mabel said canned strawberries are like summer in a jar," she told Hobo as she spooned sauce over the vanilla ice cream in her bowl. "She said all the work would be worth it. I believe she was right."

* 21 *

"Doesn't seem very heavy for its size." Glenn Hanson frowned and double-checked the post office's scale. He tapped the side of the cardboard box and gave Melinda a curious look. "What's in here, anyway?"

She tucked away a smile and shrugged. Weren't mailed materials confidential, once it was determined the items weren't dangerous? But she had expected Glenn to be nosy, and had her story straight before she came in the door.

"It's just something for a friend. I've meant to get up to Minneapolis to give it to her in person, but the weather's been terrible, you know?" Glenn was nearly as obsessed with the weather as Auggie, and she knew that would distract him.

"You're right about that." He shook his head as he printed out the bar code. "All this freezing and thawing, warm days and then snow. The gravel's a mess these days. Pete about busted an axle just yesterday. It's his truck, of course, but such things come out of the department's budget. Terrible hassle." He shuddered, recalling some past bureaucratic nightmare. "Well, any special instructions on this one?"

"It's fragile. I packed it well, but I'd like to get it there as fast as possible. The fewer days on the truck, the better."

Glenn's eyes widened, but he refrained from pushing for more details. "Sure thing. I can have it there by Saturday. Do you want insurance on it? How much?"

She wasn't sure what to say. How could anyone put a price on what was packed in that box?

"Let's say ... a hundred. Yes, that sounds about right."

"Can do. Might as well, the insurance is cheap. And despite what you see in those awful videos on the internet, it's amazing how many packages the post office gets to their destinations without a scratch. And on time," he added for emphasis.

Melinda reached in her purse for her wallet. "And, oh yeah, I've got some special deliveries coming." Glenn looked up with interest.

"I ordered some flower bulbs and starter plants yesterday. Looks like they're coming through the postal service. I should have put the store's address on them, but I forgot. If you see them come through, can you give me a call? I'd like to step over here and pick them up, rather than have them chilling on the porch steps until I get home."

Glenn reached for a sticky note and tacked it to the inside ledge of the counter, where he kept an ever-changing string of special requests. "It does my heart good to hear you talk about planting flowers. Just look at that fine sunshine! We're not out of the woods yet, but it's already the tenth of March. Every day brings us a little closer to spring."

Melinda pushed through the post office's door and stepped out into the unusually warm afternoon. She didn't have to be back at Prosper Hardware for another fifteen minutes. Bill was there and Aunt Miriam was minding the counter, visiting with customers before she started her weekly balancing of the books.

There was time for a walk around the block, a few moments to bask in the bright sunshine flooding Main Street. And to revel in the relief that her task was finally completed.

The truth was, she never had any intention of delivering the box's contents herself. Elaine Ainsworth was someone she never expected to see again, and hoped she was right.

The day after the last lamb was born, she called Horace and asked him when he wanted to sign the papers for the farm. She could only spare a few thousand dollars more, but urged him to take it.

"Don't you worry about us." Horace had shooed away her concerns. "Wilbur and I are getting by just fine. You'll take care of the place, that's what matters. What would we do with all of Elaine's money? And the tax man would take most of it. We come into this world with nothing, and we leave the same way. She hasn't figured that out yet, but it's the truth."

Kevin's cousin Ron volunteered to handle the sale, and promised to push the deal through within a month. Ron gritted his teeth through several tense conversations with Elaine, as Horace now refused to pick up her calls. But when Elaine threatened to drag an attorney into the family drama, her husband put his foot down. Bitter but defeated, she reached out to Ada with a different request.

"I need you to do something for me," Ada had told Melinda the other night on the phone.

"For all of us. For yourself, too. There's a set of cut-glass berry bowls in the china cabinet. Elaine says she wants them more than anything."

"More than she wanted the house?"

Ada snickered. "I tell you what, it's the easiest peace offering anyone could ask for. If you can buy her off with a few dishes, it's more than a fair trade, don't you think?"

With her phone tucked under her ear, Melinda had popped open the buffet's glass doors and rummaged among its contents. She found the six bowls stacked in the back of the cabinet.

"They certainly are pretty. But not very flashy, or large. Doesn't seem like Elaine's style. I hope I have the right ones."

"If they have starbursts on the sides, then we're good." Ada was clearly relieved.

"I guess Mother got them out every time Elaine and George visited the farm. In the winter, she filled them with gelatin salad. In the summer, it was strawberries and cream. Sometimes, she made her shortcakes, too. You're right, they aren't fancy, but it's the memories that matter."

Finding a box for the dishes was easy, but the note Melinda wanted to add was a struggle.

She tried to explain how much the farm meant to her, and wanted to remind Elaine that memories can never be taken away, never be lost. But the words wouldn't come together, and Grace and Hazel were thrilled with the crumpled balls of paper Melinda tossed to the floor. She settled for writing out the shortcake recipe tucked in the antique recipe box.

Elaine desperately wanted those dishes, and Melinda would make sure she got them. Maybe there wasn't anything else to do. Maybe there was nothing else to be said.

As for Ada, all she wanted was the recipe box. She promised to copy its contents for Melinda, but planned to take it with her the next time she visited the farm. "No one else has raised their hand, and I'm not about to remind anyone that it exists."

"It definitely should go to you. And if anyone asks, I'll shrug and act like I don't know what they're talking about."

Melinda walked down Third Street, crossed the gravel drive for Prosper Hardware's back lot, and passed homes where muddy patches of dead grass decorated the thin layer of remaining snow. A few small drifts clung stubbornly to the shadowy spaces where the pavement met the curbs.

Even in the bright sunshine, the tiny town looked a little weary and barren. But as she turned the last corner, Melinda remembered how Main Street had been before, and how it would be again: The flowers back in bloom, lush grass carpeting the community's lawns, and the trees bursting with fresh leaves.

She could just make out the little bend in the road to the west, before the co-op and the railroad tracks, and catch a glimpse of the now-barren fields that started as quickly as the little town ended. They were brown now, and sleeping, but would also spring back to life.

Lost in her musings, she jumped back just in time as a truck cruising down Main splashed through a muddy puddle. The stranger behind the wheel grinned and waved, and she returned the greeting. A woman across the way was walking her dog, the hood of her parka defiantly pushed back to soak in the sun's surprising warmth.

Melinda was almost back where she started, the green overhang of Prosper Hardware reaching her way with welcoming arms. Before she could push down the handle of the store's oak front door, Miriam's cheerful face popped out.

"Guess you're done at the post office, huh?" Her aunt gave a wicked grin, and they both laughed.

Although her friends and family had heard about Elaine's demands, only Doc knew how close Melinda had come to giving up. But he'd apparently filed her confession away under the header of patient-doctor confidentiality, and never said a word to anyone. She knew it was true, as any whisper would have come back to her in a town this small.

While she was still pondering that one, and feeling thankful for all the kind people in her life, Miriam beckoned her inside.

"I'll go up and get started on those purchase orders," she called over her shoulder as she hustled toward the stairs.

"And we had a rush of customers come in while you were away. Melinda, I'm so glad you came back when you did."

The little brass bell over the front door announced her arrival, and the comforting scent of lemon floor polish greeted her as she wiped her shoes on the mat.

"So am I, Aunt Miriam." Melinda quickly removed her coat and stepped behind the oak counter, adding her purse to the shelf below.

She couldn't keep the smile off her face. "So am I."

WHAT'S NEXT

"Songbird Season": After all the hard times Melinda faced during the winter, you might be wondering: Will spring ever arrive? Of course! Melinda has big plans for her little farm. And Prosper might only be a dot on the map, but there's always something for the coffee guys to gossip about in the mornings. Read on for an excerpt from "Songbird Season."

Get on the list: Sign up for the email newsletter when you visit fremontcreekpress.com. Click on the "Connect" tab and fill out your info, and you'll get updates on when future books in the series will be available. Book 6, "The Bright Season," will arrive in late 2019.

Recipes: The collection is really growing over on the website! Click on the "Extras" tab for a few more sweet treats and hearty suppers that'll make winter fly by!

So ... what did you think? If you've got something to say about "Waiting Season," please hop on to Amazon.com and leave a review. Or, share your thoughts with your friends on Goodreads.

Thanks for reading!
Melanie

Sneak peek: Songbird Season

Late March: Prosper Hardware

The painted bench needed to move the right, Melinda decided, so the store's gleaming new garden shovels would be more visible from the street.

Prosper Hardware's two plate-glass windows were impressively wide and tall, but there wasn't much room behind them to set out merchandise. That didn't stop her from creating seasonal displays, her creativity kicking into high gear as she plotted how to showcase the store's must-have items.

"OK, that's better." She stood back, checked the grouping for balance and scale, then slid the old varnished dresser to the left. "I can drape those lattice-patterned dish towels over the edges of the open drawers. And that vintage iron rack, once it is stocked with garden seeds, will look perfect on top."

A selection of shiny, waterproof boots would be cute lined up on the bench. She reached for one pair each in yellow and navy, then the dark gray that was always so popular.

At the last moment, she picked up the canary-colored set and checked their price tag. "Just the right size. Hmm." She subtracted her employee discount, and set them to the side.

"Good thing there's more of these upstairs. They're just so pretty, even though I know they'll get muddy soon enough. I've always been a sucker for a cute pair of shoes."

It was a beautiful day, the sunshine streaming in so warm that Melinda almost removed her sweatshirt. Aunt Miriam, in a rush of spring fever, had just switched off the furnace and propped open the store's heavy oak front door. A soft breeze, carrying the invigorating scent of thawing earth, brought fresh air into Prosper Hardware for the first time in months.

Miriam reached for the broom kept just inside the entrance, and attacked the dirt and now-dry mud that came through on customers' shoes earlier that morning. "Well, would you look at that?" She pointed across the street. "Look who's here!"

Melinda saw flashes of orange, and then heard the sweet songs of two robins as they flitted among the still-bare branches of the volunteer bushes between City Hall and the vacant building on its left.

"I saw my first one out at the farm yesterday. Seems a bit early, but I'm glad they're back. The cardinals and jays that hog my feeders at home will have to start sharing."

Miriam glanced at the clock. "How about we get lunch from the Watering Hole? I'm buying. I'll run back and get Bill's order. Frank's busy at City Hall, working on that history project. I'll text him."

Melinda nodded her approval, then reached for the carton of vegetable seed packets, thrilled by the possibilities waiting inside. "This day keeps getting better. Aunt Miriam, you just saved me from some boring leftovers. I can't wait for a cheeseburger smothered with ranch!"

She filled the display rack until it was a rainbow of greens and yellows and reds, then made herself put the rest of the packets away. Trays packed with dozens of young plants already filled her canning room's table. She had to rein in her enthusiasm, or give away half of everything she grew.

"Here you go." Miriam pulled some cash from her purse. "Bill wants his usual, that pizza burger thing. Frank wants a burger, no cheese. I'd like a chicken sandwich. Grilled would be better, of course, but fried is fine if that's all they've got."

Melinda raised her eyebrows. Frank and Miriam were trying to eat healthier.

"Don't look at me like that. We ate fish last night. I'm overdue for something good. And don't forget the fries."

Melinda had barely made it out the door when movement across the street caught her eye. Uncle Frank burst out of City Hall and dashed across Main, still clutching a stack of yellowed papers in one hand. Melinda wondered if he felt guilty about the burger, and now wanted a salad.

"Don't worry, Frank, there's still time to change your order." She laughed, then stopped when she saw the agitation on his face.

"Melinda!" he gasped, his cheeks brighter than they should be. "I just can't believe it! I can't believe that map!"

"What's going on? You shouldn't be getting worked up like this, with your heart and all. Is everything OK?"

"Miriam won't be, if what I just found out is really true!"

Frank was still trying to catch his breath. Melinda gently pushed him down on the bench in front of the store. Before she could get any details out of him, he was back on his feet.

"Bill's here, right? We've gotta get ..."

Frank's words disappeared as the screen door slammed behind him.

"What's all that racket?" Glenn Hanson came out of the post office, pulling on his windbreaker as he hustled down the sidewalk. "I saw Frank barrel across the street like his pants were on fire."

"I have no idea." Melinda threw up her hands. "He ran over here, babbling something about a map. He just ..."

The screen door banged again. Frank was gesturing wildly to a perplexed Bill, who had a large metal spool in his hands. "I'm sure there's just an error, Frank, especially if the map's that old."

Frank snatched the spool and made Bill take the end of the measuring tape. He pointed at the far edge of the post office, which was on the corner of Third and Main. "Go to the curb, we'll measure from there."

Bill sighed and shook his head, but did as he was told.

"Good Lord!" Miriam popped out the screen door. "I go up to the office for five minutes ... What's this all about?" Glenn and Melinda could only shrug.

"Honey, stop it!" she called after Frank, who was backing down the sidewalk, shaking his head and muttering. "Tell me what's going on!"

Frank lined himself up with the double wall that marked the end of Prosper Hardware and the start of the vacant, rundown building next door. He swore as he figured the measurement, then checked it again. His flushed face suddenly turned pale.

Glenn rushed to his old friend's side, beating Melinda and Miriam by mere seconds.

"Now listen, you need to calm down." He wrapped a supportive arm around Frank. "Whatever it is, it's not worth all this fuss. You're going inside to rest. Or I call an ambulance. It's up to you."

"Calm down? I can't calm down!" Frank was in tears as Miriam reached for his hand. "You have no idea. Honey, it's the lot! I can't believe it!"

"What?" she gasped. "Whatever do you mean?"

"This family's owned Prosper Hardware for a hundred-and-twenty years. But if that map I just found is correct, we don't own all the land under it."

"Songbird Season" is available in Kindle, paperback and hardcover editions

ABOUT THE BOOKS

*Don't miss any of the titles
in this heartwarming rural fiction series*

Growing Season (Book 1)

Melinda Foster is already at a crossroads when the "for rent" sign beckons her down a dusty gravel lane. With her job gone and her prospects dim, it's not long before she finds herself living in a faded farmhouse, caring for a barn full of animals, and working at her family's hardware store. And just like the vast garden she tends under the summer sun, Melinda soon begins to thrive.

Harvest Season (Book 2)

Melinda's efforts at her rented farmhouse are starting to pay off. But even in Prosper, nothing stays the same. One member of the hardware store's coffee group shares a startling announcement, and a trip back to the city makes her realize how deep her roots now run in rural Iowa. As the seasons change, Melinda must choose between the security of her old life or an uncertain future.

The Peaceful Season (Book 3)

As a reflective hush falls over the fields, Melinda turns her thoughts toward the coming holidays. She has a list of what will make the season perfect: Prepare her acreage for the coming winter, host her family's Christmas dinner, and use her marketing smarts to upgrade Prosper's holiday festival. But when a mysterious visitor arrives, she is reminded there is so much more to the Christmas season.

Waiting Season (Book 4)

Melinda finds herself struggling to keep the worst of winter's threats from her door. She pushes on because Horace's offer still stands: He'll sell her the farm in the spring. But as winter tightens its grip on rural Iowa, Melinda's biggest challenges are still to come. A series of events threatens to break her heart and shatter her hopes, and it will take all of her faith to see the season through.

Songbird Season (Book 5)

The first blush of spring finds Melinda filled with great expectations. But as the songbirds return and the garden's soil is turned, not everything's coming up roses. When Uncle Frank makes a shocking discovery in the town's archives, the fallout threatens to dim Prosper Hardware's bright future. As friendships are tested and family ties begin to fray, can Melinda restore the harmony in her life?

A TIN TRAIN CHRISTMAS

Travel back in time to Horace's childhood for this special holiday short story inspired by the "Growing Season" series

From the author of the heartwarming "Growing Season" novels comes this old-fashioned story of family and faith to brighten your holidays!

The toy train in the catalog was everything two young boys could ask for: colorful, shiny, and the perfect vehicle for their wild imaginations. But was it meant to be theirs? As the Great Depression's shadows deepen over the Midwest, Horace and Wilbur start to worry Santa may not stop at their farm. But with a little faith and their parents' love, the boys just might discover the true spirit of Christmas.

"A Tin Train Christmas" is available in Kindle format as well as a paperback version that's perfect for holiday gift giving!

And there's more: At the end of the story, you'll discover three holiday recipes handed down in the author's family!

CPSIA information can be obtained
at www.ICGtesting.com
Printed in the USA
BVHW030436060520
579278BV00001BA/3/J